FALLOUT

PART 3

OF THE TRILOGY

BETWEEN THE MOUNTAINS

AND THE SEA

FALLOUT

BETWEEN THE MOUNTAINS
AND THE SEA

RUTH SUTTON

HOAD
PRESS

First published in United Kingdom
by **Hoad Press** in 2014
2 Lowther Street, Waberthwaite, Millom, Cumbria LA19 5YN
www.ruthsutton.co.uk   ruth@ruthsutton.co.uk

ISBN–13: 978-0-9523871-6-9

A CIP catalogue record for this book is available from the British Library.

Prepared for publication by Aldridge Press
enquiries@aldridgepress.co.uk

Editorial: Charlotte Rolfe
Design: John Aldridge
Cover design: Kevin Ancient
Cover photos: John Aldridge: Seascale beach; Daily Mail/REX: men in protective suits at Windscale nuclear plant, 1957
Text photos: John Aldridge: Seascale 1, Drigg beach view towards Sellafield/Windscale 66, Solway Firth 117, Wastwater screes 216, St Catherine's church Boot 238, Drigg 292; Neil Kendall | Dreamstime.com: Maryport harbour 38; Daily Mail/REX: Windscale in 1957 19 & 173
Typeset in Bulmer 11.5/14.5pt

Printed and bound in UK by TJ International, Padstow

Acknowledgements

Many people in my community have shared with me their memories of the times and places at the centre of this story, for which I am very grateful. The local history library in Whitehaven has also been a great source of information for this book, as for the others in the trilogy.

Charlotte Rolfe and John Aldridge have contributed their friendship as well as their professional skills as editor, photographer and book designer as *Fallout* has taken shape. And thanks again to our cover designer, Kevin Ancient, for his sensitive use of photographs.

Above all, I am indebted to my partner Mick Shaw, for his careful reading of the text, his ideas and feedback, and for his unfailing support and encouragement throughout the project.

RS, Waberthwaite, April 2014

Author's note

Fallout is a work of fiction, but its location is real and an essential part of the story of Cumberland's west coast. The fire at the Windscale nuclear reactor in October 1957 is also part of this story. In its portrayal I have referred to the following individuals who played key roles at that time: Gethin Davey, Windscale Works Manager; Tom Tuohy, Deputy Works Manager; Tom Hughes, Assistant Works Manager; Huw Howells, Health and Safety Manager; Ron Gausden, Pile Manager; K. B. Ross, Group Director of Operations, based at Risley and visiting Windscale at the time of the fire; Sir William (Bill) Penney, member of the Atomic Energy Authority Board and Chair of the enquiry into the fire; Sir Basil Schonland, Deputy Director of the Harwell nuclear establishment and a member of the enquiry team. However, the main witness to these events in the story, Dr Lawrence Finer, is a fictional character, and bears no resemblance to any real person, living or dead.

For the facts concerning the Windscale operation, I am indebted to the official account and documents presented by Lorna Arnold in *Windscale, 1957: Anatomy of a Nuclear Accident* (2007 edition). Other factual details have been drawn from first-hand accounts in *Sellafield Stories* edited by Hunter Davies, published in 2012.

CHAPTER 1

SEASCALE, CUMBERLAND: NEW YEAR'S EVE 1956. Someone was knocking on the door. In the small sitting room of the upstairs flat, Jessie Whelan was asleep in a chintz-covered armchair by the window. Her head was bowed, grey hair falling across her face. On the verge of waking, sharp dreams glittered behind her eyes: a young man stood on a wide, tide-soaked beach, his arms outstretched. Dark hair blew in soundless wind but the face was blank.

The landlady, Mrs Sharp, knocked on the door again, louder, more insistent.

'Miss Whelan, Jessie, are you there? It's me, Betty. There's a policeman downstairs to see you.'

Jessie raised her head, listening.

'He says it's urgent.'

Jessie struggled to her feet, feeling the usual ache in her knee. Anxiety thumped in her chest. 'I'm here, Betty,' she called to the

1

closed door. 'Hang on a moment.' She peered at her image in the small mirror on the window sill and ran her hand through her hair, coaxing it back into shape. The face that stared back at her was strained. She looked away and turned to open the door.

Betty Sharp was standing on the second stair down, looking up. 'It's a constable, that new one. He says he knows you.'

'What does he want? Is it Judith?'

'He didn't say. Just asked me to fetch you down.'

Jessie pushed past her, gripping the rail, her heart beating fast. Not Judith, please not Judith. As she turned down the last flight of stairs into the hallway, the young man standing there looked up and smiled at her. He was bare-headed, holding a helmet in his hands.

'Miss Whelan,' he said. 'It's Jamie Carruthers. I was in your class at Newton School.'

Jessie squinted into the light that streamed through the window above the front door. 'Jamie? Let me look at you. You've grown up so.'

'Twenty-five now, miss. Just joined the police,' he said, holding up his helmet. 'We got a call to find you, and I recognised the name, so I came meself.'

'Thank you, constable,' said Jessie gravely. 'You said it was urgent?'

'There's been an accident, miss,' the young man continued.

Jessie felt her stomach turn. 'The bus, did something happen?'

'Not a bus, miss,' he said, puzzled. 'It were a car, up Moota way, on that long stretch. A car and a lorry. The car driver was 'urt bad. In th' hospital at Whitehaven. She's asking for you, miss.'

'Who?'

'Miss Plane, from Newton. Can you come with me? I've got the car.'

They drove east through Seascale, past the stacks and chim-

2

neys of the power station and the Windscale plant, to the main coast road and then north to Whitehaven. Jessie sat in the back. She didn't want to have to talk to Jamie. A car accident; it was New Year's Eve and plenty of people on the road had been drinking, but not Agnes. In times past, Jessie would have been staying with Agnes on New Year's Eve as she often did when they both lived at Applegarth, but since that last time… Jessie hung her head, remembering what had been said, the bright eyes so close to hers, the tears.

'You alright, miss?' The constable was looking at her in his mirror. She could see his young face. 'Do you want me to stop?'

'No, no,' she said. 'Can you tell me what they said, the people who rang you?'

'It was the police who went with the ambulance. They said Miss Plane was hurt and she was asking for you.'

'And you're sure it was me she wanted?'

'Oh yes. That's what she said, before…'

'Before what?'

'Before she, you know, before she passed out.'

Oh, God, thought Jessie, please let me talk to her. Don't take her away yet, not like this.

The car surged north into the darkening afternoon. To the west the sun rested on the horizon, its last rays catching the tops of trees and houses, leaving the road in shadow. As they passed the turning to St Bees Jessie thanked God that it wasn't Judith lying in the hospital. They'd spent the afternoon together, walked on the beach, talked. How she loved that child. Not a drop of shared blood between them, but she'd loved her from the start. How did that happen? Maybe that was how Agnes had felt, from their first meeting so many years before. Had Jessie been too preoccupied to see it, too blinkered by work and selfishness? And then there was Andrew, who drove such a wedge between them.

'How many years ago was it?' asked Jamie Carruthers.

His voice cut through her thoughts. Had she been talking to herself? 'Was what?'

'Since I was in your class? I've been trying to remember.'

Jessie made herself respond. 'You're twenty-five now, you said. So ten years ago you would have just left school.'

'Ten years,' he said. 'In 1947. Things have changed a lot. We had no electric in the village then, and now look at us. Power coming out of a nuclear plant. Who'd 'ave thought it?'

He turned the car into the main entrance of the hospital in the centre of Whitehaven. 'We're 'ere, miss. Not sure where Miss Plane will be.'

'That's alright, Jamie,' she said, pulling her coat round her. 'Someone will know where she is. Thank you for the ride. I can get back on the train when I need to. You go now, I'll be fine.'

When she found the ward, a doctor met her, stethoscope round his neck, peering at her over his glasses. 'Miss Whelan?'

'I came as soon as I could,' said Jessie as the man steered her into a small office next to the ward. He hesitated, but only for a moment. 'We did all we could, but I'm afraid she's gone.'

'Gone where? To Carlisle? How bad is it?'

'No,' he said. 'Miss Plane is here. She died, just a few minutes ago.'

Jessie stared at him, unbelieving. 'Agnes died? Can I see her?'

'Best not,' he said, leaning forward. 'The windscreen, you know. Rather a mess.'

'I want to see her, I must see her,' said Jessie, wiping a tear that ran down the side of her face.

The doctor got up and left the room. It was hot and airless. She took off her coat and folded it on her lap, numb, waiting.

'Come with me,' he said from the doorway, and she followed his white coat through the ward and into a separate room. A nurse stood back from the bed on which a figure lay. That's her body, thought Jessie, the life has gone. Her friend's face was torn and bloodied despite the efforts of the nurse who stood quietly to one side.

'What happened?' she heard herself ask.

'A lorry,' said the doctor's voice behind her, 'coming out of a lane onto the main road. Right in front of her, the police said, no chance to avoid it. She went through the windscreen.' Jessie looked again, trying to see the calm familiar face beneath the ravages of the impact. 'Are you a relative?' asked the voice.

'No', said Jessie. 'Just a friend, an old friend.'

* * *

It was late when she turned the key in her front door. Betty Sharp heard the door creak and came out from her kitchen, light spilling into the dark space.

'Is everything alright, Jessie?' she asked.

Jessie could hear dance music on the radio. 'What time is it?'

'Just gone seven. Do you want to come in with me for a while? You look very tired. Cup of tea, or something stronger? Was it bad news?'

Jessie nodded. 'May I?' she said. 'Don't think I could face the flat just yet.'

'Come away in. I'm going down the club shortly to see in the New Year, but didn't want you coming back to a dark house. You've been away a while.'

Jessie unbuttoned her coat in the warmth of the kitchen. The range oven door was open and she put her hands to the glow. 'Do you know Miss Plane, from Newton?'

'Can't say I do,' said Betty. 'Is she…?'

'Yes,' said Jessie. 'She died before I could get there. A car accident. I was just too late.'

Betty murmured some words that Jessie did not hear.

'She was my oldest friend.' Jessie spoke as if talking to herself. 'The first person I met when I came to Newton for the job at the school. That was nearly thirty years ago. We were neighbours, and then I lived at her house for a while when I left the school, before I came here. Agnes was working in London during the war, and then stayed on, so she was away a lot. I wish I'd seen more of her recently. So much left unsaid.'

Betty nodded sympathetically, glancing at the clock by the curtained window. 'What can I get you? A brandy, maybe? You've had a shock.'

'No,' said Jessie. 'No brandy, thank you. Just a cup of tea. That's all I need.'

Betty busied herself with kettle and teapot, leaving Jessie sitting at the table, trying to remember the words that had pushed her out of the comfort of Applegarth and into three rooms in this house. They had been words of love and hope, and Jessie had turned away. In all the years since, they had never mentioned it, and now it was too late.

John, she thought, I must tell John, and cousin Hilary in London, and the Leadbetters in Cockermouth. Her mind raced. She had always hated the phone. Maybe a telegram. Or a letter. If she could get letters into the box before midday...

'Here you are,' said Betty, putting a cup and saucer on the table in front of her. 'Have you eaten?'

Jessie shook her head, and a slice of dark fruit cake appeared on a small plate. It tasted like cardboard. The two women sat in silence for a while. Jessie was thinking about Agnes. Betty was thinking about how close she could get to Bill Southgate at the midnight countdown, to make sure of the kiss she'd been waiting for since last year.

Later, as the excitement in the Windscale club mounted, Jessie sat alone in her room, writing letters. Before work tomorrow she would contact the undertaker. The rituals of mourning and funeral arrangements would keep her occupied, for a few days at least. She did not write to John, but went downstairs early the following morning to phone him at home before he left for work. Maggie picked up the receiver.

'Happy New Year, Jessie,' she said. 'You're up very early. Is everything alright?'

'I have some bad news,' said Jessie. 'Agnes Plane was in a car accident yesterday. I'm afraid she died. It was too late to call you when I got back from the hospital, but I wanted to tell John myself.'

'Oh, how dreadful. I'm so sorry, Jessie. Let me fetch John.'

A minute passed, then, 'Jessie?' said the familiar voice. 'Maggie says Agnes has died. What happened?'

Jessie told her son as much as she knew.

'Are you going to work?' he asked.

'Yes,' she said. 'I'll need to talk to the undertaker, but all the letters are written, and there's nothing more to do today. I need to be at work, not sitting here.'

'Let me come and fetch you,' said John. 'Don't go on the bus, not today. I'll be there in twenty minutes or so. Please, Jessie, let me do this.'

* * *

Punctual as ever, John unfolded his tall frame from the car and walked round to open the passenger door for his mother. They sat for a minute side by side. He reached out and took her gloved hand.

'I'm so sorry, Jessie,' he said. 'It's a terrible shock for all of us. And for you...' His voice tailed away. He looked across at her but she faced resolutely ahead. 'She was always so kind to me. I think she knew about me being your son, even before I knew myself.'

'I showed her a photo of Clive,' said Jessie, remembering. 'She'd had a good look at you that day she picked you up from the hospital, and she could see the likeness straight away.'

'But she didn't say anything to me,' said John.

'Nor to me,' said his mother. Jessie looked in her handbag for a handkerchief and dabbed at the corner of her eyes.

'She always tried to do the right thing,' John said. 'I can't believe she's gone, that we'll never see her again.'

'I'll need to go to Applegarth, today if I can,' said Jessie. 'There are more addresses I need, if I can find them. I think I know where to look.'

'I can take you there after work if you like.'

How kind he is, Jessie thought, turning to glance at him. We're so different in many ways, but he is a good man. Agnes had said that he was a credit to her, even though he'd been raised by strangers after she had given him away. When John had turned up to claim her as his mother twenty years before, Agnes had been more pleased than she was herself. She hung her head.

'Shall we go?' he said.

* * *

After work, in the winter gloom of late afternoon, John inched the car down the steep drive at Agnes's beloved Applegarth and pulled up by the garage. Jessie badly wanted to sleep as the impact of the shock sank into her eyes and limbs, but she knew she had to be there. The spare key was in its usual place. John took it from her as she hesitated and opened the front door. He stepped into the dark hall and she followed, stumbling against the umbrella stand before John found the light switch. The house was cold, the air stale. Any minute, Jessie thought, the kitchen door would open and Agnes would bustle towards them, solicitous, welcoming, pleased beyond words to see the two of them together.

But there was no sound. John broke the silence. 'We won't stay long, not now. Nellie will come and do anything necessary. Have you told her?' he asked.

Jessie shook her head. 'They've no phone. I was going to write her a note.'

'We'll drive up there,' he said. The last time he'd been to the Kitchins' cottage was on the night he found his mother. Memories swamped his mind and he sat down on the little chair by the telephone.

'I'll get the address book,' said Jessie. 'You wait here.'

A few moments later she was back, the book in her hand. 'That's all I need for now,' she said. 'I'll do the rest of the letters and phone calls tomorrow.'

When they reached the Kitchins' it was John who knocked on the door to break the news. From the car Jessie could see Nellie's hand go to her mouth. One of the daughters spoke to John, then guided her distraught mother back into the house. The rectangle of light disappeared as the door closed.

'How's Maggie?' she asked, somewhat belatedly, as John drove down the valley towards the coast road.

'She's fine,' he said. 'Shocked, of course, like the rest of us, but she didn't know Agnes very well.' He hesitated. 'I think she and the McSherrys were a little afraid of Agnes. She was very posh by their standards. Maggie likes to see herself as pretty posh too, these days,' he added, smiling, 'but she still found Agnes intimidating.'

'Did you?' said Jessie.

'No, I didn't actually. Different, a bit exotic. All those trips to London, her war work, all that. I was very fond of her.'

'And how are the boys?' Jessie continued.

'Lively as ever,' he said. 'They love living so close to the beach, even in the winter. And they seem to be doing well at school. I wish I saw more of them, but by the time I get home, they're ready for bed.'

'So why send Judith away to school?' asked Jessie. She knew it was Maggie's idea.

'Maggie believes that where we grow up defines us,' said John carefully. 'Judith's had plenty of time with her mother and now with me and her brothers. She's quite independent enough to manage away from us for a couple of years and it could make such a difference. We're lucky enough to be able to do it, so why not give it a try? If she hates it we can think again. I don't think she will.'

'I'll miss her,' said Jessie.

'We all will, but that's the decision we've made,' said John firmly.

They drove the rest of the way in silence. He's my son, she thought, but it seems we can't talk about anything that matters.

As they neared the village the lights of the power station and the reactor across the river lit up the great chimneys topped with their clumsy filters. At the front door of her lodgings Jessie got of the car. 'Goodbye, John, and thank you,' she said. He didn't respond. She watched the car pull away down the quiet street. A faint mist hung in the air. Dust from the past, she thought. It seeps out of memories and pollutes our lives. Dangerous invisible particles, like nuclear fallout.

Chapter 2

THE HEARSE WAS COMING. Jessie and John stood side by side in the porch at Applegarth, she in her best black coat, he tall beside her, coat collar turned up against the cold and a soft-brimmed hat shielding his eyes from the low mid-morning sun. In the front room of the house they could hear voices, but it was quiet in the porch. Their breath hung in the air. He spoke without looking at her.

'I remember the first time I came here.'

Jessie did not turn her head. 'Please John, not now. That was a long time ago.'

'We never talk,' he said.

'I know, but not now.'

Lionel Leadbetter's voice rose, unmistakeable, in the front room. 'He may be in a wheelchair,' said Jessie, 'but the voice is as strong as ever.'

'Too strong,' said John. 'Maggie can't stand him. I hope they can get through the day without an argument. She promised me, but you know what she's like.'

'Where are the children today?'

'Apart from Judith, you mean?'

'Judith's not a child.'

'Judith said she wanted to be here, to support you. Frank and

11

Vincent are at school. They'll have their share of funerals when they're older. Maggie wanted to keep things normal for them.'

'Bit overwhelming for them anyway, all these people they wouldn't know. Hannah and Fred Porter were asking about them. Maybe when it's warmer we could all go up to Boot to see them.'

'How did those two manage to get here?' asked John.

'Someone brought them down on their way to Egremont, and will be coming back for them later. People are very kind.'

'They all thought well of Agnes,' said John. 'I expect the church will be full.'

The church was full. The hearse had crept down the lane towards the river, and in the car behind Jessie caught her breath as the back end slid slowly on a patch of ice. The coffin did not move, but the simple spray of holly and Christmas roses did, coming to rest against the back window. Jessie took John's hand and squeezed it. On his other side, Maggie Pharaoh straightened her new hat. From the churchyard gate they could see people already standing in the porch, keeping out of the wind until they moved aside to make way for the coffin.

Only three men in the party were fit enough to be coffin bearers: John, Agnes's old friend Dr Dawson, and Adrian Plane, a nephew from Carlisle, with three others from the undertaker's to make up the numbers. When they entered the tiny church by the river, the congregation, sitting in tight groups in the old box pews, shuffled to its feet.

Jessie was pleased that Adrian Plane had agreed to say the necessary words about his aunt. She did not think she would have been able to do it. He made them smile with stories about Agnes's passion for shoes, and made some of them cry too as he recalled her many kindnesses to people less fortunate than herself. Jessie glanced across at Maggie, but the lovely face betrayed very little, except her concern for her husband. Maggie had always fought for John, thought Jessie, whether he wanted her to or not. The first time she and Maggie had met, the young woman had berated her in her own home for, as she put it, abandoning John as a baby and then passing him off as her nephew. Jessie knew that this still lay at the root of their regular disagreements, and resolved – yet again – not to make John a reluctant referee between his mother and his wife.

Later, they stood at the graveside after the hymns had been sung and the prayers intoned, while a shower blotted out the view of the sea, rattled over them and disappeared up the valley. The January landscape was a palette of brown, grey and rust, the trees bare apart from the three cedars that had stood behind the church for two hundred years. The tide was ebbing, chased by the river's flow, bubbling over the mud banks where the old ford had been. Romans, Celts, Vikings, they'd all been here, their successors watched by the weathered sandstone cross in the churchyard. A curlew warbled over the estuary as cold, dark earth thudded onto the coffin. Ashes to ashes, dust to dust.

Jessie looked out towards the sea, her eyes full of tears. She had lost a true friend, who had loved her longer and more dearly than any man.

'Thank heaven it wasn't that dreadful vicar they sent us after the war,' whispered Caroline Leadbetter to Jessie as they picked their way across the muddy farmyard to where the cars were parked. 'Mr Bailey may not have known her very well, but at least we were spared a rant about the iniquities of private property, and all that.'

'Ah yes, Gideon Barker,' said Jessie, remembering. 'It was he who convinced me to leave the school, you know. Him and Mr Crompton the teacher, the one who'd been in the navy, they ganged up on me about Crompton needing the job and the schoolhouse more than I did.'

Caroline shook her head. 'I remember,' she said.

'I was angry at the time,' Jessie went on, 'but now I'm glad I got out when I did. I'd been at the school for long enough. Agnes put the idea of working at Windscale into my head, even before they started building it. She persuaded me to start on the shorthand.'

They stopped by the cars, where people were standing in small groups, coats pulled round them against the wind.

'Working at Windscale's been a whole new life for me, but I'm not enjoying it much at present.'

'Really?' said Caroline. 'What's bothering you?'

'Making bombs, mainly. That's all it seems to be about these days, and as fast as possible. I don't trust Macmillan.'

'Don't mention any of that to Lionel,' said Caroline, taking Jessie's arm. 'It would set him off again about Suez and the Americans, and I've heard quite enough about that.'

'I promise,' said Jessie, smiling.

In fact it was a different topic that threatened the peace at Applegarth when they had all assembled for their lunch. In the kitchen, helping Nellie with the sausage rolls, Jessie heard first Lionel's voice and then another, female, and loud. It was Maggie Pharaoh, whose irritation had boiled over, encouraged by two glasses of sherry. As Jessie emerged into the hall, Maggie was putting on her coat, and her mother, Violet McSherry turned towards Jessie to speak her mind.

'I'm sorry but we 'ave to go,' she said. 'Mebbe 'e's in a wheelchair, but that's no excuse for being rude.'

'What happened? Can't you stay a while longer?' said Jessie.

'No offence, Miss Whelan,' said Violet. 'But our Maggie can't stand to hear people slagging off the miners, and nor can I. That old man knows nowt about it.'

'What did he say?'

John was with them now, shaking his head. 'I knew this would

14

happen,' he said. Maggie jammed her hat onto her auburn hair. 'That man,' she said with emphasis, 'the old one with the loud voice, he said that Windscale is full of ex-miners who just went there for a soft life and take orders from the union, not the management.'

John rolled his eyes. 'Lionel is a liability,' he said.

Maggie went on, undeterred. 'God knows what our dad would say about that.'

Judith emerged from the front room. Her face was flushed. 'Do I have to go too? Why can't I stay? I've got the whole day off school.'

'You too,' said John. 'Get your coat. Your mam has to be home for the boys, and we'll all go together. I'll come back for you, Jessie, in an hour or so.' He winked at his mother and steered the three women out of the front door.

Jessie provided the company with a necessary distraction by handing round the sausage rolls. Funerals and weddings, she thought. Things always bubble up. Families with old scores to settle, a bit to drink. That'll do it every time.

Caroline squeezed her arm and whispered, 'I'm so sorry, dear. It's his stroke you know. He can't help it. Thank heaven Andrew isn't here. He and his father could shout at each other any time.'

'How is Andrew?' Jessie asked, knowing that she would be expected to enquire.

'Who knows?' said Caroline. 'Not a single letter since I was in Toronto for the wedding. Such a lovely girl, and quite devoted to him. I was hoping there might be some news, you know. If they're going to have a family it's time they got on with it. She's quite a bit younger, but he'll be forty-five soon. He finds writing hard since his injury. Have you heard anything?'

'Not a word,' said Jessie, and this time it was true.

Jessie had tried hard to avoid talking to Matthew Dawson and his wife, but in vain. He insisted on helping her when more coal was required, despite her protestations that she could manage.

'You're looking well, Jessie,' he said, as she held the lid of coal bunker open for him.

'I am well, thank you. Never felt better, actually.'

He smiled. 'This independent life of yours seems to suit you.' She ignored the unspoken critique of her decision not to marry him.

'And married life must be suiting you too,' she said.

'Brenda's a wonderful girl,' said Matthew. 'I'm a very lucky man.'

Girl, indeed, Jessie thought to herself. 'And how are your other girls?' she asked. The inference was lost on him, as she knew it would be.

'They're both splendid, thank you. Emily and her husband have produced another grandchild, a boy this time.'

'Lovely,' said Jessie.

'And Anne looks well, too, don't you think? She's happily married of course, but her husband couldn't get away. She'll be heading back to London this afternoon.'

'I expect she and Brenda get on very well?'

'Like a house on fire,' said Matthew happily. 'They even look alike, have you noticed?'

'Really?' said Jessie. She smiled as she opened the back door for him, and hoped he didn't see it.

* * *

When John arrived back at Applegarth, he waited until Nellie had gone home, poured himself a small glass of whisky and sat down at the kitchen table. 'Can you sit with me a minute, before we go?' he said to Jessie. 'There's something I need to ask you about.'

Jessie had heard this tone before, and it was not good.

16

'When we were in the car just now, Judith referred to you as Jessie, not Granny Jessie,' John continued. 'Maggie corrected her, and Judith claimed that you said it was alright. Is that true?'

'Oh dear,' said Jessie. 'I thought that could cause trouble. It was on New Year's Eve, when Judith was with me, before we heard about Agnes. Judith just asked me, out of the blue, if she could call me Jessie. I couldn't really see why not. She's old enough now to make up her own mind about things like that, isn't she?'

John shook his head. 'Couldn't you back us up about this? Is it so important?'

'No', said his mother, 'it's not important. That's the whole point.'

John said nothing. He swilled the remaining whisky round in his glass before he finished it.

'Maggie thinks you're undermining her, with Judith.'

Jessie groaned. 'I thought we were through this. Why does she have to find fault with me?'

'She doesn't "find fault", and she knows that Judith is fond of you –'

'And I'm fond of her too,' Jessie interrupted.

'Let me finish,' he said, with obvious irritation. 'Look, you and Judith are not related in any way. Maggie is my wife and Judith's father never even saw her before he was killed in the war. So you have no right to – to influence her, none at all. That's down to Maggie and me.'

'What's that got to do with her calling me Jessie?'

'Maggie feels it's just typical. You know we want Judith to call you Granny, as a mark of respect, but you go against that. And there's another thing.'

'More?' Jessie rolled her eyes.

'Don't look like that. We know you've criticised our decision to send Judith away to school.'

Jessie was angry now. 'That's just not true,' she said, 'whatever Judith has told you. We had a discussion about it, about the ups and downs of that choice, and I ended up encouraging her. I said it was a great opportunity to see more of the world.'

'You also said it could stop Judith having friends at home.'

'That was part of what we talked about, that's true, but I didn't know that you and Maggie had just presented it to her as a *fait accompli*. She's old enough to be talked to sensibly, she's not a child.'

'She's not quite sixteen, and she is our child. We make the decisions about her and deal with things the way we see fit. You're my mother, and Judith's grandmother by marriage, that doesn't give you the right,'

'That's enough, John. You've made your point. Or you've made Maggie's point, I should say.'

John stood up. His face was red. 'Maggie is my wife and I love her. If she's upset by your behaviour towards her daughter, I will support her. I do support her.'

Jessie pushed her chair back from the table. 'And now you've said your piece and put me in my place, yet again. You'd better go, before we rake up any more of the old stuff. I'll get a taxi home. You go back to the family.'

He looked down at her, wishing that things could be different.

'I've said I'll take you home, and I will,' he said. 'It's on my way.'

They drove back to Seascale in silence. As Jessie got out of the car, John looked across at her. 'Goodnight,' he said. She shut the car door and went inside.

18

Chapter 3

'Mr Pharaoh's office.'

'Is Mr Pharaoh available?'

'He's very busy this morning, may I give him a message?'

Jessie hesitated. 'Could you ask him to call his mother. I'm at the office.'

'Does he know how to contact you?'

'Yes, he does.'

'Very well, goodbye.'

Jessie put down the phone and finished her lunchtime sandwich. She rarely went to the canteen these days, since she felt she couldn't talk openly there. Now that the idea of leaving the plant was in her mind, it was hard not to question everything she saw and heard. Maybe she was absorbing more of the tension in the place. Too much going on, too quickly.

She was surprised when John appeared in her office only a few minutes later. He was looking as smart as ever, in his grey wool suit, red scarf loosely round his neck, and his familiar hat. A good looking man, she thought, now that he'd filled out a bit. So like his father.

'I got your message when I was going for lunch, so I walked over here on the way out. Did you want something?'

She glanced around. Nothing was private in this glass-walled room.

'I'll walk back over with you,' she said. 'Might as well take advantage of the day.'

Outside the wind was biting, but the sky was cloudless above the chimneys.

'Northerly,' he said. 'The fells looked so clear and close this morning. Made me want to drive up there and climb something instead of coming to work.'

She hesitated, rehearsing what she's planned to say to him.

'I'm sorry about the other day,' she said finally. 'I should have been more clear with Judith, and backed you and Maggie up more definitely. And when you asked me about it, I got defensive. I don't know why I react like that.'

'Has that been bothering you all this time? It must be three weeks ago.'

'Well, I want you to do something for me, and I realised that I shouldn't assume that you would want to see me, never mind help me with something.' She stopped and looked at him. 'Is Maggie still angry about it?'

He looked up at the sky. 'It's like an itch she wants to scratch, ever since we first met and she heard about you and me. And I think she's a bit afraid of you too, you being a teacher and all that, when she was just a screen lass.'

'But –' Jessie began.

'I know, I know,' he said. 'She was never "just a screen lass". She's an amazing person and always has been, but I can understand where that feeling comes from. Those women on the screens were treated like untouchables. So when Maggie, or Violet come to that, gets even a whiff of someone putting them down, it just sets them off. Look how they reacted to Lionel at the funeral.'

'But she still thought I was undermining her, didn't she?'

'Probably.' He smiled. 'And I think Judith wound things up a bit too. She feels as if we're pushing her into this boarding school business.'

'I do love Judith, John, even though we're not related. Maybe that's the teacher in me. She has such spirit, and she's funny too. Great company. I know she's just a child, but it's hard to treat her like one.'

'She is great kid, isn't she. I hate the idea of her being away for weeks at a time, but I'm sure it'll open up her world in a way that just won't happen if she stays at home.'

'I still think Maggie disapproves of me.'

'Is that what you want to talk to me about? I feel like I'm caught between the two of you, have been for years.'

'It's not that. It's about Agnes's will.'

'What about it?'

'Mr Brownlee's written to me, Agnes's solicitor. He wants me to go over there, to Broughton, and I don't want to go alone.'

'You want me to drive you?'

'I want you to be with me. You and Agnes were always very close, especially in the last few years. She was Frank's godmother, all that. It must be about the will. I'd feel better about it if you were with me.'

He stopped and looked down at her. 'You're always so strong, Jessie. It never occurs to me that you might want help with anything. You don't ask and I don't offer.'

'And Maggie thinks I'm a bad influence. Not very good, is it?'

He smiled. 'Of course I'll come with you to Broughton. We'll go in the car. And I'll tell Maggie you never meant to undermine her, but I won't apologise for you. If you want to do that you'll have to do it yourself.'

He watched her walking back across the river to the plant. Even after twenty years, it was hard to see Jessie as his mother. There were still great gaps between them, but they'd been apart for the first half of his life, so maybe that was inevitable. He knew what bothered Maggie more than anything was that Jessie had given him away, to strangers. 'Twice she turned her back on you,' Maggie had said to him. 'Once when you were born, and again when you tracked her down. How dare she?'

* * *

The following Friday afternoon John told his secretary he had important family business, picked Jessie up in the works car park and they drove to Broughton together. The cloud was low on Corney Fell so they went the long way round, down the coast and then up the winding road through the Whicham valley to the little town that sat surrounded by green hills. Smoke from a hundred chimneys mingled with the cloud, hanging over the town like a shawl. Lights were on, although it was only early afternoon. On auction days the streets were busy with wagons and farmers, the sounds of cattle and sheep in their pens echoing off slate walls, until the business was over and the pubs were full. But it was quiet today; they parked the car in the square and walked across to the solicitor's as the clock struck three.

Mr Brownlee's office was lined with wooden shelving, displaying dozens of identically bound volumes. A fire burned in the small grate. Mr Brownlee himself was a sprightly figure in a tweed suit, half-moon glasses perched on his nose, thinning hair parted in the centre and combed carefully into place on either side of his face. A tray of tea appeared almost straight away, even before they had taken off their coats and sat down on the hard, high-backed chairs at his desk.

'I've heard so much about you over the years, Mr Pharaoh,' he said to John. 'Miss Plane always followed your career with great interest. She was very proud of you, but I'm sure you know that.'

John blushed.

'And Miss Whelan and I have met before of course. Agnes's wonderful hospitality … well, well.' He leaned back, holding the tips of his fingers together as if in prayer. 'A sudden and tragically early death,' he said, lowering his eyes to the file on his desk, 'but you won't be surprised to learn that Miss Plane left everything in order. Her will is clear and straightforward.' He opened the file.

'She left the house, Applegarth, and all its contents entirely to you, Miss Whelan. There were various other bequests to friends rather than family.' He glanced again at the file. 'Do you know a Mr and Mrs Porter, in Boot?'

John and Jessie looked at each other and smiled.

'They inherit a tidy sum,' he went on, 'and a Mr and Mrs McSherry in Kells?' He looked up, eyebrows raised.

'My parents-in-law,' said John. 'They'll be astonished that she should remember them.'

'Good people, all of them, that's what she told me when we discussed these bequests, and fully deserving of some benefit from her personal good fortune. I had the impression that Miss Plane's family are quite comfortably off already.'

He looked back at the file.

'You and your wife have three children, I believe, Mr Pharaoh?'

John nodded.

'There's something for each of them when they reach twenty-one. She told me they were like grandchildren to her and she wanted to give them a bit of a present when they are heading off into the world.'

Jessie took John's hand and squeezed it.

'I'll read the full terms to you both, but those are the main head-lines, so to speak. Oh, and there's one other thing, Miss Whelan. Miss Plane left an envelope with me, very cleared marked to be given to you, in person, in the event of her death. If unfortunately you were to have pre-deceased her, it was to be destroyed. Here it is, as per my instructions.'

He passed a large envelope across the desk into Jessie's hand.

'More tea?' he said.

* * *

John waited until the younger children were in bed and Judith up in her room with the radio on before he told Maggie the details of the will. 'She seemed to think of our kids as her grandchildren, sweetheart,' he said. 'I had no idea she felt like that.'

'She was always so fond of you,' said his wife. 'I can understand that. I'm very fond of you myself.' She leaned across the table and kissed him.

'Did I ever tell you that Agnes wanted the three of us, she and Jessie and me, to live together at Applegarth, like a family? That's what she said that first time, when I had tracked Jessie down. I was in such a state I couldn't think straight.'

'And yet she left the house to Jessie in the end. Nothing for you.'

'Of course she did. Jessie lived there with her for a while, before she got the job at Windscale and moved up there. And Agnes knew how well I'm doing now. She wanted to leave most to people who don't have much. There's nothing for her family. They're all rich.'

But they don't have three children, Maggie thought to herself. She got up to clear away their supper plates.

'Jessie and Agnes didn't see much of each other after Jessie moved out, did they?' she said.

'Well, Agnes was in London most of the time, and they were both so busy. They must have meant a lot to each other, for her to leave Jessie the house.'

'I wonder,' said Maggie.

* * *

Back in her rooms in Seascale, Jessie put the unopened envelope on the table and looked at it. Agnes's instructions were written on it, in her own hand. When did she write this, Jessie wondered? What was in her mind when she did? She poured herself a glass of this year's sloe gin and pulled up a chair to the table. Then she opened the envelope carefully with a knife, so she could close it back up again easily if she wanted to. Or maybe she would have to burn it in the fire that crackled in the grate behind her.

There was single sheet of paper in the envelope. She drew it out carefully and began to read.

My dear Jessie,

I've asked my solicitor to give you this should anything happen to me, and to treat its contents with confidence. No one but you and I know what passed between us that night, when I made the mistake of telling you how I much I love you. I still do, but I know – as I did the moment I'd said it, – that you could not return my feelings in the same way. I should have understood that all along and said nothing, but I was foolish and a little tipsy, and there it was.

The price of that foolishness was that I frightened you away, my dearest friend, and I have missed you terribly.

Jessie put the letter down for a moment, to find a handkerchief. It was a moment before she could read on.

*As I write this, several years have elapsed since that night.
We've both been lucky to have such engaging work. For me,
being in London has kept me busy and interested in the
world, but I've never met anyone who could replace you in
my heart. I've left you the house, as I always intended to do.
My hope had been that you and I, and John too, would live
there together, but now I just want to think of you there, in
my place when I have gone. That may not be what you want,
and Applegarth is yours, to do with it whatever you want. If
you sell, please find someone who will love it as I have done
and look after the garden.*

*Whatever has happened, don't feel sad. My faith has
always been strong and I have no doubt a better place awaits
me. I wish you had such certainty for yourself.*

Please remember me with love, if you can.

Your friend,

Agnes

She let the paper fall to the table and leaned her head back. She
could see Agnes's face as it had been that night, so full of hope, and
then so distraught. Agnes had offered her love, as rich as anything
Jessie could ever have had from a man, but she had rejected it
without hesitation and lost so much. Since then, there'd been
nothing. And never likely to be now, she thought.

The sloe gin helped to blot out the images and regrets that
trampled through her brain, churning up the ground. When she
woke with a start the following morning, she suddenly wanted to
talk to Pat, the one person who knew and understood her secrets,
as close to her as Agnes had been. Pat O'Toole was a dear friend.
He liked her, she knew that, and always had done, even before he
broke his vows and left the church. He had supported her through
very difficult times. And what about Applegarth, she thought as

she lay in bed, delaying the feel of the cold floor on her warm feet. She could live there, comfortable and content, working in the garden, walking by the river or on the beach. With the money she'd saved, and the bits of pension available to her, she could survive financially, and earn a bit extra from tutoring, or even a bit of teaching. She was healthy and reasonably fit, apart from the aching knee. But she would be alone in Newton, away from the friends she'd made in Seascale, and the school and the shops and the club. She didn't need a car here, with the train and the bus so close by. She could keep her independence. And if she sold Applegarth, she could buy a place here in the village and have money left over to keep her going for a while,

It was only later, in the crowded bus that rumbled down the straight road to the plant, that another thought came to her. She could buy a house like Betty's, make the top floor into a flat and rent it out, using the money as an income to live on. No debts, owing nothing to anyone, close to the village she enjoyed. All day at the office she relished the thought, anticipating the fun of making a house her own. She would need help, and began to think of people at the plant who she might persuade to do some jobs for her, things that she couldn't do herself. It could be a project, real and demanding, that would change her life, and the idea delighted her.

Chapter 4

'Jessie's asked me if we want the house,' said John. 'I said I would talk to you about it.' He'd waited until their quiet time to tell her, the time he loved most with Maggie, between the boys' bedtime and their own, when he could forget about work and responsibility for a while. They were sitting together on the sofa in the living room of the house in St Bees.

Maggie turned to see his face. 'For nothing?'

'No, not for nothing, for a proper price. But we get first refusal and if we want it we save all the fuss of looking for a place, agent's fees, all that.'

'Do you want to live there?' She was still looking at him.

'I love the house, but I'm not sure about all of us living there. It has a lot of memories for me, old memories, some of them not so good.'

'Well, it's certainly big enough,' said Maggie. She snuggled into John's shoulder. 'Who'd have thought it, me living in a house like that, after starting off in West Row? Mam would be over the moon. Wouldn't want it for herself, like, but it would be good to tell her friends about.'

'But do you like it?' said John. 'We want a bigger house, but it doesn't have to be there.'

Maggie turned the idea over in her practical mind. 'The boys

28

would have to move school. And you would need the car, so I would be stuck there during the day.'

'Not necessarily,' he said. 'I could get the bus up, or bike to the station and get the train.'

She sat up and looked at him again. 'You're the Finance Manager of a big power station, John Pharaoh. You're not going to work on a bike like some poor bugger who works in th' office. You've worked hard for years, earned everything you've got.' She settled down again beside him. 'And anyway, I don't want to be beholden to your mam.'

'I thought that would come into it somewhere,' he said.

'Well, I don't,' said Maggie. 'Never have. No matter what she says, it's all about her. She's never done right by you, John, that's what I think.'

'I know, love,' he said, kissing the top of her head. 'Putting herself first is just a habit. She's had to do it, to survive all these years. If I can accept that, why can't you?'

'Because you're too soft. I had to struggle too, early on, but I never let it affect our Judith. She was first in my life, right from the start, and she still is, and the boys of course. That's why I want to see her at a proper school, away from here and all the stuff that pulls us down.'

She was quiet for a while, thinking. The clock on the mantelpiece ticked. He could feel her heart.

'Do you remember we had a talk one time, about the way we speak? We were up a mountain somewhere, before we, you know, got close.'

He laughed. 'Got close? You sound like your mam. I remember it, we were on top of Harter Fell, looking out at the view.'

'Well I want our Judith to be around people who don't talk like us, not even like you. People like Agnes, posh people. Then at least she has the chance to make more of her life. And the girls she meets, they'll live different, too. She's bright enough to make a good living but it's about who you know, not what you know.'

John smiled. 'So Judith was right when she said we want to make her posh. But she doesn't want that.'

'She's too young to know. What did you want for yourself when you were her age?'

John thought for a while. 'I wanted not to have to go to church and go climbing instead. That was it really. What about you?'

'All I wanted was to leave school, get a job somewhere for a while and then get married and have some kids. And that's what I did, the getting married bit, to the first lad who asked me and he turned out to be pretty useless. If he'd come back from the war and we carried on I think I'd've gone crackers.'

John laughed and held her a little closer. 'Poor Isaac,' he said. 'He didn't have a chance.'

'And then you came along,' she said. 'Couldn't believe it, a man with a clean job and manners and his own house. Did you know then how hard we tried not to tell you I were a screen lass? I thought that would be the end of it.'

'And look at us now,' he said. 'We're very lucky.'

'It's not luck,' she said. 'You've worked hard, and I do too, with the kids and the house and everything.'

He hesitated. 'Jessie admires you, you know.'

John felt his wife shaking her head. 'She may say that, but I know better. She looks down on me, always has.'

There was silence for a while. In the street outside a dog was barking.

'What shall we say about the house, then?' said John finally.

'Tell her thanks for the thought, but we'll find our own place.'

* * *

We were both very pleased to have the chance to buy Applegarth,

Thank you for thinking of it, John wrote in a letter to his mother. He didn't want to phone her at work and the phone at Betty Sharp's was downstairs where anyone could overhear. *In the end we decided that we need to stay in St Bees, for the boys' schooling. I'm sure you'll find a buyer if you decide to sell. There must be lots of people who would love the place as much as we do.*

'That's what we told her,' said Maggie to her mother Violet McSherry on the following Saturday morning. They were walking down into town from the house in Kells where Violet lived with her husband, Frank, and her brother, Tom Pickthall. Both men had been miners, and one way or another the pits had ruined both their lives. Frank had been caught in an underground explosion many years before and had lost the use of his legs. His skill in manoeuvering the wheelchair round the cramped house in West Row was a source of unspoken admiration for any visitor. Tom was luckier, in a way. He had survived one of the worst mining accidents in Whitehaven's history just after the war, but a lifetime of coal dust had seeped into his lungs. Like many other men on the street, his coughing was inescapable and would kill him. Violet cared for them both with a loyalty matched only by her devotion to the Catholic church, in the person of Father Price. Her respect for the desiccated local priest was unique in the family. Maggie remembered how difficult Father Price had been when she and John wanted to marry, which she neither forgot nor forgave.

'But how much would Jessie 'ave asked for it?' asked Violet. 'It's a grand house, our Maggie. Plenty of room for you and the kids and for me too, like, if I came to stay.'

'We never asked about the price,' said Maggie. 'I knew I didn't really want to live there, and it's not that big. Four bedrooms. The boys would have to share when a visitor came.'

'Listen to yourself,' said Violet, stopping on the steep hill to look hard at her daughter. 'Time was when you thought yourself

31

lucky to share a bed with our Judith, never mind everyone 'ave their own room.'

'But we've moved on from that, Mam, and thank God for it. You and I don't have to work in that freezing filthy screen shed any more.'

'You know I miss it sometimes,' said Violet. 'The work was 'ard but we were strong enough and we 'ad a good laugh, stuck together.'

'We 'ad to stick together,' Maggie responded, lapsing back into Kells speech from the more careful accents of St Bees. 'Remember that time when the dog got stuck under th' floor and we dug it out? That were a grand day. Anyway, we're not moving to Newton, our Judith is going to that fancy school in Casterton and if we need a bigger house we'll find one near where we are.' She took her mother's arm. 'You know, Mam, this is the first time in me life when I really feel in charge of things. I don't 'ave a job or me own money but John earns enough for us all to live well, and 'e's so generous. Keeps some for 'imself and hands the rest over, so we decide together how to spend it. I must have done summat good in this life to find 'im, Mam, no matter what Father Price might say about it. Anyway, that's what we decided, and John wrote it down in a letter so he didn't have to see 'er. He says he still doesn't know what to say to 'er sometimes, or how to say things.'

'She's a clever woman, that Jessie,' said Violet. 'People are scared of 'er. Not you, Maggie, you're scared o' nowt.'

* * *

By the time the letter from John arrived the following day, Jessie had gone out to see her friend Kath Attwood at the school in the village. They were standing in the doorway, watching the children playing in the yard, and talking about houses.

'You could have had an authority house to go with the job at the plant.' said Kath. 'They offered you one, didn't they?'

'Yes they did,' said Jessie. "But I didn't want one, not after all those years at the schoolhouse. And anyway, someone told me the authority houses are all damp, something about the bricks being upside down.'

'Sounds fairly typical,' said Kath.

As she spoke, driving drizzle swept in from the sea, blotting out the hills and forcing the two women further back into the doorway.

'Better get them in,' said Kath. She leaned into the rain to blow a whistle and the children began to line up in the yard, damp and red-cheeked, before filing past them into the building. Jessie remembered how much she loved being around children, and even more now that she didn't feel responsible for them. She followed the last child into the corridor and closed the door on the miserable afternoon.

'Don't go out again in this,' said Kath, taking Jessie's arm. 'Come in my office for a bit, I'll make us some tea.'

Jessie looked at her watch, and decided she did have half an hour to spare.

'This place has changed beyond recognition since I came here three years ago,' said Kath, pouring water into the special teapot she kept for visitors. 'About half the children's parents work at the plant, with degrees in God knows what. Must be the brainiest village in England by now. We tried to find a science teacher earlier this year but none of them knew as much physics as the kids.'

'Good for your exam results though,' said Jessie.

'That's true,' said Kath. 'Of course it's all down to wonderful teaching,'

'Of course,' said Jessie.

'So can you come back and help us, when you've finally left Windscale?' Kath asked, nodding at Jessie, hoping to persuade her. 'We need you, not forever, just a year or two. We need your experience of working with children and parents from away.'

Jessie laughed. 'That's a pretty weak argument, and you know it. My children "from away" were evacuees from Newcastle during the war. A bit different. And their mothers, well, they were a bit different too. They went in the pub, on their own. The old boys in Newton nearly had heart failure.'

'Well, we need you anyway for whatever time you could spare.'

'No, Kath, I'm not changing my mind about that. I loved my teaching, but that was years ago and I've moved on. Can't go back. Not now.'

'So what will you do all day?'

'What do sixty-year-old landladies do all day? Read the paper, play golf, work in the garden, walk on the beach. Maybe a wee bit of home repairs, some light dusting.'

'You'll get bored stiff.'

'Maybe,' she said. 'I've been working all my life and I'm tired of it. I worked in a factory in Chorley during the war, the first war, did I ever tell you? And then to teacher training and after that teaching in Liverpool, and then up here. No break. I've been lucky with my health, so far at least, but I just want to stop.'

Kath looked at her friend. Was it possible that Jessie was feeling her age? 'Have you sold the house in Newton yet, the one Agnes left you?'

'Not yet. I offered first refusal to my son and his wife and haven't heard back from them yet.'

'And what about buying a new place? Will you look here in the village?'

'Probably,' said Jessie, 'but I want a view of the sea, not those damn chimneys and cooling towers. Somewhere big enough to set up the top floor as a flat, like I have at Betty's. Bit of privacy, toilet, wash basin, even a sink and a hot plate or something for cooking. There must be people who don't want a house to themselves and don't want to live at the hostel. Someone older maybe. Have to sell Applegarth first though, and then find the right house to buy.'

* * *

Jessie read John's letter when she got home. Poor John, she thought, still stuck between me and his wife. But at least now she could go ahead and put Applegarth on the market as soon as the probate was settled. And it wasn't just the house she had to sell. She spent a while that evening making lists of the Applegarth furniture, room by room. She started with the upstairs rooms and landing, picturing each piece that she knew so well. Some had come with her from the schoolhouse, and would probably move again. Others were just too grand or big, or both. And then there was the piano. She had only ever heard it played once in all the time she had spent there. The sunless room at the back of Agnes's house had been cold that day, so cold their breath was visible, and Piotr had rubbed his hands together to warm them before he began to play.

She had thought of Piotr during Agnes's funeral, and probably would do so at every funeral for the rest of her life. He had come to visit her at Applegarth from the Displaced Persons' camp where he lived and had played that piano for her. Chopin. So beautiful, and with such longing. A few days later he had filled his pockets full of rocks, clutched a heavy cross to his chest and walked into the sea until he drowned, while she had watched helpless from the shore. She hung her head as the memory swept over her. At his funeral the Polish men from the camp had sung their Polish hymns and she'd thought her heart would break. Pat O'Toole had given Piotr a proper Catholic funeral, even though his death was clearly suicide, and Jessie had loved him for it. Pat didn't tell her what the bishop had said, but she knew it was one of reasons he'd finally left the Church. The other reason had something to do with his housekeeper, but he never talked about that either.

Pat was a good man, she thought. Was it possible? Could they ever be more than the good friends they had become in the past few years? She couldn't imagine being in love with him, feeling about him the way she had felt about John's father, Clive, or Andrew, but that was so long ago. Did women of her age fall in love like that? Had she already felt all the love she would ever feel for a man? Probably, she thought, and was both relieved and disappointed. All she really wanted now was a quieter life, in her own home by the sea, with undemanding friends, and time to enjoy herself without having to get up every day for work. She was getting older and heavier, her hair was going grey, and her knee hurt sometimes, but nothing to complain about. It was years since she'd seen a doctor, and she wanted to keep it that way. She was content, especially now that her anxiety about working at the plant could die away.

To celebrate this imminent freedom, Jessie put on a warm jacket and hat and went out, down towards the station and the beach. The days were getting longer now, but the afternoon was drear, low cloud obscuring the tops of the Windscale chimneys as she turned away from them and down the hill. The beach had the hue and sheen of old pewter, and pale light gleamed on the horizon. Shortly the sun would fall just below the ceiling of cloud and flash across the sea towards her, but it was too cold to sit and wait for that to happen. She quickened her pace and took the road that led up the hill, to have a good look at the houses that faced out over the beach. There was a *For Sale* sign outside one and she stopped and turned, looking up at the steep façade. The window on the top floor was quite big, which meant the rooms up there might be the size she had in mind. And the front room on the first floor with the shallow bay window could be her bedroom, filled with light, and a view changing hour by hour with the tide and the cloud and the seasons. She wrote the name of the estate agent on a scrap of paper and walked on.

Chapter 5

Only three more weeks to go at work. It hadn't really hit her yet, but on the train to Maryport at the weekend Jessie realised that this would be the kind of thing she would be able to do any time she wanted, on a weekday when everyone else was sitting at a desk or getting suited up to work in the reactor buildings. She and Pat took it in turns to visit, and this time it was her turn to travel. He was taking some of the Barnardo's children he worked with out for the day, and she was looking forward to that as well as to seeing him. They would have plenty of time to talk, and she had always been able to talk to him in a way that she couldn't with other people, even close friends. He and the Porters – Hannah and Fred – were the only people who would never judge her, or so she thought.

From the station at Seascale the train hugged the coast for most of the way, apart from between St Bees and Whitehaven, where it turned inland past the boarding school and then through a tunnel before emerging on the far side of the harbour. They passed the old sandstone buildings of St Bees school, and Jessie thought about Maggie's determination to send Judith away to Casterton school as a boarder. Jessie still struggled to know how to deal with her daughter-in-law. Whatever she did or said seemed to be misconstrued and held against her. Or was she just not trying hard enough?

Pat was there to meet her at the station. He was looking his age, she thought, although he was only a year or two older than her. But he'd lost some weight and it suited him, although it might be a sign that he wasn't well.

'You're looking thinner, Pat,' she said to him. 'Is Mrs Foster not feeding you properly, or is it all the exercise you're getting with the kids?'

'Well,' he smiled, 'I was convinced that my trousers had shrunk in the wash, and then I had a look in a mirror for the first time in years and saw what the problem was. I asked Mrs Foster to go easy on the big breakfasts for a while, and now the trousers seem to be a bit too big. It's a miracle! You look as well as ever, Jessie,' he said. 'You haven't aged a bit in all the years I've known you.'

'Go on with you,' she said. 'There's grey hair under this hat, and I've got some of those brown spots on the back of my hands already. It's the beginning of the end. Now tell me about these children we're meeting later.'

'They've had a rough start, some of them. Parents dead or in jail, or too sick to keep them. Not had much love, and it shows. Are you sure you don't mind spending the afternoon with them?'

'Mind? Those days at school during the war when we were crowded out with kids from Newcastle were the happiest times for me. Made me feel that the effort was worthwhile. I knew I could make a difference.' She thought about it. 'It was the same with those men in the camp. They needed people to pay attention to them, and you and I both did that. You were wonderful with them, you know.'

'No more than they deserved,' he said. 'They were stuck in that place through no fault of their own.'

They were walking up hill towards Pat's lodgings near the cliffs where the old drill hall looked out over the Solway Firth. It was a bright, clear day, with enough breeze to chop the sea into foamy spikes as the outward flow of the river met the incoming tide. Ragged clouds slid across the sky. Pat took Jessie's arm. 'Mrs Foster insisted that I bring you up home for a spot of lunch, before we meet the children. I think she wants to have a good look at you.'

* * *

Mrs Foster certainly had a good look at Jessie, with the discriminating eye of a small-town widow. 'I've heard so much about you, Miss Whelan,' she said. 'So glad to meet you at last.' Her voice betrayed roots on the north side of the Solway, across the border. 'Wigtown,' she announced, 'not Wigton. I came south with my husband, God rest him, and here I am still.'

'And I'm from Ireland, so you're the only English person here, Jessie,' said Pat, winking at her.

They spent a busy afternoon with seven lively children, on a hunt around the town for evidence of the Roman presence there centuries before. Pat had planned their route with care and given the children a list of questions they needed to have answers to. When they stopped at a café on the main street he and Jessie helped the children recall what they had seen and learned. Jessie was impressed, yet again, with Pat's patience, and his knowledge of the history of the town.

'How long have you lived here now?' she asked him as they walked back up the hill in the gathering darkness. Mrs Foster had insisted that they return for a while before Jesse went for her train.

'About eight years,' he said. 'Came here not long after that time at the camp, after I'd decided to leave the Church. It was a difficult time, and Mrs Foster has been a great help, just by being here, you know, and letting me be. She was curious about you today.'

'She certainly was,' Jessie interrupted.

'Ah, well,' he said, 'She knows how much you mean to me.'

'And you to me, too,' she replied.

After they'd drunk more tea and eaten some excellent macaroons, Mrs Foster left them alone, and they sat for a while in companionable silence listening to damp logs hissing on the fire.

"May I ask you something, Pat?'

'Ask away,' he said.

'It's about what happened, why you left the Church.'

'Oh, that,' he said. 'Well it's the age-old story. I fell in love with someone, but she was married. I never told her, and she never guessed. But if she'd been willing, I would have broken my vows in an instant. I knew I couldn't stay a priest after that. It was just a sham.' He got up to put some coal on the fire. 'And there were other things too that I wasn't happy with. That business with Piotr's funeral, you remember?'

'I do indeed,' she said. 'In fact I thought about it just the other day,'

'Aye, well, the bishop wasn't pleased. I'd tried to convince him it was an accident, but we both knew it was a lie. I prayed for a long time after that, but couldn't shift the thought that I needed to live my life differently. Still as a believer, but not as a priest. They were probably glad to see the back of me.'

'Your parishioners still remember you. And my son, John, too. You were prepared to take him on before he married Maggie, to make a Catholic out of him for her sake.'

'It was for her mother's sake, if I recall,' he said. 'How is Violet?'

41

'Just the same,' said Jessie. 'Still as staunch as ever.'

'Bless her,' said Pat. He looked at Jessie. The only light in the room was from the fire and a small table lamp. 'And you, Jessie? How are you, in yourself?'

She didn't look at him. He always seemed to know when something was troubling her. 'I still can't believe that Agnes has truly gone, that I will never see her again. And I regret not seeing her more in the later years. We used to be so close. Sometimes I just wish I could pick up the phone and hear her voice, or go and sit with her at Applegarth, quietly, like we're sitting here.'

Pat said nothing, watching.

'And now,' Jessie went on, 'now she's dead and the house is mine. I'll sell it to be able to leave Windscale. I've wanted to for quite a while.'

'Why would that be?' he asked.

'Well, at first I thought it was so exciting, creating cheap, clean energy after all those years of coal. And everything happened so fast, no time to consider what we were really doing. But the last few years have been different. Being Mr Meadow's secretary, I've picked up what's been going on. Not allowed to talk about it of course, and I shouldn't be telling you now.'

'Pretend I'm still a priest,' he said, 'and this is the confessional.'

'It feels a bit like that. I'm not certain whether all the cutting corners is really a problem. It's been alright so far. Now they're sending someone else up from Harwell, that's the big research place down south. It'll be just like the other times they've sent people to sort us out, and everyone gets tetchy. The Windscale men, the local ones, they prefer to do things their own way.'

'That's the way it works up here, isn't it?' he said. 'Most of the men were in the pits, or in the army. They don't sit around discussing things. If they think something needs doing they just get on with it.'

'Maybe we all need to ask more questions, be more awkward. The nuclear stuff is so new, I'm not sure we really know what we're doing. First the uranium, now that other stuff, tritium I think they call it, and all for bombs to show the Americans that we can keep up with them. Even worse since Macmillan came in.'

'And since Suez,' said Pat, nodding his head. 'It felt like Britain had something to prove after that.'

'Well, the past few months at the plant have been worse than ever,' she said. 'Now I've got the chance, I can't wait to get out.'

Pat looked at her, and the determination in her face. 'Let me tell you something,' he said. 'I've been going to meetings in Carlisle, with some people who feel like you do, not just about Windscale but about the whole nuclear business. We've had speakers from London, and Glasgow. There are similar groups all over the place. Can't be long before we all link up.'

Jessie shook her head. 'Won't get much of a following round here,' she said. 'So many jobs wrapped up in the plant, and no one wants to go back to the pits.'

'That's why I've not mentioned it to you before, Jessie. Didn't want to put you in an awkward position, but now you're leaving –'

'Are you trying to recruit me into something, Pat?' she said, smiling at him.

'Maybe I am,' he said. 'We need people who are able to speak out against what's going on, people of courage, who understand what's happening and where it might lead.'

'And you think I am such a person?'

'I know you are,' he said. 'I've seen your courage, haven't I? Now that you're leaving the plant, you could join us. We have supporters in the plant itself actually, but you won't know who they are. They have to keep quiet about it.'

'I bet they do,' said Jessie. 'They'd lose their jobs pretty quick if they started talking like that.'

'I'll write their names down for you, in case any of them get in touch. If you want me to, that is? I can't force you into anything, I know that.'

'Let me think about it,' she said.

Later he walked with her down to the station, and they sat together on the platform, out of the rain.

'Are you going to stay in Seascale?' he asked. 'No need to stay there now is there, if you've left the job? Maybe you could move up here.'

Jessie looked across at him. He was serious, she could see that. But what was he really asking her?

'Pat –' she began.

'Don't say anything,' he interrupted, holding up his hand. 'Not today. Think about it. Even if you can't agree with me about the political stuff, there's the work we could do with the children here.'

He put his hand on hers, and she did not pull away. 'You know how fond I am of you,' he said. She nodded. 'We're both not getting any younger,' he went on, his head close to hers, speaking softly with the faint Irish accent that she loved. 'We could be very happy, working together, doing something worthwhile. Will you think about it? Promise me?'

On the rattling train back to Seascale, Jessie tried to picture a future with Pat O'Toole. He had never said outright what he had in mind, but she thought she understood. He had loved before, in vain, and wouldn't want to risk being hurt like that again. She was not in love with him, but admiration and respect mattered just as much, didn't they? She and Pat could work together in Maryport, in a new place where no one would know or care what she had been before. If more developed, so be it. If not, the politics and the work with the children could be a new adventure, something that could make a difference. Did she really want to spend her time doing what she'd said to Kath, fiddling around, waiting for age and illness to catch up with her?

The house was cold and dark when she let herself in and climbed the stairs to her flat as quietly as she could. Even so, an opening door leaked light and she heard Betty's voice. 'Is that you Jessie?' She always says that, thought Jessie, smiling. Who else would it be? 'Yes it's me, Betty. I'm back.'

Betty was standing at the foot of the stairs, looking up.

'Did you have a good day? Not too wet?'

'Not much rain up there,' she said. 'We were lucky.'

'And Father O'Toole, is he well?'

'He's not a father any more Betty, hasn't been for years.'

'Mm,' said Betty.

'And we had a good time with some of the children he looks after.'

'Mm,' said Betty again. 'Well, goodnight, Jessie.'

'Goodnight.'

Jessie had been a single woman all her life. Even now, she seemed unable to have a man as a friend without someone assuming it was more than that. Maybe all women believed, as Jessie's mother Cora had, that friendship between a man and a woman was impossible, and that sex would always be part of it. 'They only want one thing,' Cora would say. 'No matter what else they tell you, that's all men think about.'

Jessie wondered about it. Surely now that we're all older, she thought, we can move on from that. Pat was her friend, one of the closest friends she'd ever had, male or female. Surely she could trust him to be honest, with her and with himself. She didn't want him that way. She wasn't sure she could ever want a man that way, not now. She made herself some cocoa, filled a hot water bottle, and went to bed.

Chapter 6

Wʜᴇɴ ᴛʜᴇ ɴᴏʀᴛʜʙᴏᴜɴᴅ ᴛʀᴀɪɴ ʙᴇɢᴀɴ to rumble across the viaduct at Arnside Lawrence Finer put down his book and looked out of the window. Pale April light reflected off the swirling water and gleamed in the carriage. Beyond the window to the west he could see the sandy flats and banks of Morecambe Bay stretching ahead in a great arc that widened as the train chugged towards the far bank of the estuary. Lawrence opened the battered briefcase that was propped against his legs, searched through a sheaf of papers and drew out what he was looking for. He opened up the map as far he could without spreading into the lap of the elderly man sitting next to him. There it was, a great bight on the north-western coast of England, and he could see the train line skirting round the northern shore of the bay all the way to Barrow before it bent north, on to the other side of the map.

He looked out again as a flock of black and white birds with bright orange beaks rose from a sandbank in a progressive wave and wheeled away to find a quieter spot.

'Oyster catchers', said the elderly man. 'Thousands of them out there, and curlews, and dippers and all sorts of ducks. There's a big flock of pintail somewhere that comes and goes between here and the Duddon flats, bit further north.' He pointed at the map resting on Lawrence's knee. 'How far are you going?' he asked.

Lawrence looked hard at the map, turning it over as his eye travelled north up the coast. 'Here,' he said, indicating with his finger. 'Seascale.'

'Going to the plant, are you? One of them scientists?'

'Is it so obvious?' said Lawrence, smiling. He'd been told that northerners were more direct, and here was the first evidence of it.

'Well you're not from round 'ere are you, not wi' that posh voice,' said the man. 'And you look like a scientist, like that chap with all the hair, and the round glasses like yours. What's 'is name? Famous, like.'

'Einstein?'

'Aye, that's the feller,' said the man. 'Foreigner, Jewish.'

'I'm Jewish myself, actually.'

'Aye, well, no offence,' said the man.

'None taken,' said Lawrence.

The train was slowing down. The man stood up and put on his coat.

'Grange,' he said. 'Getting off 'ere. Good luck to ye.'

Lawrence watched the old man step stiffly down onto the platform and acknowledged him as the train pulled slowly away. He didn't miss much, thought Lawrence. I might as well have a label written on my forehead: "Mad Jewish scientist from down south. Handle with care." On the promenade that had opened up next to the railway track people were strolling in the afternoon sunshine, and a group of children sat on the fence waving at the train as it passed. He followed the route on his map, checking off the stations – Kents Bank, Cark – and watching the expanse of the bay widen. The far side was barely visible, and still no sign of the open sea. He noticed a lighthouse on a steep hill, and the train crossed a canal before stopping at Ulverston. After that the line turned inland to Barrow, where he had to change trains. The station was crowded with men and women on their way home from work, and Lawrence found a space in the corner of the station buffet to get a cup of tea. He wanted coffee but decided against it, glad that he'd remembered to bring his own little coffee jug with him. Good coffee was something he was not prepared to do without, and he was not optimistic about finding it so far north. He'd lived in an isolated area before, and didn't expect much. But the first sight of Morecambe Bay had challenged his assumptions about the landscape; he'd not expected anything so glorious.

Most of the men fell asleep as soon as the next train pulled out, while the women chatted to each other. Lawrence listened to their voices, but couldn't make out what they were saying. If he couldn't understand their accents, what would the Windscale people make of his, he wondered. After fifty years or so there was no trace in his speech of the Russian he'd heard at home as a child, but still it was unmistakably southern. Posh, the old chap had called it. How could it be anything else after all those years in London, and then Cambridge and now Oxford? He'd come back from Canada with a few North American sayings, but they'd mostly faded. What would Rebecca say if went back to Harwell talking like the two women sitting behind him? He looked at his watch, reminding himself to ring her when he got to Seascale.

It had been a long day and an early start, and he dozed for a while, waking when the train rumbled across yet another viaduct. The sun had sunk lower, turning the underside of the clouds pink and orange. Lawrence stared out of the window. In the crowded carriage, he was the only one mesmerised by the unexpected beauty of the open sea on one side and the dark shape of mountains to the east and north. No one had told him that this place was so beautiful.

The train slowed again, and he scrambled to pull down his suitcase from the luggage rack as they stopped at Seascale station.

A driver would meet him there for the short drive to the hostel. He would have liked just to stand for a while, watching the sky as it deepened to rose and purple over the nearby beach, but he was tired and hungry and walked instead to the exit. The suitcase wasn't heavy, but his briefcase was weighed down with papers and files.

'Dr Finer?' said a man in a dark overcoat and peaked cap.

* * *

They turned off the main road into a complex of brightly lit buildings and the car pulled up outside one of them. Lawrence picked up his bags, pushed open the door and rang the bell at the hatch marked 'Reception'. A door opened almost immediately.

'Dr Finer?' said a smartly dressed woman, looking down at a paper in her hand. 'We're expecting you. I'm Mary Tyson, the manager here. Welcome to Greengarth.' She glanced down again. 'From Harwell, isn't it? You've had quite a journey. Just in time for dinner though, so you've timed it well. We'll get your room sorted in a jiffy. Just for one?'

'Yes,' said Lawrence, giving up the idea of any further explanation. 'Just for one.'

'Grand,' said Mary Tyson. 'You won't be short of company here, that's for sure. More scientists than farmers in Seascale these days. A young crowd mainly, plenty going on. Friday night dance right here later on, but they'll be done by midnight. Can be a bit noisy.' Lawrence was relieved to realise that he could understand most of that she was saying. Maybe he would get used to the accent after all.

She led him down a corridor and up a staircase to a room that was fairly sparse but better than he'd anticipated, with hot water in the small hand basin, and a work desk that looked almost new. A single bed, but it felt reasonably comfortable. Like being back at university, he thought. And the noisy dining room felt like that, too. Most of the men and women there had to be at least thirty years younger than him, but the voices and subjects of conversation were reassuringly familiar.

'Been here before?' asked an athletic young man sitting next to him, who had introduced himself as Bill Fletcher.

'No, never,' said Lawrence. 'I did a couple of years at Chalk River, but I've not been here before.'

'That's near Ottawa, isn't it? Water-cooled plant?'

'That's right, Bill,' Lawrence replied. He'd learned the trick of remembering names by repeating them early and often. 'I was there just after the war, in the early days, then back to Harwell. They've seconded me here for a while to work on the energy release from the piles. Not been working as well as it should, apparently.'

'Not my field,' said Bill, 'but the reactor chaps will be glad of some help. Too much work and not enough people to do it, that's the story here, between you and me. They're pushing us really hard, trying to keep up with the Yanks.'

'So I've heard,' said Lawrence. 'I've got the weekend to find my feet and then start properly on Monday.'

'I'm going in tomorrow morning for a while,' said Bill. 'Fancy coming along, just for a look around?'

Lawrence nodded. 'Yes, I'd like that. Thanks.'

Two hours later, after a filling meal and a couple of pints at the bar, Lawrence was very ready to sleep but the Friday night dance was just getting started. He remembered his promise to call Rebecca and found the phone by the front door. Fortunately he could close the door, as young people came and went noisily outside. He dialled the number but no one answered. He tried again, but again there was no response. Where was she, he thought? Had she forgotten that he'd said he would call? He felt very alone, wondering whether to go to the dance after all. But he needed to rest and went back to his room. By the time he'd reached it, loneliness had turned to irritation. The least she could do, surely, was to wait for his call before going out. He found some paper in his briefcase, took the familiar weight of his fountain pen in his hand and sat down at the desk.

My dear,

Train journey was long but it all worked well. The room here will do for a while, but the place is full of people half my age and I suspect it will be pretty noisy. You suggested in the note you left for me that I might need to find somewhere else to live and I think you're right. I'll give it a week or so and then see what else is available. Seascale looks like an over-grown village from I what I could see on the way through. Must have been pretty sleepy before the plant came. The views from the train were quite lovely, surprisingly so. Right on the coast of course, and quite big mountains close by. Fells I think they call them. I saw a notice for the hiking club on the board downstairs, and bridge and all sorts of things to get involved with.

I do hope you can re-consider, dear. The children don't really need us do they, now that they're grown? I know you say Helen will need her mother close by when the new baby arrives, but you could always go back to London for a while when that happens, couldn't you? And David's twenty-two now, so he should be leaving home soon. Of course we wouldn't sell the house, and it wouldn't be more than a year or two here. When the test ban treaty comes in next year, if it does, then things might slow down a bit and I could go back to Harwell. It could be fun, couldn't it, for a little while? Like the early days.

Tired now dear. Let me know a good time for us to talk on the phone one evening.

   Love you,
   Lawrence

He read the letter over. Part of him wanted to go back to those early days in Cambridge when they first met. Everything was new and exciting and they'd been so much in love. But then the children came, and after David was born Rebecca seemed to lose interest in him. She denied it of course, but that's how it felt. When he'd been sent to Ottawa the children were younger and couldn't be left, he understood that. But she'd never once offered to come and visit, and when he came home on leave he felt like a visitor in his own home. And now? Maybe that's just what happens after thirty years together. Passion fades. Now they had separate beds. It was months since they'd made love, that time after Henry's wedding, when they were both a little drunk. She'd complained about being dry and uncomfortable but refused to talk about it and he felt as if he'd forced himself on her. Lying on the narrow bed so far from home, listening to the energy and the music downstairs, he felt like an old man.

* * *

The short visit to the plant with Bill on Saturday morning was instructive, and Lawrence enjoyed a walk on the beach later in the day, but Sunday was drear and cold. He slept late, missed breakfast and lunched early. Playing bridge helped to while away the afternoon, followed by another meal. His weight had stayed the same for many years, but that was likely to change, he thought. More beer in the hostel bar with his fellow bridge players was on offer, but he declined and went to bed early. No point in ringing Rebecca again until he'd heard from her. She was probably away with Helen. By Monday morning interest in the work was having its usual effect, pushing doubts about anything else to one side. But Lawrence's first day at the plant started badly.

'Who are you again?' said a tall man with a moustache and a pipe in his mouth.

'Lawrence Finer. From Harwell. They said you wanted someone to help with the Wigner release process.'

'Who said that?' said the man. 'I'm one of the blokes that manages the piles and we never asked for help.'

'I only know what they told me,' said Lawrence. 'Bruce Immingham sent you a letter about it.'

The tall man was unrelenting. 'Not to me, he didn't.' Lawrence had an almost irresistible urge to turn round, pick up his suitcase from Greengarth and go back to Harwell on the next train.

'Wait here,' said the man, and he was gone, leaving Lawrence standing uncomfortably in the office, watched by a young woman who was trying in vain to close a filing cabinet drawer. She turned towards him. 'Don't worry about Fred,' she said. 'Nothing personal. It just keeps 'appening. People arrive, like you, from Risley or somewhere, but no one seems to know why.'

'I've got a copy of the letter,' said Lawrence, remembering that he'd left it at the hostel.

The office door opened again and another man appeared.

'Tim Fahey,' he said, extending his hand. 'Sorry to have kept you waiting. Looks like you met Fred Bottomley already. Bit of a mix-up. We are expecting you, and very pleased to see you, I have to say. We've been looking for advice about the Wigner release for some time. We'll head down to the reactor building and I'll take you through it.

'Right,' said Lawrence. 'Lead on.' The young woman abandoned the over-full drawer and went back to her desk, giving him a thumbs-up sign as she did so.

'You've been in this business a long time. Nothing I can tell you about the theory of the release process that you don't know already,' said Tim, as they walked across to the reactor building. Lawrence wanted to explain that he'd worked on nuclear energy all his adult life, but decided against it.

'Well, like a lot of other things round here,' Tim went on, 'the release doesn't always work exactly how it should. Sometimes the temperature in the core goes up uniformly, like it's supposed to. Sometimes different areas of the core behave differently, and we don't know why. We've done it eight times now. Mostly it works in the end, but one time the temperature started dropping half way through and we had to start again. That worked eventually, as well, but we still don't really know what was going on. Next release is scheduled for October, and that could be different again.'

'What about the instrumentation?' Lawrence asked.

'Good question,' said Tim. 'We're never as sure about the actual temperature in the core as we would like to be.'

'Why not?'

'Basically thermometers are in the wrong places. Never really designed for the job. Like the chimneys, outside. Filters should have been built in, but by the time they realised that, the stacks were half built so they had to fit those big filters on the top at the end. And the fuel cartridges to hold the uranium in the reactor, that was another cock-up. You know we had to trim the aluminium, to thin them down?'

'That was a few years back, wasn't it?'

'Yes, 1950.'

'I'm afraid it was my team at Harwell that suggested it, but we thought you'd send the job back to Lancashire where the fins were made. Never thought you'd have to do the job yourselves.'

'No time to send them all back to Springfield. Gaffer worked out what we 'ad to do and how long it would take and we just did

54

it, working down there at the charge hoist right by the reactor. Took us three bloody weeks. A million strips we cut off those fins. Nearly bloody killed us.'

'Who's the gaffer?'

'Tom Tuohy, Deputy Works Manager. He gets things done, I'll say that for 'im. Doesn't just issue orders like some I've worked for. Gets in there 'imself. You'll see 'im around. Can't miss 'im.'

'And what about the tritrium yield, what happens there?'

'Your job to ask hard questions, I suppose. Well, there's no good answer to that one either.'

Tim's explanation of the various problems in the reactor was detailed and technical, but during the day, through this and several other conversations, Lawrence gathered that the response to most problems at Windscale was short-term and pragmatic. When people like him, the physicists, identified a potential problem, possible solutions were passed down the line, ending up with the people like Tim at the sharp end who did what they thought was needed, as fast as possible. They had no practical experience to draw on, because there was none. Windscale was a first, and ever since it was built most nuclear specialists like Lawrence regarded it as almost obsolete. There was more effort going into designing the next generation of reactors than there was in making the current ones work properly. Like many of his thoughts that day, Lawrence kept this one to himself. He was trying not to talk as much as he normally did, unaware that his quietness would inevitably be perceived as typical offcomer disdain.

At lunchtime Tim took Lawrence across to the canteen, which involved changing back into their own clothes.

'Tekking the boffin 'ere over for lunch,' Tim had said to the young woman in the office. Lawrence still didn't know her name and no one had bothered to introduce him. Boffin, he thought. God knows what they call me behind my back.

At the far end of the canteen there was small group sitting apart, listening to someone who appeared to be making a speech.

'What's going on over there?' Lawrence asked. He couldn't hear what was being said. There was smattering of laughter and applause.

'Looks like somebody's leaving do,' Tim replied, looking across. 'Aye, that's Miss Whelan, standing up now. She's worked 'ere ten years, since the beginning, in one of the bosses' offices. She must know a thing or two. Came into some money, they say, and decided to pack it in.'

'Lucky for some,' said Lawrence.

Chapter 7

REBECCA WROTE BACK THE FOLLOWING WEEK. Lawrence read the letter while he ate his breakfast in the canteen one morning, and then folded it up and put it in his jacket pocket. As he suspected, she was spending most of her time at Helen's house in London, probably outstaying her welcome but no one would ever dare suggest that. If he wanted to talk to her on the phone, best to call her there, she said. Not a word about coming up to see him, and certainly no hint that she might be prepared to stay with him before his secondment was finished. He wondered if there was any chance of cutting it short and going back to Harwell and home, but he had to stay until the next controlled release of stored energy in the reactor, the Wigner release as they called it, and that wasn't due until October. He needed to find somewhere else to live, away from the crowded noisy hostel, but couldn't look for a place until he knew whether Rebecca would join him there. Now it was clear he would be on his own.

A few days later, on his way out to work, Lawrence glanced at the notice board near the front door and one of the items caught his eye: *Rooms to let, Drigg Road, Seascale. Newly renovated, own facilities. Reasonable rent. Apply J. Whelan.* There was a local phone number and address. He would find the place and have a look before he did anything else. Didn't want to move more than once. And who was J. Whelan? Someone at work might know. He'd known a few landlords in his time, and some of them he would not want to meet again.

Someone at work did know. 'J. Whelan,' said Tim Fahey, when Lawrence told him about the rooms to let. 'That'll be Jessie Whelan. Remember that first day in the canteen, there was someone having a leaving do? That was her. She worked for Gordon Meadow for years. Then she came into money. Must have bought a place and now she's renting rooms. Tidy income, that, with housing in such demand round here. She could be a problem though.'

'What sort of a problem?'

'Well she's not an easy woman. Used to be a schoolteacher, clever, always has something to say, likes her own way. Bossed Gordon around apparently, but he let her.' Tim leaned towards Lawrence, conspiratorially. 'Lazy bugger, that Meadow, between you and me. She did the work and 'e took the money. No wonder she left when she could.'

'Nothing wrong with her leaving, is there?' said Lawrence.

'Nay, not in itself. But since she left, she's been talking about a lot of stuff she couldn't say when she were 'ere. Safety, all that. She says we're too busy keeping up with the Yanks, that's it's all about bombs, not the power station, that kind of stuff.'

'Standing on a soapbox somewhere, you mean?' asked Lawrence, trying to picture the grey-haired woman he'd glimpsed in the canteen becoming a wild-eyed radical.

'Nay, no need for that round 'ere,' said Tim. 'She just talks, you know, at the shops, or the library or wherever. Word gets around. Folk don't like it. Feels like letting the side down.'

'Are you saying I shouldn't stay there?'

'Up to you, Lawrence,' said Tim. 'You might get a lecture or two, and you'd 'ave to keep real quiet about what we're doing, all the checks we're doing on the Wigner process, stuff about the fuel rods and how many of them get damaged. I'm not happy about some of that, and nor are you, but we can't 'ave that getting around outside the plant. Too much being stirred up already. That Canon Collins feller, the anti-nuclear chap in London, he needs to keep his mouth shut.'

'So what should I do about the rooms?'

'You do as you please. It's a free country, but tek care, that's all I'm saying. And don't tell 'er anything.'

What the hell, thought Lawrence, as another noisy Friday dance kept him awake. I'll have a look at the rooms, and the fire-eating landlady. It's only for a while, and I can keep *shtum* about the work. Just a place to sleep. I could probably get meals here at the hostel if I wanted to.

* * *

The following Monday, after another frustrating meeting with Fred Bottomley, Lawrence walked round to look at the rooms he'd seen advertised. He found the house easily enough, standing tall above the shore. On the horizon, the Isle of Man was clearly visible. What a view, he thought, and if the rooms for rent are upstairs it must be even better. He rang the doorbell and waited.

'Coming,' cried a voice, and a few moments later the front door opened.

'Miss Whelan?' he asked.

'That's me.'

'I hope you don't mind me calling unannounced.' He put out his hand, which she grasped firmly. 'My name's Lawrence Finer. I saw a notice on the board at the hostel, about rooms to let.'

'Oh, that,' she said. She glanced at the watch on her wrist. 'I'm expecting company, but it won't take long to show you the rooms, will it? Come in, please. Straight through. The rooms are at the top of the house.'

Jessie led the way up two flights of stairs, to a door at the top, which she unlocked.

'I had this door put in,' she said, 'for privacy, you know, and fixed some other things to make it more of a separate space. Not easy to find men to do those jobs with all the work on offer at the plant, but I called in a few favours. There's room for two people, one bedroom at the front and one at the back. Washbasins in each room, hot water of course, and the front room has a hot plate and a little sink.'

'Oh,' said Lawrence. 'I'll probably be here on my own. Most of the time at least.'

'Well you could take both rooms if you wanted,' she said. 'Up to you.'

'Actually, my wife may be coming up from Oxford, we're not sure yet. Having both rooms would be useful.'

'I have a double bed that would fit in here if you needed it,' said Jessie.

Lawrence went into the front room and walked across to the window. He blinked against the glare. 'What a view,' he said. 'I had no idea it would be like this up here. It's a revelation.'

'Bit too bright in the afternoon sometimes,' she said, 'but you can always close the curtains if you have to. And anyway, you'll be at work won't you? Are you at the plant?'

'Isn't everyone round here?'

She smiled. 'Feels like that. I was there myself until recently.'

'Is that right?' said Lawrence, not wanting to reveal that he knew anything about her.

'Office work,' she said, 'Pretty lowly stuff. You?'

'On the physics side,' he said, non-committally. 'Just here for a while, from down south. A project, won't last long, that's why I want somewhere to rent.'

'How long?'

'Not sure. To the end of the year, at least, I should think.'

'That would work,' she said. 'This is my first foray into land-ladying. Not sure how I'll feel about having someone else in the house. Gives me a chance to test it out, so to speak. Nothing personal, you understand.'

'Of course,' said Lawrence. So, I'm on probation, he thought. Nice.

'I would definitely want both rooms,' he said. 'I'd use the back one for work if I needed to.'

'Would you like a desk in there?'

'That would be splendid, thank you, if it's not too much trouble.'

'No trouble at all. More furniture than I know what to do with actually.'

Lawrence could see why Gordon Meadow had found this woman useful, and why he might be frightened of her too. Quick, confident, no nonsense. Tim's assessment was pretty accurate so far. She'd been a good-looking woman once, he thought. Pity she'd let herself go.

He followed her back down the stairs to the big kitchen on the ground floor where she obviously spent most of her time. They agreed on the rent, and Lawrence said he would think about it and get back to her later in the week.

'Before next weekend, please,' said Jessie. 'Other people have asked about the rooms.' That was a lie, but a useful one. She'd always known how to lie when necessary. She edged round him to open the front door. A man standing right outside with his hand raised to ring the bell stepped back in surprise.

'There you are,' she said. 'Perfect timing. Mr Finer is just leaving.'

Lawrence and the man nodded at each other.

'I'll be in touch about the rooms,' Lawrence said to Jessie. As he walked up the hill to explore the village he was trying to think where he'd seen the man before.

* * *

'You must be Mick,' said Jessie, beckoning to the man on her doorstep. 'Pat O'Toole wrote to me about you.'

'Mick Porter,' he said. 'I've seen you around the plant, but you probably wouldn't remember me, just one of the workers.'

'Now, now, Mr Porter,' she said, ushering him into the kitchen. 'We don't do the workers and management thing here, not on a Saturday afternoon. I chose this house because I couldn't see the chimneys from here. Out of sight, out of mind.'

'But that's the point, Jessie. May I call you Jessie? And you call me Mick, please.'

'Call me anything you like Mick, apart from "comrade".' She smiled at his intensity, the way his pale hair flopped over his eyes, and the deep furrows where he wrinkled his forehead.

'Well, that's my point, Jessie. The plant can't be out of mind, can it? If anything happened there, this whole village could be wiped out.'

'Ah,' said Jessie. 'Pat said you're very worried about safety. I'm more bothered about the bombs. Twelve years since Hiroshima but I still dream about those poor children, vaporised, nothing left but a shadow on the floor.'

'I've got two kids of my own,' said Mick, 'and I worry about them. We each have our own reason for taking a stand, Jessie. I could leave the plant, I suppose, and move away, but it's more important that I stay. We need information about what's really going on. When the time comes, I'll leave, like you did, but for the time being –'

'You think I left because of the bombs? Well that was part of it

I suppose, but I'm a realist. I needed the money, so I stayed until I could afford to do without it.'

She sat down at the table and invited her earnest visitor to do the same. 'Now, let's talk about what you came for. Pat said you would have some information for me, about a meeting in Newcastle?'

'Next month, yes. It's a meeting of all the anti-nuclear groups in the north, the real north, not the Manchester folk. It'll be us from Cumberland, the north-east, maybe even a few from north of the border. We have to make a lot of noise about the nuclear test ban treaty, and about Macmillan and the Yanks. No good thinking local any more, that's not going to be enough.'

'And how can I help?' said Jessie. 'Do you want tea, by the way? I was just going to make some before that other visitor came.'

Mick looked at her again, questioning. 'Do you know who that man is?'

'Lawrence Finer, he said. Works at the plant, on some kind of project. He's been at the hostel, poor chap. Looks about thirty years too old to fit in there.' She put the teapot on the table between them and sat down opposite him. 'Why? What about him?'

'Well, it's Dr Finer, not Mr Finer, for a start, and he's from Harwell. Some kind of research egghead. Fred Bottomley told me about him. Just turned up saying that he'd come to help with the reactor, where Fred works. Fred wasn't happy about it.'

'Not the first time that's happened. And Fred Bottomley was always a grump. What's the word, "curmudgeonly"? That's a great word, don't you think?'

Mick looked unimpressed. 'So what was he doing here?'

Jessie stared at him. 'That might be none of your business, Mick, to be honest. I know we have a cause in common, but it has no bearing on who comes to my house.'

Mick Porter leaned forward in his chair. The furrow on his forehead deepened. 'I'm sorry, er, Jessie, but it might have. There's a few of us at the plant thinking of forming our own group, like, to help with the campaign that's going to start with that meeting in Newcastle. We need somewhere to get together. Can't be the pub or the club, and we don't want our kids or even the missus listening in. Wouldn't be fair, if anything happened.'

'Like what?' Jessie asked.

'Well, the police might be interested, or the bosses here. National security stuff. They're all paranoid about spies.'

'So we have to be paranoid too?'

'Well, yes, I think we do.'

Jessie sighed. 'I think I'm too old for that, Mick. Macmillan may be a despicable old man but this was still a relatively free country the last time I checked. They can't stop people meeting to talk to each other.'

'I came to ask you if we could meet here, in this house, but how could we, if that man moves in here? He could overhear, turn us in. He might have been sent here deliberately…'

Jessie held up her hand. 'No more, please. Let's keep our feet on the ground. Dr Finer, if that's what we have to call him, is looking for a place to sleep. He's not moving in *with* me, if you can see the difference. This is still my house. There's a door to the flat on the top floor and I've no doubt he or anyone else up there will keep it shut. Who visits me in the rest of the house is my business. I would be quite willing for you and a few others to meet here from time to time, if that would help. Pat O'Toole and I have discussed this before and I'm happy to make a contribution to the cause, so to speak, and to learn more, too. There's clearly more going on than I was aware of.'

Mick hesitated. 'I can't tell you how to live your life, Jessie,' he said, 'but I have to say I'd be unhappy about that man living here, and so would the other blokes in our group. I'm surprised you'd even consider it.'

Jessie put down her cup carefully on the saucer and looked at the young man. 'I think I need to make something very clear. I've not let anyone boss me around in the nearly sixty years I've been on this earth, and I don't intend to start now. This is my house, the first house I've ever owned, and I decide who steps through that front door.' Her voice was quiet. She was looking at Mick intently. 'I have known Pat O'Toole for many years and have the highest respect for him. He would never try to tell me how to live my life, and you should learn from that, Mick, if you and I are going to continue this conversation. Is that clear enough for you?' Mick said nothing, looking down at the pattern on the plastic table-cloth. 'If it is, let's talk a bit more about the other people in your group, this meeting in Newcastle, and how I can help. Otherwise, I'll ask you to leave, right now.'

Mick didn't leave until he and Jessie had agreed a date and time for the group to meet at her house. He was no match for her, and they both knew it. As for the other one, she thought to herself, I probably won't see much of him, and that's fine with me. The money will be good, for both rooms, and he wouldn't be staying long. Just as well, as she didn't much like what she'd seen. Scientist, southerner, married, and his head's too big. And those glasses! He must be trying to look like Einstein. Science had a lot to answer for, she decided.

CHAPTER 8

IT WAS THE LAST WEEK IN MAY, less than a month before the longest day, and Jessie noticed that Lawrence was closing his front bedroom curtains to let less light into the room. When he'd first moved in a few weeks before, he hardly ever closed the curtains. He said he couldn't bear to hide the view and there wasn't much chance of being overlooked up there. No mention or sign of the wife coming to stay, Jessie noticed. Maybe other people lied just as she did, for convenience and to keep unwelcome questions at bay. Nothing to do with me anyway, she thought. Thank heaven for a lodger who seemed utterly self-sufficient and demanded nothing from her. If Mick had been right and Lawrence was a spy, he was a most incurious one.

John's car arrived at the house at exactly the time he'd said. Punctual as ever. Jessie heard the car doors slam outside and glanced quickly round. She'd done her best to tidy up and made up a bed in the room next to hers for Judith, who was staying for two nights. She'd even mopped the floor, cleaned the bath and wiped the window sills, in anticipation of Violet's search for evidence of domestic laxity. Maybe if I'd grown up with coal dust in every pore I'd worry more about it, she thought. And to confirm the good impression, she'd had her hair cut, the annual shearing Agnes used to call it, and bought a new blouse in Carlisle when she'd been there for another meeting of the Cumberland anti-nuclear group. That was something she wouldn't be mentioning today. John was embarrassed by rumours of his mother's interest in such things, apparently, and there was enough tension between them without adding to it.

She'd left the front door open to the warm sea air, and Judith came running in, catching Jessie as she tweaked her new hairstyle in the mirror in the kitchen.

'Let me see,' said Judith, standing beside her to look in the mirror. 'Look, I'm as tall as you now. And your hair is lovely, Jessie. Who did it for you?'

'Just the same place I always go to,' said Jessie, giving her granddaughter a hug and a kiss on her freckled cheek. Judith had her mother's colouring, reddish hair with pale skin and green eyes. She was growing into a very lovely young woman.

'Here we are,' said Maggie, tapping the open front door as she entered. 'We've got a few things for a picnic. John and the boys will bring them in. Violet's waiting to be invited, by the way, Jessie. First time in your new house, and she said she couldn't just walk in. I've brought a cake – where would you like me to put it?'

'I'll show you, Mam,' said Judith.

'Mum, not Mam, pet,' said Maggie, 'or Mummy or even Mother.'

Jessie didn't hear Judith's response as she hurried out of the house. Violet was standing by the car, both hands gripping her handbag. She was wearing a hat that Jessie recognised as the one she'd bought last year, when the Queen came to open Calder Hall power station.

'Violet,' said Jessie. 'Welcome. How lovely to see you here, and in your best hat! Come in and I'll give you a proper tour. It's a bit different from the other houses I've lived in while I've known you.'

'Very pleased to see the place at last, Jessie,' said Violet, taking her arm. The two women, Judith's two grandmothers, were always scrupulously polite to each other, in public at least.

'After you, dear,' said Jessie. She turned back towards the car. 'Are you coming in John?'

'In a minute,' he called. 'Just listening to the cricket.' The two boys waved at Jessie from the back seat.

'Cricket already?' she said to Violet.

'If it's not that, it's rugby, or football. I tek no notice,' said Violet.

'Let me take your hat, dear. Would you like a drink, or shall we do the tour?'

'Tour first, then a nice cuppa. And I'll keep the hat on, if you don't mind.'

'Right-ho, we'll go right to the top and work our way down to the kitchen,' said Jessie. 'I asked my lodger if it would be alright for me to show you around. He's gone to the club for a while.'

Jessie unlocked the door at the top of the stairs.

'Not as young as I was,' said Violet, standing behind her and breathing quite heavily. 'Time was I'd have climbed them stairs and not even noticed. Our Tom couldn't manage them at all, poor man.'

'How is he?' Jessie asked. 'I've not seen him or Frank for too long.'

'They don't get out much, neither on 'em,' said Violet. 'Company for each other, though. Now, let me look. John told me what a lot of work you'd done up 'ere.'

She stood and looked right round the room, checking the

carpet, the curtains, the tidy bed, books and papers piled neatly on the table. Then both women edged across the room to the window. The view was never the same, and always special. Only when the sea fret blew in was there nothing to look at. Today the wind was hardly more than a breeze from the east, and the high tide below them was unusually flat, like a pond rather than the ocean. The swell rose and fell slightly, and they could hear the shirring of water on pebbles through the open window.

'Listen,' said Jessie. 'Can you hear the sea?'

Any chance of doing so was lost when Frank clattered up the stairs and into the room.

'Who lives here, Granny?' said the boy, looking round the room. Violet couldn't resist straightening the blue counterpane on the bed.

'Keeps it nice,' she said, 'for a man.'

'My lodger lives here,' Jessie said to Frank, before turning again to Violet. 'He's quite domesticated. I've never met his wife but she's trained him well. In fact I hardly see him. He's at the plant all day, and Saturdays too sometimes. Has most of his evening meals at the hostel or the club.'

'He has lots of books,' said Frank, picking one off the pile on the bedside table.

'No, Frank,' said Jessie sharply. 'Put that back, please. This is Dr Finer's room, and we mustn't touch anything.'

'Dr Finer, is it?' said Violet. 'A proper doctor?'

'No, more's the pity. He's a doctor of physics, I think. Very clever man. Looks like it too.'

'Finer. That's a funny name. Is he Jewish?'

'I think so, yes. I really don't know much about him. We keep ourselves to ourselves.'

'Best way,' said Violet.

They peeped into the back room where Lawrence kept the

things he didn't use much. The suitcase was there, ready for the trip back to Oxford, which he'd said he intended to make but never did.

'Good view from up here too,' said Jessie, 'if you try not to notice the towers and chimneys.'

'Our John's started going climbing again,' said Violet, 'up in those hills we can see, probably.'

'Can I go to the toilet, Granny?' asked Frank.

'Of course, dear,' said Jessie. 'But downstairs, in my bathroom not up here. I've told you, this is Dr Finer's place, not ours.'

The tour of the house continued slowly, as Violet examined every curtain and cushion. She ran her finger surreptitiously along the mantelpiece in the living room, and Jessie was glad she'd spent an hour or so making sure everywhere was clean. In the kitchen, John was sitting with young Vincent, just seven and devoted to his father, on his knee. Jessie bent to give the boy a kiss, and patted her son on the back.

'Thanks for bringing everyone over, dear,' she said. 'I think Violet's given the house her seal of approval.'

'Very nice, Jessie,' said Violet. 'The view's almost as good as ours at West Row, but we see more of the Scottish coast, on a good day at least. And the man upstairs seems like a good lodger. Neat and tidy. No dirty clothes all over the place.'

'I've never asked about his washing,' said Jessie. 'Not sure what I'd say if he asked me to do it for him.'

They sat at the crowded kitchen table to have a drink, saving the cake for later. The main event of the day was to be a picnic further down the beach at Drigg, where the old armaments factory used to be. The dunes there made a great spot for 'setting up camp' as the children called it, which meant the adults sat and talked while the young ones ran in and out of the sea on a good day, or built castles in the sand. Jessie filled a couple of thermos flasks, and they set off, everybody carrying something, even little Vincent striding out with his towel and swimming trunks rolled up in his arms.

It was the most pleasurable afternoon with the family that Jessie could remember. Maggie was in a good mood, John was clearly enjoying time with his boys and even Judith let herself play like the child she still was, despite her protestations about being grown-up. All contentious issues, Judith's schooling, Jessie's views on the nuclear issue, Violet's devotion to Father Price, were carefully avoided and the sun warmed them benevolently as they sat in the soft sand, watching the children play. As the tide approached towards the end of the afternoon, Jessie and John joined the children in their sand boat, built with its prow facing the oncoming waves. Together the five of them vainly mended crumbling walls, screaming with delight as the water finally broke through and swamped them, sending them splashing towards the shore and the last of the sandwiches. At last they all headed slowly back along what remained of the beach.

'We'll get the boys home,' said John, after sandy legs had been sluiced in the bath and sandy clothes and towels gathered into various bags.

'And I'm staying here!' cried Judith, 'Just me and Granny for two whole days.'

'Behave yourself, pet,' said Violet. 'I'll sleep in your bed in St Bees while you're here. Me and your mam can have a reet good chat, and your granda and Tom will just have to manage without us.'

'Thanks, Jessie,' said John, giving his mother a peck on the cheek. Maggie did the same. I am honoured, thought Jessie. Maybe this would be the way from now on, which would be a great relief after the tensions of the past. It was what she'd always hoped for, quiet acceptance of each other.

71

When Lawrence arrived back from the club well after ten o'clock, it was still light and Jessie and Judith were sitting together playing cards. Judith was relishing her grandmother's company and being treated as a grown-up, as she put it. Instead of going straight up to his room as he normally did, Lawrence knocked on the kitchen door and pushed it open. The smell of beer and cigarettes entered the room with him.

'I heard voices,' he said, smiling at Judith.

Drunk, Jessie observed. The great scientist has drunk too much, would you believe it?

'Had a good evening, Lawrence? This is my granddaughter Judith. Judith say hello to Dr Finer.'

'Hello,' said Judith, holding out her hand, which Lawrence took in both of his and gripped warmly.

'Delighted to meet you, Judith,' he said, 'but you're far too grown-up to be Jessie's granddaughter, and she looks far too young to be, well, you know.'

'We get the picture, thank you,' said Jessie. He'd certainly had a beer too many, and he looked quite different too. Younger, less earnest.

'By the way, Jessie,' he said, still smiling. 'I'll be going back to Oxford next weekend. Just for a few days. I'm a grandfather too, you know. They're coming to visit…' His voice tailed away. 'So, anyway, good night to you both.'

They heard him clumping unsteadily up the stairs.

'He's drunk,' said Judith, wrinkling her nose. 'And he smells of cigarettes. Does he have to live here? I don't like him.'

'You don't know him, dear,' said Jessie, 'and neither do I really. He's very clever I'm sure. Something to do with the reactors at the plant. And he doesn't smoke, so that must just be the smell from everyone else smoking, at the club.'

She picked up the cards from the table. 'Time for us to go to bed, too. It's late. Don't tell your mother I kept you up playing cards. We'll see what the weather's like tomorrow and then we'll decide what to do.'

'Will that man be here?'

'I don't know, but he's very quiet, and he often goes out to the golf club on Sundays. Says it's much easier to get a game here than where he lives, near Oxford.'

'I'm glad he's going out,' said Judith. 'That means I can have you all to myself.'

Jessie was pleased about that too. One of the great regrets about losing John as a baby had been missing his teenage years. In school she'd always enjoyed her pupils in their final years before they left. She loved the mixture of hope and confusion, and the fun you could still have. With Judith the pleasure of her company was unalloyed by anxiety or responsibility. The times they had together were few and treasured, with all the hard decisions left to the parents. One of those was about sending Judith away to school. Maggie had always wanted for Judith all the advantages that she herself had been denied. Nothing wrong with that, Jessie conceded, so long as Judith was happy about it. But Judith wasn't happy about it. It could not be mentioned, along with sundry other sensitive topics.

Judith's question to Jessie the following day raised another problem.

'I know you're my dad's mam, but John isn't my real dad is he?'

'Of course he is, dear,' said Jessie. She'd wondered how long it would be before Judith asked about this. 'What's made you ask about it now after all this time.'

'A girl at school said that John's not my real dad. My real dad was called Isaac and he was killed in the war. And I was called Judith Lowery, before John, when I was little. But no one will talk to me about it. They still think I'm a child, but I'm not.'

'You growing into a fine young woman Judith,' said Jessie. 'We're all very proud of you.'

'So why won't they talk to me properly? I want to know how John met my mam. And there's another thing. If you're John's mam, who's his dad? What happened to your husband?'

Jessie's heart sank. After all her hopes of leaving the past alone, it was going to be stirred up again by adolescent curiosity. This time she really didn't want to lie, not again, not to Judith.

'I never had a husband,' she said, sitting down at the table. Sunlight slanted into the room. 'John's father was called Clive, Clive Whelan. He died before we could be married, before John was born. I couldn't bring up a baby on my own, and my mother wouldn't help me, so I gave him away.' She looked up. Judith was staring at her.

'You gave him away?'

'Yes. He was four days old.'

'Who to?'

'People who lived in Barrow. They wanted a child and they couldn't have one of their own, so they raised John as their son. They were called Mr and Mrs Pharaoh.'

'So what happened?'

'When John grew up, older than you are now, he found out that his parents weren't his real parents, and he then he found me.'

'How?' said Judith.

'Well, there were one or two things he knew, and he just tracked me down.'

'Wow!' said Judith.

Jessie smiled. 'Yes indeed, wow. John is a fine man. I'm as proud of him as I am of you. His father, Clive, was a fine man, too.'

'Do you miss him?' said Judith.

'To start with I did, terribly. But it was a long time ago. That feeling faded.'

'And did you miss your baby, when you gave him away?'

Jessie hung her head. There was nothing she could say. But Judith continued. 'Why won't they talk to me about it?'

Jessie shook her head. 'Maybe they will, when they're ready. Maybe they don't like the idea of John being given away, never knowing his real father.'

'But that wasn't his fault,' said Judith.

'Of course not,' said Jessie. 'But people still worry about things like that.'

'So can I still call you Jessie?'

Jessie looked at Judith and smiled. 'When you're here with me, just the two of us, you call me Jessie if you want to. But not when there's anyone else there. It's our secret. I don't think your mother would like it, nor John. They think that calling me Granny is more polite, more respectful.'

'But you don't mind, do you?'

'No, I don't. Come and give me a hug.'

The two of them held each other for a long time. Jessie would miss the child more than she could say.

They were standing in this way when Lawrence walked into the house. He was carrying a bag and let it slip noisily onto the floor.

'I'm sorry,' he said. 'I didn't realise.'

Jessie eased herself out of Judith's arms, wiping her eyes with her sleeve as she did so. 'Judith and I were having a little talk,' she said. 'She'll be going away to school soon, won't you, Judith, and we won't be able to see as much of each other.'

'I'm sorry,' he said again, picking up the bag and climbing the stairs.

'Oh dear,' said Jessie, closing the kitchen door. 'That's the trouble with having someone else in the house. You never know when they're going to walk in.'

'I don't like him, not at all,' said Judith. 'I hope he doesn't stay here much longer.'

Before John returned to pick up Judith the following morning, Jessie reminded her not to talk at home about what had been said, any of it. Lies had been always been so necessary, and now the truth felt like a threat.

CHAPTER 9

IT WAS A MONDAY MORNING, EARLY IN JULY. Jessie had seen the rain coming when she opened the curtains. It hung like a grey veil over the sea, moving closer as she watched, and now the gutters were full to overflowing. She was sweeping the floor in Lawrence's bedroom. He'd packed a suitcase and left quite suddenly on the Saturday morning, saying he'd be away for a week, but he would pay her the rent regardless, so not to worry. No problem, she thought, and quite convenient too as Pat O'Toole was coming for one of his regular visits on Wednesday. She had shaken out the two rugs as best she could during a short break in the downpour and now had most of the moveable furniture piled on the bed so she could get into all the corners with the mop. At least she didn't have to carry the bucket full of water up the narrow stairs. Lawrence's gramophone, an impressive item that he'd bought in Canada, was too heavy to move, and Jessie took advantage of his absence to try it out. She told herself it was an acceptable interference with his things as she was in the room for an acceptable purpose, not mere curiosity.

She looked through his records to find something to accompany her housekeeping duties. Beethoven, Shostakovich, some American blues singer she'd never heard of. And what was this, *Salad Days*? She was surprised that he should have bought something so light and inconsequential. It must have been a gift. She loved the songs, and sang along with them as she worked, masking the sound of the telephone ringing in the hall. By the time she'd lifted the needle from the record and rushed downstairs the phone had stopped, but it began to ring again almost immediately and she picked it up.

'Seascale 249.'

'Jessie?' She'd expected Pat's voice, but it was not.

'Lawrence?' she said. 'Is that you? I thought you were in Oxford.'

'I was,' he said. 'I'm in London, at my daughter's house. I thought you might want to know that I'm coming back earlier than I expected. I should be there on Tuesday, late afternoon all being well.'

'Is everything alright?'

There was a short pause. 'Yes, yes.I just decided, well, for various reasons really, that I needed to come back. Is that OK with you? I'll try not to get in your way. It'll be a chance to catch up with a few things, maybe a round of golf...' He said something she couldn't catch.

'What was that? I didn't quite hear...'

'Nothing important... So I'll be back Tuesday. I'll have a meal at the hotel if I'm not too late.'

'Don't worry about that.If it's late you can eat here.'

'Well, goodbye then.'

She put down the phone. The man was a mystery. He sounded anxious, but maybe he disliked the phone as much as she did. 'Other people's lives,' she said to herself as she climbed the stairs back to the top floor to finish the job. She couldn't work him out, and he seemed unwilling to talk. But as long as he paid his rent and kept to himself, that was really all she wanted. She just hoped he would be out somewhere when Pat came to visit.

Back in Lawrence's room, Jessie lingered longer than was necessary. There was a photograph propped up behind the small mirror on the chest of drawers. She picked it up. It was Lawrence with a young child in a park somewhere. He was smiling, his hand on the child's shoulder. A dark jacket hung easily from shoulders that were square and straight. His intelligent, confident gaze held her attention and flickered round her mind. She replaced the photograph carefully and left the room, closing the door firmly behind her.

It was late, past nine o'clock, and the light was fading to grey twilight on Tuesday evening when Lawrence arrived back. Jessie heard his key in the front door and went to meet him. In the light from the kitchen door he looked pale and very tired. He put down his suitcase and stood up, stretching his back.

'Too many hours sitting down,' he said. 'We were running late from Lancaster, not sure why, and missed the connection in Barrow. Had to wait there for almost two hours.'

'Well, you're back now,' she said. 'It's too late to eat at the hotel. I've some lamb stew from earlier and I can do more potatoes while you take your bag upstairs and have a wash or whatever you need. And there's a bottle of beer in the pantry if you want it.'

He smiled. 'That's very kind,' he said. 'I don't have to work tomorrow, so the beer sounds as good as the food. Thank you.'

Jessie laid a place for him at the kitchen table and sat with him as he ate the stew and mashed potatoes with obvious relish. When his plate was clean he lifted the glass of beer in a grave salute. 'I can safely say, Miss Whelan, that was the best lamb stew I've eaten in a very long time.'

'Local meat,' she said, 'and a good butcher. Now there's a wee bit of rice pudding if you want it? Otherwise I'll finish it myself.'

'We'll share it,' he said, and they did. She cleared the dishes from the table.

'So, what brought you back so early?'

The question seemed to catch him off guard, and she turned to look at him when he didn't answer. 'Ah,' he said. 'Well it turned out Rebecca was only expecting me to stay for a little while. She'd arranged, or, well, she decided to go and visit our daughter Helen in London, to help with the baby, so I went with her, but there wasn't really room for us all, and they had things to do, so, well, I just thought I could come back here and get out of their way.'

Jessie didn't know what to say. The poor man had spent seven hours on a train to see his wife and must have expected to stay a little longer. He seemed uncomfortable even talking about it.

'The new baby's due, you see,' he went on, 'and they had such a lot to do, painting the nursery and so on. I wanted to help, but "too many cooks", as they say. And getting the train back from London was easier than coming from Oxford, so … well, here I am.'

'I was busy too,' she said. 'I took the chance to clean your room properly. You keep it very tidy, I must say.' She hesitated. 'And I hope you don't mind, I had a look at your record collection. *Salad Days* was a surprise. I didn't think that was your style.'

'Too frivolous for the serious scientist?'

'Well, yes.'

'We all have our secrets,' he said.

Jessie leaned against the sink and looked at him. 'You look tired,' she said. 'Anything I can help with?'

'No,' he said without looking up. 'I'm feeling a bit lost, rootless, somehow. It happens sometimes, doesn't it? For me anyway.'

'I know you don't want to talk about your work,' she said.

'Work's part of it, but … being away from the family, that's part of it too. They move on, you know, when you're not there. You miss out on things. It was the same when I was in Canada.'

'How long were you there?' she asked.

'Two years, almost. I was in Chalk River, it's near Ottawa. Canada's first nuclear plant. Very exciting for me, but the family couldn't come over. The children were at school, you know, and Rebecca needed to stay with them...' He hesitated. 'Actually, they could all have come. Other people had their families with them, but Rebecca wouldn't hear of it.'

He paused again, and she waited, seeing that he had more to say. He went on, still looking down. 'I wanted her to come with me up here, but she was just the same. She thinks civilised life stops somewhere around Birmingham. I've tried to persuade her, that's what I went back for this time, but, well, I think her mind's made up.' He took off his round glasses and looked up at her. His eyes looked different, smaller, and sad.

'Couldn't you go back home? Do you have to stay?' asked Jessie. She could see how upset he was.

'Until October, certainly.'

'Why October?'

He paused, wiping his glasses and putting them back on. 'Just something I have to do, at the plant. I'm not supposed to talk about it.'

'No, of course,' said Jessie. She wondered whether he'd been warned not to tell her anything. She thought about what Mick had said, and that reminded her about Pat's visit.

'I have someone coming to see me tomorrow,' she said, 'an old friend. He was a great help to me when I was unhappy for a while. You'd like him. He used to be a priest.'

'So long as he wasn't a rabbi,' said Lawrence, smiling. 'Had enough of rabbis over the years.'

* * *

On the train from Maryport early the next morning, Pat O'Toole was looking forward to having the whole day with Jessie. Mrs

81

Foster had washed and pressed his old corduroy trousers, the ones that went well with the tweed jacket. The black uniform of a priest had been so easy, but he enjoyed thinking about clothes and how he looked, even though he could never spend much. In his jacket pocket was a list of things that he and Jessie would need to discuss, but just being with her was what raised his spirits. Ever since he'd first met her all those years ago, he'd loved… what? What was it about her? Her openness, mainly, the way she seemed to know what she wanted and went after it with energy and courage. She must be nearly sixty now, he reckoned, but age seemed to have enlivened her rather than slowed her down, at least since that dreadful time after Piotr's death and the trouble with her son. She was lucky with her health, but perhaps that wasn't luck. As a priest he'd seen many sick people, and sometimes it was hard to tell whether sickness of the soul had been the product of bodily illness, or its cause.

Pat had heard from his young friend Mick Porter that Jessie had taken a lodger, someone who worked at the plant. Mick's note had made the man sound rather sinister, but he did tend to exaggerate. That was another thing Pat admired about Jessie. She had a very rational mind; she never lost her bearings. He'd never heard her speak in public, but if she was as articulate in front of an audience as she was in private she could be a huge asset to the cause. And the cause, as he liked to call it, was growing. There were rumours of a national anti-nuclear coalition being established fairly soon, probably based in London like everything else. They needed to discuss that too.

There she was, at the station to meet him, as she promised. This would be his first time at her new house, and even though he knew roughly where it was, she wanted to escort him in person, and he was happy to let her do so. The morning was warm, and she was wearing a dress he'd not seen before, blue flowers on a white background, with a full skirt. She looked lovely. He kissed her cheek, as he always did when they met.

'Well, my dear,' he said, 'home ownership obviously suits you. That's a lovely dress.'

Jessie smiled and took his arm. It was only a few minutes' walk up to the house, but before they reached it Jessie stopped and tugged at his sleeve.

'I was hoping it would be just you and me today, Pat,' she said.

'So was I,' he said, wondering.

'But my lodger arrived back unexpectedly last night. I'm not sure what happened but he seemed upset. As he's not working today, I asked if he would like to meet you. Hope you don't mind.'

Pat did mind, acutely, and felt the disappointment run through him. 'No, of course I don't mind,' he said. 'This must be the chap I've heard about, from Harwell?'

'Did Mick Porter tell you? He tried to warn me off taking Lawrence as a tenant. I wasn't happy about being told what to do.'

'I can imagine,' said Pat, grinning. 'Mick should have known better than that.'

'But it's been fine,' said Jessie. 'Mick and the others meet at my house in the early evening and Lawrence is always out or in his room, or maybe he makes himself scarce when he knows I have company. It's hard to tell what he's thinking. Mick thinks he's a spy for the police or the bosses. Anyway, you can make up your own mind. I think he's rather a sad soul. You'll like him.'

'What does that say about me?' said Pat.

They were laughing as they walked into the house. Lawrence was coming down the stairs, still wearing his dressing gown.

'Oh dear,' he said. 'Sorry. I woke up when I heard you go out. You're back so soon.'

'This is the friend I told you about,' said Jessie. 'Pat O'Toole, meet Lawrence Finer.'

Lawrence stepped down a little further to shake Pat's hand.

'I'll put the kettle on,' said Jessie, 'and leave a cup of tea outside your door. You were so tired last night, no need to rush.'

'Thank you,' said Lawrence. In the relative darkness of the hallway Jessie realised that he was blushing as he turned and went back up the stairs.

'What does he do at the plant?' asked Pat, once the kitchen door was closed.

'I'm not even sure,' she said, filling the kettle at the sink. 'I think someone at the plant may have warned him off saying too much to me. "That Jessie Whelan, not to be trusted. Tell 'er nowt in case she tells 'er Commie friends all our mucky secrets".'

Pat laughed at her mimicry. 'Sounds about right,' he said.

'He has mentioned something to do with the reactors that will keep him here until October. I think he'd go back to Harwell tomorrow if he could.' She rinsed out the teapot with hot water. 'Anyway, it doesn't matter what he does. It's none of my business, or yours. We know things aren't right at the plant and it's the pressure for bigger bombs that's the problem.'

'Is he Jewish?' Pat asked her. 'There are lots of Jewish people in the movement, especially down south. Not surprising they don't want another war, not after the terrible time they had in the last one.'

'He said something last night about having had enough of rabbis. I'm not sure what that was about. I'll take him his tea up. He has a little coffee pot, but I don't know how to use it, so this will have to do.'

Pat weighed things up in his mind while she was out of the room. It was clear she hardly knew the man, and that he wouldn't be staying long. The relief surprised him.

'I've been wondering,' he said, when Jessie returned, 'whether you'd be prepared to speak on behalf of our group, when we go

84

to Newcastle in September. There could be quite a lot of people there.'

'What would I say?'

'Just what you believe, what you've said to me so often, about your fear of nuclear war.'

'I wouldn't want to say anything specifically about Windscale. I think I've upset a few people there already. People work at the plant because they have to, not because they necessarily believe in nuclear weapons. My son, John, firmly believes that nuclear energy is what it's all about. Cheap power for the people. He's as passionate about that as I'm concerned about the weapons. We don't talk about it of course, just like we don't talk about most important things in our lives.' She hesitated. 'John said that to me, at Agnes's funeral. "We never talk," he said, and he's right, we don't.'

'It's been difficult for you both,' said Pat, remembering.

'Well, just lately it feels much better,' she said. 'We had a lovely day together a few weeks ago, as a family. Maggie and John, and Violet, all day with never a cross word, or even one of those looks they give me when I'm saying the wrong thing. I just hope we can make it last.'

They both heard Lawrence's step on the stairs a little while later. He knocked on the kitchen door and waited until Jessie called, 'Come in, Lawrence. Make yourself at home.'

He came in carrying his coat and hung it over the chair before he sat down, nodding at Pat. Jessie poured more tea and made toast for them all, which they ate with the last of the plum jam. 'Plums from Agnes's garden,' she said, remembering the smell of the ripe fruit on her fingers.

'Tell us a bit about yourself,' said Pat to Lawrence. 'Not about the plant, I know you wouldn't want to do that, but about you. Start at the beginning.'

Lawrence smiled. 'Jessie said you used to be a priest,' he said. 'You haven't lost the knack. Well, before I was born, my parents came here from Russia when things were really bad for the Jews there. I was born in London in 1902, too young for the first war, thank heaven. Went to school in London, then Imperial College, then Cambridge. They were just starting on nuclear research and I got in right at the ground level and kept going. Exempted from the second war because of the work we were doing. Spent some time in Canada while the war was still on, then came back to work at Harwell. That's it really. I'm the stereotypical Jewish physicist with the round glasses and the big hair. Except that I'm going bald.' He ran his hand over his forehead and laughed. He was a different person when he laughed.

'You make it sound pretty humdrum,' said Pat.

'Some of it's been exciting, of course, but some I've not been so happy about.'

'The weapons?' said Jessie.

'Of course,' he said. 'But once that cat was out of the bag, so to speak, the only chance we have is to create such a stalemate that nobody dares actually use them.'

Jessie stared at him. 'That's absurd,' she said. 'You're risking nuclear war and millions of lives lost on a supposition.'

'Hang on,' said Lawrence. 'I'm only putting the case, it's not my personal decision.'

Jessie's voice rose a little more. 'Well, whose decision was it to build even bigger bombs than the ones that wiped out the Japanese? You do it just because you can, without any thought for the consequences.' She sat back from the table.

'But that's the whole point,' Lawrence replied, surprised at his own irritation. 'They have to be hydogen bombs, with unthinkable consequences. That's the only thing that would stop people being tempted to use them.'

'You hope,' she said, leaning forward again. 'What about the finger on the button? People make mistakes, accidents happen.'

'There are safeguards, of course. We scientists know how to build in safeguards.'

'That doesn't fill me with confidence,' said Jessie. 'I've watched what's happened at the plant over the years. Those reactors were built far too fast. What did that chap Hinton call them, "a monument to ignorance" wasn't it? That made us all feel much better!'

'That was just the first reactor,' said Lawrence. 'We all know it won't last much longer.'

'And then what?' said Jessie. Frustration and fear was bubbling out of her. 'What mad scheme will they think of next?'

'Not sure,' said Lawrence, trying not to rise to the anger he could see in her face. 'It's up to the politicians in the end.'

'Wonderful!' said Jessie, leaning back again, her face flushed. Lawrence was surprised by her strength of feeling and remembered what Tim Fahey had said about her. It was time to calm things down.

'I'm putting my faith in the test ban treaty,' said Lawrence, 'to slow the whole business down, and then we have to hope the Russians don't go off their heads.'

Pat sat silently, watching.

'Just the Russians?' Jessie retorted. 'What about the Americans, or us? There's nothing that the generals of this world like better than a good war, whichever country they're in.'

'I just hope it never happens,' said Lawrence. 'And I do really think war is less likely with these ghastly bombs than it would be if they didn't exist.'

Jessie looked away and shook her head. For a minute or so, nobody spoke. Lawrence was not going to back down, Jessie was clearly furious and Pat looked from one to the other. His heart was beating faster. Every instinct told him to calm things down, to find the common ground, but he didn't want to do so.

'Excuse me,' said Jessie. She stood up, gathered the empty teacups and put them in the sink, before she walked out of the room. They heard her going upstairs.

'Well,' said Pat finally. 'I think we know where she stands.'

'And you too, I suppose,' said Lawrence. 'I must say I wasn't expecting a grilling like that, not here, where I live. This is where I come to get away from work pressures, not walk straight into them.'

'Ah, yes,' said Pat.

'Best if I go out,' said Lawrence, pushing his chair back from the table. 'You've come to visit and I seem to have put my boot in it again.'

'Not at all,' said Pat, smiling. 'We can have our disagreements about things that matter to us, surely. No harm done.'

'I hope to see you again, Pat. Unless I've had to find different digs by then.'

'I'm sure it won't come to that,' said Pat. 'Jessie may even decide to settle a bit further away from the plant, now that she doesn't have to be close by. We've talked about the possibility of her coming to live in Maryport, to help with my Barnardo's work.'

'I see,' said Lawrence. 'Just as well I probably won't be here after October then, when my project finishes.'

'October. Is that so?' said Pat.

Lawrence picked up his coat from the back of the chair and put it on. 'I'll get out of your way,' he said.

'Don't worry about Jessie,' said Pat. 'She'll calm down.'

Chapter 10

Jessie waited upstairs until she heard the front door open and close.

'Pat?' she called down from the first landing. 'Has he gone?'

Pat put down the tea towel he was holding and turned from the sink towards the kitchen door. 'He's gone out, you can come down now.'

'Thank God for that,' she said, as she came down the stairs.

'Are you OK?' Pat asked, looking at her.

'I am now that he's gone. I don't expect to be lectured like that in my own home. He's just like all the others, pompous, thinks he knows everything.

'Well, you held your own well, my dear,' said Pat, smiling at her. 'I can see you now on a big stage somewhere speaking with such passion.'

'Do you think so?'

'I do, truly. Most people don't think quickly enough to argue a case like you can. You find the words, so eloquent. It's a gift, Jessie, and you have it.'

She thought about that. 'Not had to do it much, really. The only time I had to defend myself, after the war when my job at the school was threatened, I just gave in. I could have fought it, but I didn't.'

'That was different,' said Pat. 'You've told me yourself you thought it was time to move on, for your own sake, not just to avoid a fight.'

'Maybe,' she said. 'Do you want some lunch? All that talk has made me hungry.'

After lunch they went for a walk, up the hill and along towards Drigg, and then down the road to where it ran out on to the beach. Behind them the Wasdale fells slumbered in the heat of the afternoon, and a skylark sang as it rose to a speck above their heads. They sat on the beach. Warm air shimmered over the stones as they looked south towards the looming outline of Black Combe.

'Ever climbed Black Combe?' she asked.

'Never,' he said. 'It was always there when I was in Millom, watching over us. But I was always busy, and not very fit.' He laughed, patting his stomach. 'Looked like too much of a challenge for a fat priest who drank more than was good for him.'

'Did you?' she said.

'Drink too much? Yes, looking back, I'm sure I did. Now I can see how unhappy I was, but it didn't seem clear at the time. I was lonely.'

'Are you still?'

'Not so much. Leaving the priesthood was a great relief, and coming to terms with the situation – with the woman I told you about. I can be more myself now.' He hesitated. 'And I have you.'

She turned towards him. 'I'm not sure I could give you what you want. I'm not sure what I want either, except a quiet life.'

'You're not made for a quiet life, Jessie. There's too much passion. It has to come out, and that will make things happen. You can't hold it in.'

She smiled. 'Maybe you're right. But I wish I could learn to think more before I speak. Too impatient, it gets me into all sorts of trouble.'

'But that's who you are,' he said. 'That's why I love you.'

She hung her head. 'Don't say that.'

'You know it anyway,' he said. 'I've always felt that way, right from the start.' He looked out to sea, to the distant line of surf where the incoming tide was creeping towards them, pulled by an invisible moon. 'I don't expect you to do anything about it. It's a force of nature, like the tide out there. We are what we are. You have choices to make and you must make them. Of course I'd like you to choose to be with me, but I can't force you. I just wanted you to know how I feel.'

'I do,' she said. 'And I'm flattered. You're a fine man.' But that's not enough, she thought. It wasn't enough for me to marry Matthew Dawson, and thank heaven I didn't. Better to be lonely than trapped.

'Come on,' he said, getting slowly to his feet. 'We can take our shoes off and walk back along the sand, easier than the stones.'

And so they did, each carrying their shoes, through the warm shallow pools, feeling the sand and water between their toes.

* * *

Lawrence walked towards the golf club when he left the house. What a mess. He wished earnestly that he was back at Harwell, surrounded by the people and the work he was used to, living in his own home, with his wife and close to his children and grandchildren. How straightforward it would be, how predictable. But instead of that he was here, having to make do and mend with a reactor that should have been scrapped by now, living alongside a vociferous woman who seem to blow hot and cold without warning. If he went back to live at Greengarth the noise would still be too much, and once he was there he was stuck, unless he had his own transport. Finding a place to stay in the village had seemed the best idea, but now he wasn't so sure. Jessie said herself she hadn't been a landlady before, and she was probably regretting it now.

He found himself outside the clubhouse but didn't go in, sitting down instead on a bench facing towards the valley and the Wasdale fells. It was beautiful day. The sun warmed his back and shoulders and he closed his eyes, letting the tension fade a little. Was she always as fierce as that, he thought? No wonder she doesn't have a husband. John Pharaoh was her son and he seemed a calm rational person. So what happened to John's father? Frightened away no doubt, by passion and vehemence. Maybe that was why Pat the priest was so attached; he and Jessie would complement each other and he would calm her down. He wondered what else there was between them, tried and failed to picture them as lovers. She was too strong for him, surely. What must it be like to be with a woman with such energy, such heat? The image came suddenly into his mind with shocking intensity. It affected him physically – he needed to sit still for a while, and have a serious word with himself. He was a married man, temporarily away from home and family, trying to do a job and live somewhere that suited him, with the kind of space and freedom that Jessie's place provided. Acting on impulse, any kind of impulse, was a bad idea. It was July already, and they'd managed well enough until the row blew up today. Instead of running away he should think about how to make the best of it. She might want to get rid of him, but he was paying for both rooms and she needed the money. For another few months they could make it work, if they avoided any talk about the plant or her political activities, whatever they were. He would spend as much time as he could away from the house and keep out of her way, for everyone's sake.

An idea came to him. He could buy a motorbike. Then he could get to Greengarth whenever he wanted without having to sleep there. And he could explore those tantalising valleys and hills that he could see but had never really discovered. He smiled at the prospect. He'd always wanted a motorbike, ever since the children came and he'd had to sell his old one. Rebecca thought that riding a bike was dangerous and adolescent, but she was far away. He didn't even have to tell her. Logically, he told himself, it made sense. It could make the difference between having to leave Jessie's or managing to stay there. And it suited him to stay there. Why should he be driven away by this woman?

Again, and unbidden, he pictured her in his arms, her face close to his, her eyes closed. He got to his feet, rubbed his face with his hands and went into the clubhouse to get a drink and some conversation, and to take his mind off her. He would buy a motorbike and be in charge of his own life for a while. Before he went back to the house he would rehearse what needed to be said. It would be all right.

The train going north was pulling out of the station as Lawrence walked away from the golf club at the end of the afternoon. He'd drunk two pints of a very palatable local beer, and had some civilised conversation with Roger Newell, one of the managers from Calder Hall.

'Do you know John Pharaoh?' Lawrence had asked him, when they'd exhausted the topic of the recent test match.

'Of course,' said Roger. 'Very capable man, sound. He was at one of the pits in Whitehaven I believe, and came here right at the start. Worked his way up. Doing well, and he'll go higher. Still quite young, forty something I would guess. Why do you ask?'

'I know his mother.'

Roger raised his eyebrows. 'Yes, that was an odd business,' he said. 'Different surname. There was some gossip about it, but I didn't take much notice. He does a good job, that's all that matters. I've seen her around, the mother. She was old Meadow's secretary, but she retired. Didn't look old enough, but you can never tell these days. Funny woman by all accounts, difficult.'

Lawrence smiled. 'She's my landlady, here in the village. And I agree, she is a difficult woman.'

'Women, eh,' said Roger. 'Can't live with them, can't live without them. Cheers, old man.'

Halfway up the hill towards the house, Lawrence realised that Jessie was just ahead of him, and he stopped to collect himself and decide what to say when they met. She must have spent the afternoon with Pat, and seen him off on the train, so chances were that she'd calmed down. If she asked him to leave, which he thought she might, he would suggest that they could work it out, but if she insisted, he would have to go. Back to Greengarth, but only for a few months. He could cope with that, and the motorbike would mean he could get away in the evenings if he wanted to. If Jessie was willing for him to stay on, they would have to agree not to talk about the nuclear issue, and he would do his best to keep out of her way. They were mature adults and had their own lives to lead. If the arrangement had practical advantages for each of them, they would make it work. He still had no idea what she was thinking, but he was prepared either way.

The front door was open when he reached it. Had she seen him behind her?

'Hello,' he called from the doorway. His voice echoed back to him. The kitchen door was open but there was no movement in the room. Then she appeared at the top of the stairs, still wearing the blue and white dress. He couldn't see her face clearly.

'You're back,' she said, as he stepped into the hall.

'Yes.'

'Pat's just gone home.' She began to walk down the stairs. 'I think we need to talk, don't you?'

'Yes, we do,' he replied, relieved that she wasn't about to throw his suitcase at him.

She led the way into the front room. More formal, he thought, as befits a business discussion. This was looking promising. He sat down on one of the armchairs in the rarely used room that glowed with sunlight. She sat on the sofa, her knees together, hands in her lap. He tried not to think about her.

'I've been thinking,' he began, taking the initiative before she had the chance to speak. 'I obviously upset you earlier on, by speaking out more than I should. This is your house after all. I would quite understand if you asked me to find somewhere else to live, but I would like to stay here, if possible.'

'I see,' she said. 'I wasn't upset earlier, just annoyed, although I should have expected that you would think as you do. It's your job, after all.'

Don't rise to it, he told himself. Let her say her piece. He looked across at her and did not react.

'I did think about asking you to leave,' she went on, looking at her hands, 'but Pat is always very sensible, and he was sure we could work this out, if it suits me for you to stay, and you too, of course.'

'Yes,' he said, wondering again about what Pat was up to.

'It is very useful for me to have the money coming in, and as I'm likely to rent the rooms to someone who works at the plant, they would probably have the same views as you.'

Very true, he thought.

She looked up. 'We would have to avoid talking about the things we disagree so strongly about. You have your work and I have my interests and activities, and we keep them well away from each other.'

'Of course,' he said, pleased with the direction this was taking. Noisy Greengarth was looking less likely by the minute. She stopped, and was looking across at him. It was time for him to say his piece.

'I'm sorry I annoyed you. I let myself get drawn in. It was a mistake, and it won't happen again. Living here does suit me, close to the plant, your lovely house, the wonderful view. If we can work this out, I would like to stay. And of course, it's only until my project finishes. October's not far away.'

'My thought exactly,' she said.

That was easy, he thought. I can mention the motorbike, and then we won't have to discuss this business any more.

'I've decided to buy a motorbike,' he said, 'to give myself more independence. Then I can go out to Greengarth of an evening or at the weekend and not be in your way. It's hard for you to entertain your friends while I'm hanging around.' She nodded. 'And I want to explore inland a bit, up the valleys. Wasdale and Eskdale, people tell me they're lovely.'

'Oh they are,' she said. 'What a good idea.'

She stood up, smoothing down the full skirt of her dress. 'Well, I'm glad we've had this chat, sorted things out. You go your way and I'll go mine.'

She smiled, a tight rather forced smile, he thought, but it was enough. Don't say any more, he told himself. Leave it. And keep out of her way.

Jessie went back into the kitchen and closed the door. She found some lemonade in the cool pantry and poured herself a glass. It had been a challenging afternoon, one way and another. Pat's declaration hadn't been a surprise. She'd picked up his feelings quite unmistakably and it was easier to have them out in the open. And she and Lawrence had cleared the air too, just enough to let him stay, keep on paying his rent and save her the trouble of finding someone else. He had behaved quite well, she thought. The educated voice wasn't annoying her so much. It would be all right.

CHAPTER 11

IT WAS ONLY A DAY OR TWO AFTER THE NUCLEAR ROW and its subsequent adjustments that the weather finally broke. For two months it had been warm and dry, hazy breeze from the south, long balmy evenings, and nights sometimes uncomfortably warm. Lawrence had kept all his windows on the top floor open to catch the draught off the sea, and slept under just a sheet. His nights were disturbed by other matters, too. He could not keep images of Jessie out of his mind. He put it down to middle-aged frustration, but why was it Jessie not Rebecca that haunted his dreams? All the more reason to keep out of her way, he told himself. Work was the answer, and there was certainly enough of that to keep him busy. The change in the weather cooled things down.

Jessie knew that she needed to keep herself occupied and live her life without being inhibited by the unusual experience of sharing a house, which she hadn't done since living with Agnes at Applegarth. That had been Agnes's house, this was hers. Now she should be able to do and say whatever she wanted. During the rainy days she tackled the long-delayed making of new curtains, spreading the material round the front room when she needed to without worrying about how messy it looked. Mick Porter's anti-nuclear group continued to meet in her home on Monday evenings, and she found herself having more to say. They listened to her too, she noticed, and suggested, as Pat had done earlier, that she might speak for them at the upcoming conference in Newcastle, which seemed to be growing in size and significance as the date approached.

'You're more free to speak your mind,' said Mick as he left the house one night. 'The rest of us have to worry about our jobs, but you – well you're more independent.'

What an irony, she thought, that her independence was paid for by weekly cash from one of their opponents. Despite Lawrence's disagreeable views, he was a reasonably polite, reasonably interesting and intelligent man – a rarity in itself –who drifted almost unnoticed in and out of the house. Jessie was quite enjoying having him around. She heard him coming and going, and sometimes heard his music from the gramophone in his room, but he had promised to keep out of the way and he was doing so. A gleaming new AJS motorbike had arrived and was parked in the backyard.

It was as if the weather had sensed the arrival of the motorbike. A trip to Eskdale or Wasdale that would have been so pleasurable on a sunny summer day felt different in the driving rain that plagued Lawrence's evenings and weekends in August. He managed to get as far as Boot after supper one night before the heavens opened yet again. He'd intended to go further, up the pass to the Roman fort at Hardknott that he'd read about, but the cloud was so low that he gave up and drove home again. Jessie had lent him some of her maps of the area: part of her campaign to keep me out of the house, he thought. He studied them upstairs, planning the routes he would take on the bike and on foot, when he got the chance to do so, if and when it stopped raining.

One lunchtime in the canteen he met John Pharoah and sat with him while he tackled a plateful of sausage and mash. 'Never tasted sausage as good as this,' he said, aware that John had chosen something half as fattening. 'This is my main meal of the day,' he said, by way of explanation. 'Saves me having to get much to eat later.'

'Does Jessie cook for you?' said John. He couldn't imagine his mother fussing over an evening meal for a man.

'Good heavens, no,' said Lawrence, with such immediacy that John laughed out loud. 'I go to the club, or to Greengarth on the bike.'

'You bought a bike? What a good idea. I had a bike when I was younger, before the children.'

'Me too,' said Lawrence. 'Your mother thought it was a good idea as well. It keeps me out of the house.'

'She likes her independence,' said John. 'She always has.' Lawrence wanted to ask more, but resisted. It was none of his business.

After a rainy week, the forecast for Saturday was a little better. Lawrence was thinking about taking a long ride somewhere, but when he encountered Jessie on the stairs on Friday evening, she stopped to speak to him instead of just the usual nod of acknowledgement.

'Would you like a cup of tea before you go up, Lawrence?' she asked. 'I was just about to make one.'

Lawrence was surprised, but decided it would be politic to accept.

'Thank you,' he said, 'that would be very welcome.'

It was the first time he had sat at the kitchen table since the argument, and he felt a little nervous. What was she going to say this time? Nothing much, was the first answer. She busied herself with the kettle and the teapot without a word. He watched her, but turned away when the troubling images pounced yet again into his head.

She sat down finally, clearly ready to say something to him.

'It's Gosforth Show tomorrow,' she said. 'The summer shows are a tradition round here, part of the local landscape. Being from down south, you might not have seen anything quite like it.' She hesitated, still not looking at him.

'I wondered if you might like to go. John and his family will be there. I spoke to Maggie about it this morning.'

Well, well, thought Lawrence. An olive branch.

'Biggest marrows and suchlike, is it?' he said.

Jessie smiled, despite herself. 'Flowers and vegetables, of course,' she said. 'And all the animals too, cattle and sheep, and showjumping. There was a Russian horse troop one year. Very exotic. Folk come from miles around.'

Lawrence felt he would have to accept the unexpected invitation, and he did so. The tea ceremony progressed politely, and they agreed to meet the following morning at ten to ten. An invitation to join him on the bike would be a step too far, and they would go instead on the special bus that was due to leave from the beachfront on the hour. 'Wear strong shoes or boots,' she told him. 'The field will be muddy after all this rain.'

Walking together down the hill the following morning felt strange: they had not been anywhere together since he moved in. He walked on the outside of her, as he had been trained to do as a boy. As they waited with others for the bus to arrive, Jessie chatted to her neighbours, who took mercifully little notice of him. The talk was about other local shows that had been cancelled because of the weather, and the state of the show field once the tractors and trailers for the animals had driven across it. 'Clarty' was a word Lawrence hadn't heard before. He surmised it had something to do with mud.

If 'clarty' meant so slippery and sticky that the mud clung to your shoes and made it hard to walk, it was just about right, he thought, as they picked their way from the bus onto the show field itself. The whole affair was much bigger than he had imagined. Huge grey and white tents, each supported by long guy ropes, stretched across the field in a line. At the far side he could see wooden fences and pens, from which came the sound of bleating and bellowing. Tractors and trailers were parked up around the edge of the field, and some horseboxes too, although the news on the bus had been that the ground was too soft for the showjumping. It all seemed very well organised, but the regular announcements on the loudspeakers were in such a strong local accent that Lawrence gave up trying to work out what was being said. Some of the tents were still closed while the judges were at work, and he followed Jessie as she headed towards the ones where the judging was complete and the handwritten cards announced the winners.

For an hour and more Lawrence followed Jessie's lead, with only the occasional comment passing between them. She met several people she knew, but Lawrence was not introduced and he was clearly intended to keep his distance. Despite the weather, which was grey and already threatening yet more rain, the show was packed, and more people seemed to be arriving all the time. Where did they all come from, he wondered? They squelched from tent to tent, seeing onions the size of footballs, gleaming leeks with green fanned leaves, dahlias and gladioli, shortbread and rum butter and knitted jumpers and crowing cockerels. Outside in the gated enclosures there were cows and calves, and big Herdwick tups, their fleeces rouged with raddle.

Lawrence was beginning to wonder if there was a beer tent that he might find without Jessie's help, when she turned to him.

'I said we'd meet Maggie and the family at the tea tent around one-thirty,' she said. 'The worst of the lunch rush might be over by then.'

'Lead on,' he said. Tea and a sandwich would be fine if beer

101

was out of the question. He still felt as if he was on trial, and that the slightest infringement would bring her wrath down on his head. It took them a while to negotiate the route to the tea tent; by now the passage of hundreds of feet had churned up the ground still further. It was only when they reached their destination that Lawrence realised how badly he needed the Gents and set off to find it. When he returned several minutes later Jessie was waving to someone, and he saw the tall figure of John Pharaoh pushing through the crowd towards them. The woman with him, who must be Maggie he thought, was strikingly good-looking. Bright auburn hair swept up into a bun at the back, with wisps framing her face, flawless skin and green eyes that he could see bright as they came nearer. She was wearing a sea green coat and looked elegant even in Wellington boots. So like Judith, Lawrence thought, but with the added beauty of a mature woman. John was holding two boys by the hand, and Judith was just behind them.

Maggie and Jessie kissed each other lightly on the cheek, and John extended his hand to Lawrence. It was the first recognition he'd had all morning and he felt curiously pleased to see John. A 'sound' man, Roger at the golf club had called him, and so it felt. John turned to introduce Lawrence to his wife, but Maggie and Jessie were already in earnest conversation about the difficulties of making curtains. Lawrence shook hands with Frank, and then bent down to speak to Vincent, who was holding John's hand.

'And you are…?' said Lawrence.

'Vincent Arthur Pharaoh,' said Vincent. 'I'm seven.'

'My name's Lawrence. Pleased to meet you.'

Vincent tugged at John's hand. 'This is my dad,' he said, 'He's a bastid.'

Maggie stopped in mid-sentence. She bent her head close to Vincent's. 'What did you say?'

'Our dad's a bastid,' Vincent repeated happily, and louder,

because his mother hadn't heard him. Some people close by turned towards the child, smiled nervously, and moved away.

Maggie bent further down and slapped Vincent hard on his bare legs. He started to cry, and pointed at Frank, who had put his hand over his mouth, his eyes wide and bright. 'That's what he said,' wailed Vincent. Maggie turned to Frank who stepped aside and hid behind his sister. 'Our Judith told me,' he said, flinching. 'She said Granny never had a husband, so our dad's a bastard. That's what she said, Mam.'

John put his arm round his younger son as Maggie looked in desperation at her children, and then at Jessie.

'What did you say?' she whispered. 'What have you done, you – you selfish…' She couldn't find the word, and turned away. Her eyes were bright with tears.

'Maggie,' said Jessie.

'Don't speak to me,' Maggie hissed at her mother-in-law, then grabbed John by the arm. 'We're leaving,' she said. 'Now.'

Judith clung to Jessie. 'I only told them what you told me,' she said. 'Tell them, Jessie. Don't let her shout at me.'

John looked at his mother. 'Did you?' he said.

'I couldn't lie to her,' said Jessie. 'I'm sorry.'

John held Judith with one hand, the other still round the weeping Vincent, and followed his wife through the crowd, which had parted for the angry woman with the red hair. Frank ran after them, frightened and excited.

Lawrence was speechless. Without warning a pleasant family encounter had blown up and now three children and two women were in tears.

'What happened?' he asked, incredulous.

Jessie shook her head. Large drops of rain began to fall, and lightning split the sky. The crash of thunder hit almost immediately. Lawrence pulled Jessie into the shelter of the tea tent, and there they stood, jostled by others seeking protection in the same way, while the canvas flapped and strained against the force of the wind. He wanted to ask Jessie about what he had witnessed, but he did not dare to. She stood beside him with her head bowed, tears still falling. He found a handkerchief in his pocket and gave it to her. She wiped her eyes without a word, then blew her nose. The storm was abating a little, and the rain had eased to a steady downpour.

'Here's the bus,' someone shouted, and the crowd began to run across the muddy field to the gate where a bus stood with its headlights on in the gloom. Lawrence took Jessie's hand and pulled her after him. They fell up the steps of the bus and stood, panting, as the bus pulled away and turned down the road towards Seascale. All around them people were laughing and sharing jokes, but Lawrence and Jessie stood side by side, silent, each looking down. Jessie wondered who might have heard what had been said, and whether the damage could be undone. Lawrence wondered about this woman standing next to him, and who she really was.

The bus emptied gradually as it stopped and started through the village and the driver tried to drop people as close as possible to their houses. The worst of the storm had moved north, but lightning and thunder were still flashing and crashing as Lawrence and Jessie stepped down from the bus at the corner by the beach. They walked in silence up the hill towards the house.

'I'll make tea,' said Jessie. 'You go and change out of those wet clothes before you get too cold.'

'What about you?' said Lawrence.

'In a minute,' she said. When he left the room she put down the kettle and cried.

Lawrence peeled off his wet clothes in his room upstairs and put them in a soggy heap in the sink. Rain was still streaming down the window, but out to sea a thin stripe of light had appeared on the horizon. He rubbed his hair with a towel and wondered what was going on. The confident woman who talked very little about herself had suddenly become a mystery to him. What could have possessed her to tell her own grandchild something so potentially embarrassing? He hoped Maggie would not punish Vincent. He was just a child, with no idea what he'd said. He'd even got the word wrong. Bastard: an angry cruel word. Poor kid. Frank could be a mischief-maker, but he was only nine. And Judith? Heaven knows what she'd really said, or why. But it didn't matter in the end. Words had been said, in a public place. Maggie must have been mortified, and John, too.

He dressed in dry clothes and went downstairs. Jessie was sitting at the kitchen table, a towel around her shoulders. The tea was steaming in the cup, but she was shivering.

'Get changed,' he said gently. 'You'll catch cold sitting there. Take your tea with you. I'll make more if we need it.'

'There's cake in the tin,' she said as she got up. He heard her shoes squelching in the hall and her step as she climbed the stairs to her room. When she came down again her wet hair was combed flat to her head and she was wearing her big dressing gown.

'This is the warmest thing I could find. I must look a real sight.'

'It doesn't matter how we look,' he said. 'Have some cake, get your blood sugar back up. We look like we've been in the wars.'

'It feels like that,' she said, sitting down at the table opposite him. 'God knows what you must be thinking about us.'

'I don't know and it's none of my business,' he said. 'All families have their ups and downs.'

She sipped her tea.

'Don't you want to know if it's true?' she asked, without looking up.

'You don't have to tell me anything,' he said quietly.

'I want to.'

They sat at the table in the darkening kitchen and Jessie told him the meaning of what he had heard. She told him about Clive, and John, and the Pharaohs, and Maggie and the screens and West Row. Lawrence listened intently but said nothing, asked nothing

'She thinks I set out to undermine her,' said Jessie finally.

'And do you?'

She looked up. 'Is that what you think?'

'Did you think about the possibility that Judith would tell her brothers what you had told her?'

'No, I didn't. Judith's a grown-up, and – '

'But she's not,' Lawrence interrupted. 'She's a fifteen-year-old child who's cross with her mother for trying to make her "posh". You gave her something she could use to prick that bubble and she used it. It's not malevolent, not really, but she must have known that Frank might blurt something out and that Maggie would be upset.'

'I was tired of lying,' said Jessie wearily.

'That doesn't really matter,' said Lawrence. 'This isn't about you. You're the adult, the one who thinks things through. I think you regret telling Judith, and so you should. You put her in a very difficult position and it wasn't fair.'

Jessie looked at him, but said nothing. She wanted to tell him to go away, but she didn't have the strength.

'What can I do?' she asked.

'You'll have to think how to make amends, if you can. I don't know how. Let things calm down, and then you'll have to say something. Otherwise…'

'Otherwise what?'

'Things just fester.' He paused, seeing her unhappiness. 'They mean a lot to you, don't they?'

'The children? More than I can say.'

'Not just the children. John is your son, yours and Clive's and he's a fine man.'

Jessie nodded.

'And Maggie is his wife. However hard it may be, you owe them an apology.'

There was silence. Jessie wanted to challenge him, to defend herself, but couldn't find the words.

'That's very hard,' she said.

'I know, but it's what I feel. Maybe there are things in my family that need to be said, and have been left unsaid for too long. Maybe I'm blaming you instead of myself.'

'But you're telling me that I shouldn't have told the truth.'

'Yes, but that was to Judith, and she's still a child. It's the adults who need to be clear with each other.'

Now it was Jessie's turn to listen, but Lawrence said no more. When he'd finished his tea, he washed up his cup, and turned towards her. 'Why don't you have a bath and warm up?' he suggested. 'There's nothing more you can do now. Things will look different in the morning.'

Lawrence climbed the stairs up to his room and pulled a chair over to the window. The sun had reached the gap in the clouds near the horizon and he waited until the glow found his face and his closed eyes. He thought about the drama of the afternoon, and then about Rebecca and the unspoken truth that their marriage was over in all but name.

Chapter 12

Jessie woke on Sunday morning when she heard Lawrence's motorbike roar into life. It was after nine, but still quite dark outside. She turned over in bed and listened to the rain on her window until she fell asleep again. Vincent's tearful innocent face and Maggie's accusations camped stubbornly in her mind. She tried all the tricks she knew to settle herself, thinking about the beach, remembering the faces of children she'd taught, but nothing worked. In the end she got out of bed and made a drink, but the empty house felt cold and damp and she took the tea back to bed. Hours later she heard the back door open and Lawrence climbing the stairs to his room. After that there was faint music, but not enough to keep her from sleeping again.

Sunday night passed like the day, in a blur, but after Lawrence went out on Monday morning she knew she had to do something. She got up, dressed quickly, lit a fire in her bedroom to ward off the damp and another downstairs in the kitchen. The sound and light of the fire warmed her as much as the heat. Shocked by her image in the mirror, she found a comb in her handbag to control the wayward hair, and a touch of lipstick. Food was the next requirement. She used up some sour milk in the pantry to make scones, and the smell of baking lifted her spirits. Things felt more normal. She tried not to think about the incident at the show, wondering who else might have heard or seen what happened. There was sure to be gossip.

When the knock on the door came at lunchtime, she knew who it would be. She'd been bracing herself for it, trying to think what she would say, what she could say. John stood on the doorstep, a dark silhouette against the grey light. It was still raining. When the door opened he folded his big umbrella and propped it dripping in the porch before he stepped past her into the house without a word and straight into the kitchen. She closed the door and followed him. He leaned back against the sink and looked down at his mother, rain from his coat dripping quietly onto the floor.

'I thought you might come,' she said. 'I couldn't come to you.'

'No. You wouldn't have got past the doorstep. I'm not sure Maggie ever wants to see you again.'

'Is she very angry?'

'What do think? And she's not the only one. The boys are blaming Judith and Judith's blaming you.'

'And you?'

'You seem intent on wrecking my family,' he said. 'How do expect me to feel? Powerless, speechless, furious, is that enough?' He bent down to look into her face. 'What gets into you? Why do you have to blurt things out, damaging things, without thinking about what might happen? It's been going on as long as I've known you, and you've never learned to control yourself.'

'What can I do?' she said miserably. There was no point in trying to defend herself against his rage. She'd told Judith the truth because she'd wanted to, at that time, in that way. She'd trusted Judith to respect what she heard, and she should have known that wouldn't happen.

'All her life,' John went on implacably, 'Maggie has wanted a better life for herself and now for her children. That's what she

109

lives for. She's fought her way up from the screen shed to what we have now, and in one thoughtless, careless act you threaten the whole thing. How long do you think it's going to be before some kid in the playground repeats what Vince said the other day, before some mother at the school gate whispers something to the others? I don't care any more, but Maggie does. And the kids, how are they going to feel when they're a bit older?'

Jessie put her hands over her ears. She couldn't bear to hear any more.

'What can I do?' she repeated.

'It's too late now. The damage is done. Maggie says we will have to move away, right away, start again somewhere where your spite can't reach us.'

'Is that what she thinks? Spite?'

'Hard to explain it any other way,' he said. 'I've told her before, many times, that you don't mean to hurt, that you just don't think what you're doing sometimes, but that's wearing thin now. She thinks, she believes, that you resent her, despise her even, and she's had enough. All she can think of now is getting away, somewhere out of your reach.'

'But what about your job, the boys' school?'

'I can find another job, and the boys would be better off with a fresh start without gossip and teasing following them around.'

She pulled out a chair and sat down. John was still standing by the sink.

'I can't stay,' he said. 'I'm on my lunch. I knew Lawrence would be out, and Maggie doesn't know I'm here. She didn't want me to talk to you, in case I "wobbled". She thinks I'm afraid of you.'

'Are you?'

'I used to be, but not any more. You were important to me then, but now Maggie and the kids are everything.'

'You're very lucky.'

'Yes I am. And I'll do anything to protect them, even move away and start again. It wouldn't have to be far. I can work anywhere there are budgets to manage and wages to be paid.'

'What will Violet say?'

'That's our business.' He picked up his hat and brushed the rain from it. 'I have to go. That's all I have to tell you.'

'Wait,' she said. He turned round in the dark hall as she got to her feet.

'You and the family should stay here, and I should go.'

'Go where? You've only just bought this house.'

'That's doesn't matter. I can sell it again. I could move north, to Maryport.'

'Why Maryport?'

'Pat O'Toole is there. He's asked me to go and work with him. And there's the anti-nuclear campaign too. They're part of the Carlisle group, well away from here.'

'That's the other thing,' said John. 'It's all very well to follow your principles or whatever you're doing, but the rest of us have to work here. No one at work's said anything to me about it, not yet, but I know what they're thinking.'

'If I was up north, it wouldn't matter.'

'That's probably true,' he said. 'Maryport might as well be the other end of the country.' He paused, then as if seeking confirmation, added, 'Would you do that, move away, just because of this?'

'You're prepared to do it.'

'It's what Maggie wants,' he said. 'She talked about it all yesterday.'

'Do you think she might change her mind?'

'She might. She was very angry. It might wear off.'

'Let's all think about it a bit longer,' said Jessie. 'It would take me a little while to sell and move and all that. I'm supposed to give Lawrence some notice, not sure how much. I'd need a few weeks.'

'I'm going to tell Maggie this so you'd better not change your mind. And for God's sake, watch what you say, about the plant and about me and my family. Old people are supposed to be discreet aren't they?' He reached out to open the front door. It had stopped raining. He turned up his collar against the wind, put on his hat, and was gone.

She closed the door after him and leaned against it. She'd never seen him like that before. Cold, unforgiving. She knew she'd done wrong, made a mistake in telling Judith, but this was an over-reaction, surely. A few mistaken words, a child's remark and their lives were changed around? It was ridiculous. For a while she sat at the kitchen table, her mind a jumble of regret, disbelief, and the practical implications of moving. She was being sent into exile. The children: the thought struck her like a blow to the stomach. When would she be able to see the children? Would Maggie keep them from her? Would John let her do that? Slowly, the only possible next steps emerged from the jumble. She must accept that she had been at fault, and begin to make amends. If they insisted on such a drastic remedy, she must offer to move away. It was unthinkable that they could jeopardise John's career at this stage, and uproot the boys, just to get away from her. It would take a while to sort everything out, time for Maggie to calm down, to get things in perspective. Even if Jessie had to move, Maryport wasn't so far. Maggie might trust her enough eventually to let the children see her.

She looked around the kitchen, at the new curtains, the changes she'd made to the first house she'd ever had. And for nothing. Suddenly she felt exhausted, shaky and bereft, as if someone had died. She pulled herself slowly up the stairs and went back to bed, fully clothed. When she woke again it was dark. Someone was tapping on the bedroom door.

'Jessie?'

It was Lawrence. She sat up. 'I'm here, Lawrence.' The door opened slowly and he put his head around to check. She waved her hand and he came into the room.

'Are you alright? I've not seen or heard you since Saturday night.' He stood looking down at her,

'Can you close the curtains?' she said.

He did so. 'It's cold in here,' he remarked, rubbing his hands.

'I lit a fire this morning, but –'

'That was hours ago. It's after five. Have you eaten anything?'

'No.'

'I'll sort the fire out downstairs and see what's in the pantry, or I could get us fish and chips. You need to eat something. And a drink. Do you want tea or shall I make some coffee for us?'

'In your little coffee pot?'

'Yes, if I haven't forgotten how to use it.'

'Coffee please,' she said. 'I'll get up.'

* * *

An hour later he cleared away their plates from the kitchen table and sat down opposite her.

'I must look a mess,' she said. 'Spent most of the afternoon in bed, after...'

'What happened?'

'John came to see me, at lunchtime. He was very angry, still. He said that Maggie wants to move away, to get away from me.'

'What?' Lawrence looked at the ceiling. 'That's crazy.'

Jessie was so relieved at his reaction she could have hugged him. 'Do you think so?'

'This is 1957, not 1857. So you weren't married when John was born, and you gave him away for a better life. That's not enough reason to uproot a whole family.'

'I thought that, but I didn't say it.'

113

He laughed. 'Hallelujah,' he said. 'Just this once you didn't say the first thing that came into your head.'

'John said that old people ought to have learned discretion.'

'Oh, God,' said Lawrence. 'Well he can be a bit pompous, can't he. And who's old?'

She smiled. 'Our children always think we're old, don't they? I don't feel old.'

'And you don't look old either, not to me anyway.'

'That's because you're old yourself.' They both laughed.

'It's good to see you laugh,' he said.

She thought about what she had to tell him. 'I couldn't say that Maggie was over-reacting. So I said that I would move instead.'

'You said what?'

'I had to. She could stop me seeing the children. And it's far easier for me to move than them, if it has to come to that.'

'Where to?'

'I could go to Maryport.'

'Ah,' said Lawrence, 'the priest.'

'Ex-priest. He's asked me before to move up there and work with him, like we used to work together at the camp. We make a good team.'

'I'm sure you do,' he said, thinking about Jessie and the priest, together.

'It's not that far on the train from there to St Bees. When Maggie feels I'm not a threat to her, or whatever it is, I could see the children again.'

'Is that what you're thinking? That she'll forgive you your sins and allow you to see her children. Is that what's she's punishing you with?'

She looked at him, confused and puzzled. 'I don't know what to think. I thought we were getting on better, but it's as bad as it's ever been. She means more to John than I do, so he has to support her. I can't blame him for that. He loves her and the children more than anything.'

'I still think this is out of all proportion.'

'But you're from the city,' she said. 'You don't know how things work up here. Respectability still matters. I've always been an outsider, but John and Maggie have to live here, hold their heads up. And the children too, they have to protect them.'

Lawrence thought about that for a while. And he was thinking about Rebecca, putting the children and grandchildren above her life with him.

'So what are you going to do?'

'I told John I would be prepared to move away if that was the only solution, but I would need a few weeks to work things out.'

'You're hoping that Maggie will calm down and change her mind, aren't you? You're playing for time.'

She blushed. 'Well, yes, I suppose I am. Is that very devious?'

'It's very sensible, if you ask me.'

'I said I had to give you notice if I was going to sell the house.'

'Good,' he said. 'How long?'

'I've no idea? How long do lodgers get?'

'A month? Could we say a month?'

'You mean make it up?'

'Of course. You're playing for time, remember. Tell them I was very annoyed and insisted on a month. That should give everyone some breathing space.'

She smiled at him. 'You're as devious as me, Dr Finer.'

'Absolutely,' he said. 'Now where's that sloe gin you keep some-where?'

It was the most comforting evening Jessie had enjoyed for a long time. They sat together by the fire in the kitchen, telling stories about people in both their lives, safe stories that made them laugh, not cry. Each of them saw behind the other's confident aura a glimpse of the vulnerability they both felt and rarely admitted to. Each of them recognised in the other a person not unlike themselves. When the bottle was empty, Lawrence said goodnight and went upstairs, troubled by his feelings. Jessie was troubled too, but her mind was too blurred to know the cause.

CHAPTER 13

JESSIE SAT ON THE BUS TO WHITEHAVEN with John's umbrella propped up beside her. Lawrence had offered to return it to John at work, but Jessie had another plan in mind. She was taking it to the McSherrys' at West Row. They would give it back to John. If that meant that John would have to tell Maggie that he'd been to see her, so be it. John and Maggie needed to talk to each other, even if neither of them wanted to talk to her.

She'd taken the bus that went the back route to Whitehaven through Kells, got off at the stop near the South Row corner and walked down the cobbled street. Ahead of her the Irish Sea glinted in September sun. It was a week after John's ultimatum. Lawrence had been preoccupied with things at work, and she'd not seen much of him, but knowing that he thought she was being sensible had cheered her up. She still felt exhausted though, and the little lump on the side of her breast felt tender. It was several weeks since she'd first noticed it, and she'd expected it to go away

117

by now. Nothing much really, about the size of a dried pea. It was probably a boil; she knew that boils happened when you were run down.

The flapping Monday washing on the drying green behind the houses caught her eye as she walked down the hill and turned the corner into West Row, and she gasped as the breeze and the view hit her simultaneously. The coast of Galloway across the Solway Firth seemed so close you could reach out and touch it. Every settlement and even the walls between the fields were sharp and clear. Children were playing in the street, making the most of the last few days of freedom before school started. A football skipped past her. 'Gi' us the ball, missus,' said one of the boys and she kicked it back to them.

The front door of the McSherrys' house was open slightly. She looked through the window and saw Frank in his wheelchair reading the paper. If Violet was there Jessie probably wouldn't be allowed into the house, but at least the umbrella would be delivered. She knocked on the window and Frank looked up, It took him a minute to recognise Jessie's face against the bright light outside. When he did, he smiled, and Jessie was relieved; she hadn't really known what to expect.

'Door's open,' he called, and she pushed on it and went in. It always took him a while to manoeuvre the wheelchair through the doorway.

'Well, by 'eck,' said Frank, stretching his hand to her. 'It's our Jessie. Come in, lass. Not seen you in God knows 'ow long.'

'Too long,' she said, sitting down to be level with him. 'I've meant to come before now, but what with moving house…'

'Aye, that's right,' said Frank. 'New 'ouse in Seascale. Violet said it's right posh, but no better view than we 'ave 'ere.'

'Looks lovely out there today, Frank.'

'Aye, after all that rain. Didn't see t' other side for most of last

118

month. What a summer! You got caught at Gosforth Show didn't you? Our Maggie and that mob got soaked just running to t' car.'

'Did she tell you any more about the show?' Jessie asked, wondering what had been said.

'Nay, just how wet they got. Violet might 'ave heard more, like, but she's not 'ere. Gone on a charra trip with the Catholic ladies and that bloody priest. She spends more time wi' im that she does 'ere with me and Tom.'

'Father Price,' said Jessie. 'He's still around then.'

'Aye, more's the pity. 'E's a miserable git and no mistake.'

Jessie remembered the umbrella and held it out to him. 'John left this at my house,' she said. 'It gave me all the reason I needed to come and see you.'

'Tom's around somewhere. I 'eard 'im coughing a while ago, upstairs mebbe. Leave brolly in th'all, Jess, and give 'im a shout. We'll have a drink.'

'You stay here, Frank,' she said. 'I'll put the kettle on.'

In the hall she called out, 'Tom, are up there? It's Jessie. Would you like a cuppa?'

Tom appeared at the top of the stairs. She was shocked by how he had shrunk since she last saw him, but smiled cheerfully.

'Well, well,' he said. 'It's our Jessie. Good to see yer, lass. I'll come down. Don't wait, 'ave to tek it slow.'

She went on into the back kitchen so as not to watch Tom's breathless progress down the stairs. From what John had told her, he might not live much longer; his lungs were in shreds.

As Jessie carried the tray of tea things back into the front room some minutes later, she noticed some evidence of Frank and Violet's small inheritance from Agnes. A new table and chairs, and some fancy crockery in a special cabinet.

'Don't get up, Tom' she said, bending down to give him a kiss. 'How are you doing?'

'Not so bad. Did Frank tell you our Violet's out all day?'

'Yes, but I've seen her recently, and I've not see you two.'

'So tell us all the crack,' said Frank as Jessie poured the tea. 'Lady o' leisure now aren't you? Busy woman like you, must feel strange to 'ave nowt to do.'

'Wouldn't say nowt,' said Jessie. 'I bought a big house that needed a lot doing. That's kept me busy. And I do some reading with children at the school, and a few other things.'

'What other things?' asked Tom.

These two don't mince words she thought. Should she tell them? Would they know already? 'Well,' she ventured, 'since I left the plant, I've got involved with a group who are worried about the whole nuclear business. There's a lot going on that I was bothered about while I was working there, but I couldn't say anything, obviously.'

'I told you,' said Frank to Tom. 'That's what our Maggie were talking about. Jessie's a "Ban the Bomber".' He turned to Jessie. 'Maggie were reet mad about it, because of our John, like. I suppose she's told you that.'

'She has, yes,' said Jessie. Mind what you say, she reminded herself. Don't make things any worse.

'Well, that's 'er, in't it,' said Frank. 'I'm 'er dad, so I can say it. She's a bit of a snob, our Maggie. Doesn't like 'owt that might show 'er up, like. Allus been like that, even when she and her mam worked on the screens. And now wi' our John doing so well, she's even worse.'

Jessie smiled. She would not be drawn. Tom's coughing went on for long enough for Frank to change the subject.

'Our Vi said summat about a lodger.'

'Aye,' echoed Tom, wiping his eyes. 'Tell us about the lodger.' He winked at Frank, who winked back.

'Roger the lodger, eh,' said Frank. 'Some feller from the plant.'

120

'Yes, he's working there for a while. Comes from Oxford, the research place there.'

'Posh, is 'e?'

'Yes, I suppose he is. He's a physicist, working on the reactors.'

'Jewish, our Vi says,' Frank pressed on.

'Long 'air and a big 'at?' said Tom.

Jessie laughed. 'Come on, Tom,' she said. 'No, he's got whitish hair, a bit bald at the front, nice face, little round glasses. Looks like a scientist more than anything else. Very clever of course.'

'Well he'd 'ave to be, wouldn't 'e?' said Tom. 'Goes wi'out saying, like.'

Frank thought for a moment. 'And what does 'e 'ave to say about you and the ban the bomb stuff?'

'Well, we disagree about it, but it's none of his business, really is it?' she said. 'I'm his landlady, not his wife.' She hesitated. 'And even if I was his wife –'

'Has he got a wife?' said Tom.

'Yes, he does actually. She's in Oxford.'

'On 'is own up 'ere then,' Tom leaned forward and winked at her conspiratorially.

'Tom,' said Jessie. 'What are you suggesting?'

'Well, fine looking lass like you, Jessie, and some posh stranger.'

'Definitely not,' she said. 'You two are worse than the women.'

'Ah, but we know what men are like, eh, Tom,' said Frank. 'Men away from 'ome, like in the war, get up to all sorts.'

Jessie got up to clear the teacups. Now it was her turn, and her need, to change the subject. She took the tray into the kitchen, washed the pots and came back to sit on the sagging sofa, twisting away from the fierce light.

'The lodger and I had an argument about the nuclear business,' she began. 'I want to see what you two think of what he said.'

'Probably too clever for us, like,' said Tom. He was wheezing,

121

but Frank took no notice and Jessie followed his lead.

'Nonsense,' she said. 'Nothing wrong with your brains, either of you, and you've got experience of things that he hasn't.'

'What things?'

'Life down the pits, for one, real work, not just faffing around in a lab somewhere. Anyway, he claimed that we have to have big hydrogen bombs to keep up with the Americans. And that when everybody had the big bombs, the ones that would just about finish everything off, they would all be so scared of using them that no one would dare start a war.'

Tom and Frank thought about this proposition for a few minutes.

'I reckon 'e's right about that,' said Frank. 'They sort of cancel each other out.'

Jessie came back straight away. 'But wouldn't that be the same if there were only smaller bombs, or no bombs at all?'

'Nay, it's got to be the big 'uns to make it work.'

'Or,' said Jessie, with a sudden certainty, 'or none of these bombs at all, small or large. Ban the lot of them. That would have the same effect, wouldn't it?'

The two men thought a little more.

'I reckon that would work,' said Tom.

Frank raised his finger, to make his point. 'But,' he said, 'only if you could get everyone to get rid of the ones they've got, not make any more and not let anyone else mek 'em.'

'That's a big but,' said Tom. 'Will they do that? Cannut trust bosses, whoever they are.'

'It all comes down to politics,' said Jessie, 'and putting pressure on governments. That's what we're trying to do.'

'Well good luck wi' that,' said Tom.

Frank was still thinking. 'It's not just about bombs anyway,' he went on. 'We need more electric don't we? Look at all the stuff that uses it now, more and more things needing more and more power. If we need nuclear for that, what's to stop them making bombs as well?'

'We can still use coal for power,' said Jessie, trying to disentangle things in her mind.

'Aye, but for 'ow long?'

'And 'ow much will it cost?' said Tom. 'I don't mean money. I mean, well look at us two. Frank's got no legs to speak of and I've got no lungs. Coal did that. 'Ow many people have died from nuclear?'

'But nuclear power's hardly started yet,' countered Jessie. 'We don't know what harm it's doing, to the air, or places like Seascale. It's vicious stuff, nuclear fallout. You can't see it, but it seeps into things, the grass and people's bodies, kills you slowly.'

'Well we can't judge what's not 'appened yet, can we?' said Frank. 'We just 'ave to wait and see. There'll be plenty of demand for coal, and plenty of jobs for them as 'as to dig it out, but that still won't be enough. That's what our John says.'

Jessie realised that she and John had never even discussed the industry that had paid both their wages, and still paid his.

'What does our John say about your ban the bomb stuff when 'e works there?' asked Tom. Jessie wished she'd never started this discussion. She'd only done so to stop them talking about Lawrence. Why weren't they talking about the weather or something safe?

'John and I don't talk about it,' she said finally.

'Not surprised,' said Tom. 'Bet 'e doesn't like it, though.'

Jessie tried another tack, knowing Frank's concern about working men being put at risk. 'But what about safety, at the plant?'

'What about it?' said Frank. 'What's not safe?'

'None of it's safe,' she said. "I'm not sure anyone really knows what they're doing. They change their minds all the time, make mistakes, then expect the men – the real workers, not the scientists – to put it right.'

'Nothing new there,' said Frank. 'It were same wi' pit bosses, wanting more profits, pushing things too 'ard.'

'Well, I don't think we've really seen the worst of it yet,' said Jessie. 'Something will happen if they carry on like this.'

'So are you safe living there?' Tom asked. 'If summat 'appens?' 'Ow far away are you?'

'A mile or two from the plant,' said Jessie. She hadn't thought much about that before.

'Well if that fallout stuff is in the wind, it could blow anywhere, couldn't it?' Tom persisted. 'Wouldn't just drop back where it came from.'

'Could blow right up 'ere, come to that,' said Frank.

Jessie spoke before she remembered her need to be careful what she said.

'That could be another reason for me to move away,' she said.

'Move away? But you've only just bought that big 'ouse. Why do you want to move already?'

Damn, she thought. 'Er, no particular reason. There's some work in Maryport I'm quite interested in, with Pat O'Toole, do you remember him?'

'He were that funny priest, weren't 'e, the one that married our Maggie and John when bloody Father Price wouldn't do it? Our Violet allus said there were summat rum about 'im.'

'Well he's not a priest any more,' said Jessie, hoping she could skirt round a few things.

'Told you,' said Tom. 'Sister Violet, right again! They chucked 'im out, did they?'

'Well anyway,' said Jessie, giving up, 'I might not live in Seascale for very much longer, that's all.'

'What about Roger the lodger? 'Appen 'e'll be pissed off,' said Frank.

'He doesn't expect to be there much longer either.'

'Whole bloody place could've blown up by then!' said Tom, at which both men laughed loudly, leaving Jessie completely nonplussed.

'Well, I seem to have cheered you both up,' she said, getting off the sofa with some difficulty.

'Nowt like a good laugh,' said Tom. 'It's a tonic seeing you.'

'Don't leave it so long next time,' said Frank, shifting his wheelchair out of Jessie's way. 'Vi'll tek John's brolly down there next time she goes. You could've taken it yourself, couldn't you?'

'Well, I was coming this way anyway,' Jessie lied again.

'Right you are then, pet,' said Frank. 'Mind 'ow you go. And tek care with these men 'anging around – mad scientists, unfrocked priests, you don't 'alf pick 'em.'

Tom laughed again, but laughter turned into a coughing fit. Jessie could still hear him after she left the house.

* * *

Going back over the conversation as she sat on the bus back to Seascale, Jessie didn't think she'd dug any more holes for herself. Maybe moving to Maryport wasn't such a good idea after all, and the thought of uprooting completely and starting again from scratch was too depressing to contemplate. And for what? Just so that Maggie would never have to encounter anyone who knew that John was illegitimate. Why should it matter so much? What did Macmillan say, we've 'never had it so good'? Well some things don't change. Same old prejudice, pulling folk down. She didn't understand it, and neither did Lawrence.

She was still thinking about Lawrence as the bus chugged down the hill into Egremont. He's not like anyone else I know, she thought, but he's a bit like me. Involved in his work, like I was at the school. On his own and lonely sometime, I expect. What about his wife? What's going on there? He was so good that day, after the show. I wanted to explain about John, and he didn't make a big fuss about it, just listened and did useful things.

When the chimneys and towers of the plant reared up ahead of them a little while later she looked at her watch. Half past four. He'll be in there somewhere, wearing one of those spaceman suits they had to wear in the reactor building, doing his work. And one day soon he'll go back to Oxford and his wife. I'll miss him, she thought. That was one more thing to keep to herself.

The conversation with Frank and Tom seemed to have cut through a puzzle in her mind. Alone in the empty house, she wrote a note to Pat and posted it straight away, before she had the chance to change her mind.

If you want me to speak at the meeting in Newcastle, I will, she wrote. *I know the others can't say anything while they're working at Windscale. I want to say that we should outlaw nuclear bombs bomb but still use nuclear power. Let me know what you think.*

Pat's response was immediate. *That's great news, Jessie,* he wrote back the following day. *We have three weeks before the meeting, plenty of time to make sure you're on the speakers' list. Leave all that to me. Can you come up here next week for us to start on your speech, or shall I come to you? I'm so pleased that you can become our voice, so confident, so clear, such a credit to us all.*

Jessie was surprised at Pat's enthusiasm, and wondered whether his expectations were misplaced, but there was excitement too. What would Lawrence say about it, she wondered? And why did she have to tell him? No matter how much she liked him, he was still a married man. Not for the first time, she told herself to be careful.

CHAPTER 14

'YOU KNOW I CAN'T TALK about what happens at the plant,' Lawrence said, leaning back in his chair. He'd come in from work on a Friday evening towards the end of September and they were sitting at the kitchen table enjoying a cup of tea.

'I know that,' she said. 'Of course I know that. I don't want you to tell me anything. I just want you to listen.' She took a sip of tea, and considered how much to tell him.

'You remember I went to that meeting in Newcastle.'

'I knew you were going somewhere with the Maryport man, but no more than that.'

'Well, it was a meeting in Newcastle of the northern groups who want to ban nuclear weapons.'

He raised his eyebrows. 'Was it, indeed? That's a big step, for you, isn't it?'

She hesitated. Was he patronising her, making out she wasn't serious? 'You know how I feel,' she said. 'I've thought about it a lot. We had that conversation…'

'I remember.' He smiled. 'You went away in the middle of it.'

'I just didn't want to say any more, to get worked up about it. I didn't know you very well then. Well, I've thought about it more since then, and I realised something.'

He didn't respond, observing the flush in her cheeks.

'We all have to stop making the big bombs,' she said. 'All of them. And soon, now, before it's too late.' She waited for him to ask or say something, but there was nothing, so she went on. 'There has to be a stalemate if we're going to survive. You said the only way to get a stalemate was to have such big destructive bombs that no one dares to use them. Small bombs won't achieve that.'

He nodded.

'So instead of big bombs we have to have no bombs. Get rid of them all. Ban the bomb.' She spoke with certainty.

'I can see that, but it's a bit late. How do you suppose we can all agree to get rid of the bombs we already have?'

'That's what has to happen, and it will if enough people, all round the world, put enough pressure on their governments to do it. Anyone with any hope for the future, all our futures, has to know that's the only way. While the big bombs exist, there's just too much risk.'

'Is that what you wanted me to listen to?' he asked, wondering where the conversation, if it was to be a conversation, would go next.

She ignored the question. 'They asked me to speak at the meeting in Newcastle.'

'Who did?'

'The organisers, Pat knows them.'

'Ah,' said Lawrence, 'so they asked Pat, and he asked you?'

'I think so. Anyway, I did. And it was ... well received.'

'What did you say?'

'I just said who I am and where I live, and that after working at the plant for several years I came to realise that things were not right.'

'You didn't say anything specific about your work at Windscale, did you?'

'I didn't need to. I just said that there were many people in the industry who believe that things had been done in too much of a rush, and that Britain should take a stand on nuclear development and not keep chasing after the Americans. Not much more than that, really.'

'If you spoke with as much passion as you did to us that day, I'm sure they loved it.'

'They did,' she said, remembering the cheers and stamping of feet that had greeted her short speech.

'What did Pat say?'

'He was pleased of course.' She recalled the look on his face: pleasure, excitement, pride. 'We talked about it on the way back, on the train. They had asked him if I could speak at another big rally, in London, in November.'

'They asked him, not you?'

'One of them said I was Pat's protégé. Pat seemed very pleased about that.'

Lawrence got up from the table and washed his teacup under the tap. He turned towards her.

'Don't get cross with me,' he said, 'but I need to ask you something.'

She looked up at him.

'Do you think they might be using you?'

'Using me? For what?'

He could see the annoyance in her face. 'To make them seem more, you know, more real, not just a bunch of middle-class lefties. And a woman, too. How many women are there are on the stage I wonder?'

'That's pretty cynical,' she said, 'even for you.'

'And another thing,' he said, stung. 'That word "protégé", was that the word they used?'

'Yes, what's wrong with it?'

'It sounds like you're his pet, that he found you somewhere and coached you for stardom. I would object strongly to that if I were you.'

Now it was her turn to be stung. 'Well you're not me, are you? If I don't mind, why should you? You're not my keeper.'

Her eyes were bright. Lawrence ran both hands through his hair, pushed his round glasses further up his nose, shrugged and smiled at her.

'We don't seem able to have a civilised conversation about this stuff, do we? You're right, forget what I just said. You deal with Pat and the ban the bomb crowd any way you want. Is that what you wanted to tell me? It's been a long day, and I'm heading out again shortly.'

Jessie wanted to ask him something else but couldn't bring herself to do so. He was obviously not interested. He was halfway to the stairs when he turned back.

'By the way,' he said. 'I won't be here next weekend, from Friday night to Sunday.'

'Where are you going?' she asked.

'Not far at all,' he laughed. 'Just to the Scawfell Hotel down the road. Rebecca's coming up for the weekend and I've booked us in there. Easier all round than her staying here, don't you think?'

It was a surprise, and for a moment Jessie didn't know what to say. 'Right, that's fine. Well, good idea, privacy, all that.' She stumbled to find the right words.

'I thought so too,' he said brightly. 'And you get your house back for a couple of days, all to yourself.'

* * *

'What's she like?' asked Kath Attwood when Jessie called to see her the following afternoon. Kath lived near the station in Drigg, well away from what she saw as the claustrophobia of Seascale,

130

and Jessie always enjoyed the walk to her house along the narrow road that was usually quiet at the weekends. It was one of those clear autumn days when the fells stood out crisply, just beginning to turn from summer green to brown. Another month and the look of them would have changed completely. Jessie preferred autumn or winter, when bare trees revealed more of the landscape beyond, and the landscape itself was more fragmented, etched with different colours and shades. Today, as she walked briskly south along the road the breeze came from behind her, blowing hair round her face. The irritating lump was still there, she realised. Maybe it was walking faster like this that made her feel it. I'll go to the doctor's, she told herself, when I'm not quite so busy.

'What's she like?' Jessie repeated Kath's question. 'I've no idea.'

'No pictures in his room, or anything?'

'I don't poke around in his room,' she said.

'But you have to clean, change the sheets and things. You'd have seen a photo.'

'Well I haven't.'

'What do you think she's like? What's he said?'

Jessie laughed. 'What does it matter? He hasn't said much, but I know she doesn't like being away from home. She didn't go with him when he went to Canada, he told me that. And they have children, and a grandchild, or maybe more. That must keep her busy.'

'Too busy to want to be with him, by the sound of it. I'll bet they don't get on well.'

'Then why is she coming up here?'

'It's only for the weekend, you said – or did he say she might stay longer?'

'Never mentioned anything except that he'd booked them into the Scawfell. That means I won't even see her.'

'Oh, but we have to,' said Kath. 'Aren't you curious?'

'Nosey, you mean? Well I suppose I am, a bit. Don't meet many people like him, so she might be a bit different, too.'

'She'll be like the other scientists' wives, only older,' said Kath, stirring the soup she had made for their lunch. 'Confident, brainy, into everything. Their kids are great, I love having them in school, but some of the mothers are a pain. Fussing on all the time. They treat the teachers like dirt, and me too, if I let them.'

'It must be hard for them,' said Jessie, 'especially the ones who don't have good jobs at the plant. All that education, going to waste.'

'Well I wish they didn't take out their frustrations on us,' said Kath.

They had finished lunch and were heading out for a walk down to the beach when Kath had a brainwave. 'I bet they'll go to the club on Saturday night,' she said. 'Lawrence and his wife, I mean. What else would they do? He's only got the motorbike hasn't he?'

'Sometimes he borrows a car,' said Jessie.

'Well I bet you a pound that's where they'll go,' Kath continued. 'So we'll go there too.'

Jessie laughed. 'We'll go to the club, just to see what she's like?'

'Why not? Admit it, you want to see her as much as I do. You can't live with a person for as long as you have with Lawrence and not be curious about them.'

Jessie admitted as much, but maintained her apparent indifference for a while before letting Kath grind her down, agreeing in the end that she would go to the club, for a change and just to keep her friend company.

'See if you can find out if they're going,' said Kath, as Jessie prepared to leave at the end of the afternoon. 'But we'll go anyway. It's ages since I went to the club. You'll have to protect me from anyone who wants to talk about school stuff.'

Jessie found no opportunity to bring Lawrence's weekend

plans into their conversation during the week. He seemed more than usually preoccupied, and she certainly didn't want to ask him outright. He borrowed the iron and ironing board one evening, but said nothing about what he was preparing for. On Friday morning he had a bag with him when he left the house, ready to check into the hotel. Jessie guessed that Rebecca would be coming by train, arriving around six probably, as most people did coming from the south. On the Friday night she washed her hair, and looked through her meagre wardrobe to find the only dress she had suitable for the club on a Saturday night.

Kath was due to call for her at eight o'clock. Mercifully it was a calm dry evening, suitable for their shoes and unlikely to ruin carefully managed hair. Jessie felt like a teenager, checking her lilac dress, putting on the only earrings that would go with it, and finding a suitable lipstick hidden at the back of the dressing table drawer. The doorbell rang before she was quite ready.

'I got a lift round,' said Kath, bustling into the hall and checking herself in the mirror by the kitchen door. 'It's a nice night. Oh, look at you, all dressed up. That colour suits you, and some makeup too. What a transformation.'

'Go on with you,' said Jessie, laughing at her friend's excitement. 'We sound like a couple of kids.'

'Well, why not? We're not dead yet, either of us.'

'You're a lot younger than me, though.'

'You've never looked your age, and dressed up like that ... you should do it more often.'

'Get dressed up, or go out?'

'Both,' said Kath. 'Can you dance, by the way? I'm hopeless. I can shuffle in time, but that's about all.'

'I learned to dance during the first war. Shared a house with a few other girls and they taught me. Decades ago, but you don't forget really, like riding a bike.'

'Well, well, hidden depths,' said Kath, squeezing Jessie's arm. 'Let's have a nip of something before we go out. Get in the mood a bit.'

Jessie found the last bottle of sloe gin that was hidden at the back of the kitchen cupboard and poured them both a generous amount.

'This should get us going,' Kath swigged enthusiastically at the full sherry glass of bright crimson liquid, 'Save us some money at the bar.'

By the time they reached the club at the other end of the village Jessie's feet were already hurting in the unfamiliar high-heeled shoes. The club was crowded and the band in full swing. They were playing something loud and modern and couples were gyrating, twisting their bodies, pushing and pulling each other round.

'Won't catch me doing any of that,' said Jessie, pushing Kath ahead of her towards a quieter corner of the hall. 'Quickstep's complicated enough for me.'

'That girl's taken her shoes off,' said Kath, pointing to a young woman with a narrow waisted full skirt, and a pony tail swishing from side to side as she danced.

'They all look so young,' Jessie said into Kath's ear as they found a couple of chairs at a small table. All around them was noise and laughter and movement; suddenly Jessie felt old and out of place. This wasn't a good idea, but she would be stuck here for a while. Kath was obviously enjoying herself already.

* * *

Rebecca had been very tired when Lawrence met her off the northbound train on Friday evening, and he suspected she already regretted her decision to visit. He'd given up asking, having been turned down so often, but this time it had been her idea.

'I'd like to see where you're working,' she said. 'The country-side you're always enthusing about, the plant. I can't picture you there. And that room of yours, looking out at the sea. It all sounds pretty wild.'

He'd booked a double room for them at the front of the hotel, which was itself quite close to the beach. He wanted to hold her when they got into bed, but she said she was too tired, and fell asleep almost at once, leaving him lying quietly beside her, hardly daring to move. He'd forgotten what it was like to sleep in the same bed, worried about disturbing the other person, trying not to touch them. He was disappointed, but not surprised, that she would not even hold him, or let him hold her. It had been a long time.

His other worry had been about the weather. On a good day the village, the sea and the fells inland would help her understand why he loved it so much. But if it was drear and viewless, or wet and windy, he wouldn't be able to share the place with her, not as he knew it. It was not the brilliant day he had hoped for, but the pale sun gleamed on a full tide as they ate the obligatory Saturday morning breakfast in the hotel dining room. Fortunately neither of them had eaten proper kosher food for some years, and the bacon was delicious, but she still wrinkled her nose at the sausage and pushed it to the side of her plate.

'No wonder you've put on some weight,' she said disapprov-ingly. 'You're not eating like this every morning are you?'

'Heavens, no,' he said, thinking of the porridge Jessie offered him most mornings, or toast and marmalade snatched from the table as he scrambled out of the house.

'She makes breakfast for me, Jessie that is, but no other meals. I have a good lunch in the canteen, and often don't bother with much after that, unless I go to Greengarth... That's the hostel,' he added, 'where I lived when I first arrived. It's a few miles away, but they do a good meal there in the evening, and sometimes I get to play bridge or see a film.'

'Who could ask for anything more?' she said lightly. 'Like being back at university.'

'I suppose it is,' he said, realising how much he enjoyed the absence of responsibility. Rebecca revelled in responsibility, he thought, being a mother and grandmother, doing things for other people, feeling needed.

'What do you have planned for today?' she asked, folding her serviette. 'I need a whistle-stop tour.'

'Well,' he said. 'We'll take a bus down to the plant this morning, I thought. Not to stay long; there are only a few places I'll be able to show you. Just so you can get the feel of the place. Then back here, and walk round to the golf club for lunch. Lovely view from there, up to the fells and out towards the Isle of Man, although some days it just disappears, as if someone's pulled it on a string down below the horizon. Then tonight we're going to the club. They usually have a good band, and some of the people I work with will probably be there.'

'Sounds like a fun-filled day,' she said, without enthusiasm.

* * *

'Look over there,' said Kath. 'In a minute, don't turn round yet. Is that him, white hair, round glasses, about your height?'

'How will I know if I can't look round?' said Jessie.

'OK,' Kath whispered, 'try now. They're sitting down, just this side of the bar. He's got up again, to fetch them a drink I expect. Look now.'

Jessie turned slowly to face the bar and spotted Lawrence straight away. Then she saw a woman sitting on her own. Lawrence turned and gestured something to the woman and she nodded her head. It must be Rebecca. Jessie looked at her between people

136

who were moving across her line of sight as the music paused. Rebecca Finer was dark, with a pale face and large eyes and nose, in profile. Her hair was swept up in a pleat at the back of her head, above a long neck. She was wearing a dark long-sleeved dress and as she got up to take the drink from her husband's outstretched hand Jessie could see a slender body, the waist emphasised by a wide belt.

'She's lovely,' said Jessie to Kath.

'I can see that,' said Kath, 'but cold looking, don't you think? Can't tell from here but she looks tall, taller than him maybe. Very London. Does she come from London?'

'He did, originally, not sure about her,' said Jessie, watching as Rebecca looked around the room. Lawrence was still standing, talking to someone. 'They live near Oxford now.'

'Same thing,' said Kath. 'Same look. Posh.'

The band began a waltz. Jessie saw Lawrence turn to his wife and extend his hand. She stood up and stepped round the table to join him.

'They're going to dance,' said Jessie urgently. 'I don't want him to see me. He doesn't know you, Kath. You watch and tell me what you see.'

Jessie turned to face away from the dance floor while Kath applied herself to the appointed task with all the skill of a professional observer.

'She is a bit taller than him,' she said out of the corner of her mouth, 'or maybe it's just the hair. Can't see if she's wearing high heels. They're holding each other, but not closely, not as if they were enjoying it. Not looking at each other.'

'People often dance without looking at each other,' said Jessie. 'Is he smiling?'

'Can't see his face. Now I can. No, he's not. Neither of them are. Look a pretty miserable pair to me.'

'He's quite cheerful, most of the time,' said Jessie.

'Well he's not tonight,' said Kath. She turned towards her friend, 'What's she come up for, did he say? He's been here for months, so why now?'

'No idea,' said Jessie. 'He's never talked much about her. Can I look yet?'

'They're talking to another couple, right on the far side. Take a quick peek. But don't stand up whatever you do.'

It took Jessie a few moments to spot them, and she craned between couples on the dance floor to catch a glimpse. Rebecca was smiling now at the couple that Lawrence must have introduced her to. The man was facing in Jessie's direction and before she could duck out of the way he recognised her, and she him. It was Mr Meadow, her old boss, and the last person, apart from Lawrence, that she wanted to speak to.

Jessie got up, but it was too late. Arthur Meadow excused himself and was heading across the hall towards her. 'Help me Kath,' Jessie whispered. 'Do something to interrupt, when this man –'

'Jessie!' said Arthur Meadow. 'Long time. I've never seen you here on a Saturday night. Angela and I never miss.' He turned and waved across to his wife. Lawrence and Rebecca had already turned away.

You're looking very well if I may say so,' he said, giving Jessie an avuncular peck on the cheek. 'Retirement obviously suits you.'

'Hello Arthur,' said Jessie. 'Have you met my friend Kath Attwood, from the school? Arthur Meadow.' Kath shook Arthur by the hand without getting up, and then leaned forward over the table until her drink overturned, splashing onto her sleeve and dripping down onto Jessie's feet.

'Goodness,' said Kath, getting smartly to her feet. 'How careless of me. So sorry Mr Meadow, has that gone on your shoes?'

'No, mine actually,' said Jessie, hiding her smile as Kath winked at her. 'I need to wipe them off before they stain. Can you excuse me, Arthur?'

'Certainly my dear,' he said, stepping aside. 'No harm done, I hope? I'll see you later. You must come and have a chat with Angela.'

'I will of course, just as soon as I've checked the damage,' said Jessie. 'Look after my seat,' she said to Kath. 'I won't be long.' She leaned over and pinched Kath's shoulder.

'You said I had to do something,' Kath hissed at her. 'And it worked, he's gone.'

'I'll be back,' Jessie smiled. 'Try not to get noticed.'

The Ladies was crowded, and Jessie had to squeeze through to get to the cubicle. One of the women looked familiar, but it was when she heard the voice that Jessie knew who it was. Mary Robinson worked in the wages office at Calder Hall, where John was in charge.

'It's alright for some people who don't have to work any more,' Mary was saying, loud enough for Jessie to hear it quite distinctly. 'They don't have to worry about jobs, and they can say whatever they like. Irresponsible I call it. Official Secrets, that's what they are, and some people need to keep their mouth shut.'

Jessie sat quite still. She heard the door into the hall open and close, and wondered if it was safe to come out. She had no doubt that the comments had been deliberately aimed at her. How many people were thinking that and not saying anything to her face? Did it matter? Surely someone had to be honest about what was happening, in the country not just at the plant, but she didn't like being blamed, not being able to explain. She waited, then opened the cubicle door slowly, relieved to see that there was no one there.

The surprise came when she opened the door back into the hall. Lawrence was standing right in front of her with Rebecca holding his arm. Even in the dim light Jessie could see him blush.

'Jessie,' he said. 'I didn't know you were here. You, I, er, this is my wife, Rebecca,' he said finally. 'Rebecca, this is my landlady, Jessie Whelan.'

'Pleased to meet you,' said Rebecca. 'You stay and talk to Miss Whelan, dear,' she said to Lawrence. 'I won't be a minute.'

She walked past Jessie into the Ladies, leaving the two of them standing awkwardly side by side.

'I didn't know you came to these dances,' he said.

'I don't normally. My friend Kath wanted to and needed me for protection against pushy parents.'

'You look lovely,' he said.

She shook her head. 'Are you having a nice weekend? At least the weather's been all right so far. I thought you might have brought her to see the house.'

'I wasn't sure,' said Lawrence. 'Would that be OK with you?'

'Of course, if you want to,' she said.

'Tomorrow morning?'

'Fine. When's her train?'

'Mid-afternoon. It takes a long time…'

'Of course,' said Jessie.

'Would you like to dance, later?' he said.

Before she could reply the door opened behind her and Rebecca was suddenly standing by his side. He smiled at Jessie, took his wife's hand, and they turned and weaved their way back across the hall towards the bar.

'What did he say?' said Kath, desperate for a report on the encounter.

'Nothing much,' said Jessie. 'He asked me if I wanted to dance, but I didn't have the chance to say before she came back.'

'Do you want to dance with him?' pursued Kath, but there was no reply.

When Jessie looked up a few minutes later and found Lawrence standing at her side, they walked together onto the crowded dance floor without speaking. He steered her as far as possible away from Rebecca who was talking to Angela Meadow.

'You look lovely,' he said.

'You said so before, thank you,' she replied. Neither of them looked at each other but their heads were close. The music was a quickstep but there was no room to dance it properly and they moved gingerly, trying to keep to the beat without doing too much.

'I love to dance, when there's room,' she said.

'So do I. Where did you learn?'

'In Chorley, during the war, the first war.'

'You don't look old enough,' he said.

'Are you having a good time?' she asked.

'You asked me that before. Not really. It feels strange, seeing Rebecca here. She doesn't belong here.'

'Do you?' she asked, glad that she couldn't see his face.

'I'm not sure,' he said, moving his hand on her back. His hand was warm, the pressure unmistakeable.

She pushed him away and stood back.

'I need to sit down,' she said. 'My feet..'

He looked at her. 'Are you sure?'

'Yes. Thank you for the dance, Lawrence. Kath and I will be heading home soon.'

'I'll see you tomorrow, after she's gone,' he said.

'I'm going,' Jessie said to Kath when she got back to their corner. 'You stay here if you want. I have to go.'

Kath could see that something had happened, and that she should not ask what it was. The two women picked up their coats and walked out into the mild evening.

Chapter 15

It was quite late when Jessie woke the following morning. Clouds over the sea were salmon pink and grey, tinted by the rising sun as they flowed towards the north. She opened the curtains and enjoyed the changing light and colours for a few minutes before going down to make a cup of tea, which she took back to bed. Her mind was a jumble of anxious questions. That woman from the wages office: was she repeating what she'd heard from John? Surely not. John might say that in private, but never at the office, not even in a careless moment. And was it what other people thought, people she knew and met around the village? Were they all talking about her?

Suddenly she remembered the feel of Lawrence's hand on her back, the pressure of his fingers, the sound of his voice so close to her ear. The same shiver hit her as she'd felt then. She knew that something had happened, unspoken but real. It had been many years since Jessie had felt the physical impact of a man. With Andrew it had always been there, that tugging tingle. Then she'd felt as if there were two of her, two Jessies in the same body. Schoolteacher Jessie was an educated rational woman, cool, careful, self-contained. The other Jessie hadn't been seen for a while. This woman was passionate, yearning for physical warmth, closeness, the touch of skin. For those few minutes, with

Lawrence's body so close to hers, the reckless passionate Jessie had returned, and in the grey light of the following day she was still here. You're back, rational Jessie thought to herself. You are why I couldn't marry Matthew. I thought you had gone forever. I've missed you so. She lay still in the early light of the room, feeling the warmth of her body, wondering.

In the Scawfell Hotel, just a few hundred yards away, Lawrence was also awake, his wife still asleep beside him. He too had opened the curtains just a little and was watching the pink and grey clouds slide across the sky. He too was thinking of the previous evening. He should never have asked Jessie to dance. As soon as he was close to her, the feeling had hit him again. He'd wanted to hold her tighter, but he hadn't dared. He wanted to tell her what a miserable time he was having, but that too was impossible. She had pushed him away and gone, leaving him to escort Rebecca back to the hotel after she pried herself out of Angela Meadow's deferential clutches. In the darkness of their hotel bedroom he had tried to embrace his wife, and she too had pushed him away.

For a while before sleep they had lain side by side. Rebecca spoke into the darkness.

'I don't enjoy making love any more,' she'd said.

He knew that all too well, but said nothing, holding his breath.

'It's uncomfortable, and…' she hesitated.

'What?' he asked. 'What is it?'

'I don't feel anything for you, not like that. We've been together a long time.'

'Nearly thirty years,' he said.

'Maybe that's long enough.'

He felt suddenly sick, but waited, saying nothing.

'Maybe it's time to face it.'

Still he waited, knowing that she had more to say.

'You have your life, your work, wherever it takes you. That's what you want. I see that. But it's not what I want. We're married but we're not really, not any more.'

'What happened?' he asked.

'Nothing happened. We just got older, separately, doing different things. We can stay married if we want, and live our own lives. Stop feeling guilty about it.'

'Guilty? Is that what you feel?'

'Don't you?' she asked. 'We've let this happen, after all we said when we married, in front of all those people.'

'Do you think they care?'

'I care. I don't want to live with you any more.'

'Is there someone else?'

'Of course not. I just want to be with me, and David and Helen and the children. That's all I want.'

'So why did you come up here?'

'I wanted to be sure. And I knew we would have to talk.'

'Are you sure about this?

'I think so. I want to talk to Rabbi Simons.'

She could not see the expression on Lawrence's face. 'The rabbi? He didn't even marry us, what's it got to do with him?'

'I want him to understand,' she said. 'It matters to me.' She moved, shifting away from him, to get out of the bed.

'No,' he said suddenly. 'You can't just go. We're not finished.'

'What more is there?' she said.

'You haven't asked about me.'

'Because I don't expect you to say anything. You never say anything. That's what I mean. There's nothing left for us to talk about.'

He slapped his hand down on the covers between them. 'But there is,' he said, loudly. She covered his hand with hers.

'Keep your voice down,' she whispered fiercely. 'There are people next door.'

'I –' he began, but stopped. He sat up and swung his legs out of the bed, sitting with his back to her. Outside the day was brightening, the clouds turning from pink to white against the pale blue sky.

'If we're married only in name, why should we stay married at all?'

'That's what I want to talk to Rabbi Simons about,' she said. 'There's no rush is there? We can think, both of us, what we should do?'

He put on his dressing gown and left the room. When he came back, Rebecca was standing by the window, looking out at the morning. A man with a dog was walking slowly along the tideline where bubbles of foam crept over the wet sand.

'We can't talk any more about it now,' she said.

'You mean *you* can't,' said Lawrence. 'You'll go back to your beloved house this afternoon, leaving me here in limbo.' He thought about the week ahead at the plant, worry and uncertainty clashing in his mind. There was pain behind his eyes. He needed water and coffee and food. He remembered saying that they would go to Jessie's house today, to see his flat, but that was not going to happen. They got dressed in silence and went downstairs together.

Little more was said before Lawrence took his wife to the station after a strained final lunch together. Outwardly, they appeared to be a quiet, well-established couple, so easy with each other that conversation was unnecessary, reading each other's thoughts, anticipating each other's needs. But beneath the veneer, Rebecca guessed that she would be blamed if the marriage failed. Lawrence didn't know what to do. He respected his wife as a sensible woman and a caring mother, but there was no more left. His heart was almost empty, and the warmth that lingered there was not for her.

Rebecca did not look up or wave as her train pulled away. Lawrence walked back to the hotel to collect his bag, and then slowly up the hill to the familiar front door. The small clouds of the morning had spread, joined into a solid moving sheet and darkened, but the band of light on the horizon could bring a gold sunset later on. He had work to do before going to the plant on Monday; he would sit at his window to read the sheaf of notes and papers one more time, watching the light on the sea.

The house was quiet as he climbed the stairs. After he reached the top he heard the front door open.

'Jessie?' he called out.

'Down here,' she replied.

He put his bag on the bed and went back down the stairs, into the kitchen.

'I had to catch the post,' she said. 'I saw you ahead of me.'

'Were you expecting us this morning?'

'You mentioned something last night, but it was just in passing. I wasn't sure, and it doesn't matter.' Jessie was standing looking at him, but he could not face her eyes.

'I'm sorry, we, well, something came up.'

'Are you alright?' she said.

'Headache. I forgot to get some aspirin. Don't feel too good.'

'Too much to drink last night?'

'Oh no, it was pretty sober evening. That Meadow chap is a bit of a bore. Not surprised you wanted to get away from him. No, I think I'm either sickening for something, or the tension's getting to me.'

'Tension?'

'Tomorrow,' he lied. 'Big job starts tomorrow. All sorts of things I have to read before I go in.'

'I'll get you some aspirin.' She poured a glass of water for him. 'You know what you said yesterday,' she said, 'About Pat?'

'Did I?' He couldn't recall what he'd said.

'You commented on someone saying I was his protégé.'

'I did? That was rude of me. I'm sorry.'

'No, you were right to notice. Well, I've been thinking about that, and then something that was said last night, at the dance, about me criticising the plant.'

'Who said that?'

'A woman from Calder Hall, from John's office. It was in the Ladies, and I'm sure she meant me to hear it. It made me wonder what people really think of me.'

'Does it matter?'

'Yes it does. I have to live here, for the time being at least. It's hard when people gossip but won't say anything to your face.'

He sat down wearily. 'Rebecca worries about that, too. Maybe it bothers women more than men.'

Jessie wanted to ask about Rebecca, but didn't dare. Rebecca was none of her business. The letter she'd posted earlier was to Pat. They had things to discuss, but with Lawrence there must be a discreet silence. Nothing else would be bearable.

'You're going to be busy at work this week, by the sound of it,' she said, as brightly as she could manage. 'So it's a good time for me to go away for the day, on Wednesday probably.'

Lawrence knew what this meant but he'd mentioned the priest once too often and couldn't do so again. Jessie was free to do whatever she wished, and he had no right to know and less to care. But he could wonder, and he did, again, what there was between her and Pat. He understood all too well what he might see in her, but she? It was hard to understand what women found attractive in a man. For a moment he envied the priest with an intensity that surprised him.

As he climbed back up the stairs, he was determined not to think any more about Jessie or his marriage. The whole purpose of his work at the plant was about to come to a head and he had to concentrate on that alone. He leafed through the stack of notes and papers, looking for a single piece. When he found it, he sat in the chair by the window to take advantage of the last of the light.

Most people would have struggled to understand the tables and figures that drew his attention, but they were pretty clear to Lawrence. Periodically the Windscale reactors needed to be allowed to overheat, to release the extra energy that built up in the graphite core over a period of time. This energy release had to be controlled carefully: it was like a slow, managed, gentle touch on the nozzle of a pressure cooker. If the energy release was too quick it could cause damage; if it didn't happen at all, the reactor would heat up too fast and go beyond their control. The process was called a Wigner release. It had been done successfully several times before, but Lawrence could see from the figures in front of him that it never seemed to happen in the same way. The theory was clear and predictable, but the practice was not. This was what he'd been sent from Harwell to advise about. This was what he'd been investigating and asking questions about in his months at the plant; this was the process he would oversee in the coming week.

Absorption in the complexities of the task, and the impact of a couple of aspirins, worked their magic for a while at least. By the time the light from his little table lamp was too dim to prevent the page from blurring and the headache was nagging once more, he gave up, put down the papers, and went to bed. The troubling events of the weekend were quickly and mercifully obscured by sleep.

* * *

The following morning, Lawrence left the house before Jessie woke, carrying the papers with him to the reactor control room.

Evidence of previous experience should have reassured him, but it did not. When he arrived, the physicist responsible for the pile was in the control room, along with the team of engineers. The atmosphere was more relaxed than Lawrence felt.

'No manual for this one, Lawrence,' said Paul Harris, the physicist. 'Eight previous anneals on this reactor. You've seen the figures. Last time was in November last year. Graphite reached 420 degrees centigrade and took nearly nearly two days to cool down again after the release. '

'What about the uranium temperatures?' Lawrence asked.

'Between 350 and 400 centigrade usually. Temperatures can be a bit patchy, hotter in some parts of the pile than others, but it works out in the end. We'll switch off the fans and do all the initial checks and then I'm going to head off for a while. Feeling really rough.'

'You too?' said Lawrence. 'I felt awful last night.'

'Flu,' said one of the engineers. 'Wife and kids all in bed at our 'ouse. A lot of kids off school apparently. Takes the young 'uns real bad.'

'And the old 'uns too,' said Paul. 'I feel like death warmed up. Let's get the bugger started.'

Once the heating was set in place, there was nothing much to do except keep an eye on the temperature as it began to rise. Lawrence took his turn helping to move the control rods: the switch had to be held down to work the mechanism and even strong men's fingers began to ache badly after a while. Most of the time Lawrence felt fairly redundant as the engineers adjusted the controls and monitored the effects. They were aiming to keep the process as gradual and evenly spread across the reactor as possible and clearly knew what they were doing. Lawrence felt he should stay as long as he could to relieve the pressure on Paul, who was still at his post despite his earlier intention to leave.

By the time Lawrence got back to the house well after seven that evening, his head felt heavy and his throat raw. Whatever it was, he'd got it.

'I'm not surprised you feel bad,' said Jessie, handing over more aspirins and some hot water with a dash of whisky. 'You've been there all day. Do you have to go in so early tomorrow? You should be looking after yourself.'

'Seems to be going OK,' said Lawrence. 'I'll not set the alarm and see if I can get a bit more sleep. '

Jessie was awake when the phone rang just after eight the following morning. Lawrence woke with a start and heard her voice downstairs.

'He's still asleep,' she was saying. 'Not well enough to come in.' There was a pause. 'Can't anyone else help?'

A moment later he heard her step on the stairs and she knocked on his door. 'They want you to go in,' she said. 'Something you need to have a look at.'

'Tell them I won't be long,' said Lawrence. His head was thick with sleep and his body ached, but he knew that Paul Harris was suffering the same way and someone would have to keep an overall eye on things. The engineers were skilled in controlling the vagaries of the Wigner release process, but it was down to the physicists if anything went seriously wrong. Jessie retreated to make him a drink and something to eat. She knew there was no point in arguing with him about it.

* * *

'There's one hot spot,' said Gordon Braithwaite, when Lawrence got back to the control room. 'But the rest of the pile seems to have stalled, and some of the temperatures are going down. Last time this happened we had to start all over again.'

''What's going on?'' asked Lawrence. He peered again at the

dials and figures, puzzled by the unpredictability of what should be a straightforward process.

'Beats me,' said Gordon. 'Could be anything. Burst capsules cause hot spots like this sometimes. There's thousands of capsules and it only takes one or two bad 'uns to bugger things up.'

'When did you say this happened before?'

'Last September, in the other reactor,' said Gordon. 'Worked OK second time around.'

Lawrence thought about it. 'What would you do?' he asked Gordon.

'Me? I'd start again like last time. Nowt else to do. Release has got to 'appen, and right now nothing's 'appening at all.'

'Right you are, then,' said Lawrence. 'Let's do it.'

A short while later, Paul appeared in the control room, feverish and worried about his family at home. His agreement with the decision to re-start, and his promise to stay at the controls for the rest of the day, gave Lawrence the excuse he needed to head back to bed. Jessie was not surprised to see him; she followed him upstairs with a hot drink, drew his curtains against the midday brightness and returned to her book by the kitchen range. She decided not to mention the letter that had arrived for him that morning, the handwritten envelope and the Abingdon postmark. It would wait, she told herself. All in good time.

At the end of the afternoon, when she was sure that he was sound asleep she picked up the phone and dialed a familiar number.

'Is he in?' she asked. 'I see. Well, when he does get back, can you tell him I won't be there tomorrow after all? I have a friend who's really sick, yes, with the 'flu, and I can't get away. Maybe next week ... yes, yes, I'm feeling fine, so far. You look after yourself too, Mrs Foster. Bye for now.'

Jessie put down the phone in the quiet house. A few miles away, deep inside the core of Pile No. 1 at Windscale the hot spot that the engineer had remarked upon earlier in the day was getting hotter, much hotter, unnoticed and uncontrolled.

CHAPTER 16

WEDNESDAY OCTOBER 9TH DAWNED GREY with a swirling wind that whined through a gap beside one of the kitchen windows. It was the first thing Jessie heard when she woke, an insistent accusatory reminder of all the jobs that still needed doing in the house. There was no other sound, no creaking of the floor from upstairs in Lawrence's room, no indication that he was awake. She tiptoed downstairs and took the phone off the hook. He'd said that the process he'd been working on was going smoothly, and if it wasn't they would just have to do without him for a while. She wanted to go and check if he was still asleep but decided to leave well alone. He had 'flu, not pneumonia, and his body would recover, given time and care.

So that any noise or smell of cooking wouldn't seep upstairs, she closed the kitchen door and made herself busy, trying without success to avoid thinking about what was happening, not at the plant but here, in this house, in herself. For the first time she had invited someone to live in her home, and it had been a mistake. She had lived alone almost all her adult life, except for the very short period with Agnes in Newton. That had ended badly, and now this. The house was physically big enough for two people but still she felt confined by another presence. Even when he was asleep he seemed to be intruding on her, and she was uncomfortably aware of him. She had no experience to compare with. Was it possible to share a house with a tenant and not feel like this?

Or was it him? Her rational mind considered this for a while. There was something about him that she couldn't place, something behind the eyes that intrigued her. She'd met clever men before: Matthew Dawson was a clever man, but she had found him narrow and conventional, predictable in a way that would have made her ultimately despise him. Seeing him at Agnes's funeral had confirmed that her decision not to marry him had been right. And those priggish daughters … she shook her head. But this man, this person, was not like that. He'd travelled and worked at the front edge of things all his life, learning, inventing, taking risks. He'd been married, he was still married, and fathered children, watched them grow and leave, and produce children of their own. But that personal life did not define him. He seemed separate, a person in his own right and not just a function of others. Like she was herself.

The perception was flawed of course, and she knew it. Until she had seen Rebecca Finer in person Jessie had encountered Lawrence as an individual only, detached from the rest of his life. Here in this shared space she'd been struck by how alike they seemed to be, seeing the same things, responding in the same ways. But she could see only a fraction of who he was. They knew almost nothing about each other, yet still she trusted him.

I trust him more than I trust Pat, she thought, which is unfair. She had known Pat O'Toole for ten years, seen him in all sorts of situations, knew details of his life and his feelings that he had probably entrusted to no one else. But now she was having doubts. Lawrence had suggested that Pat might be using her for his own ends, to raise his standing among his peers. She did not want to be his mouthpiece, or anyone's. And she wasn't even sure about what 'the cause' stood for any more. Some of the anti-bomb campaigners extended their hostility to the whole idea of nuclear power, and Jessie didn't agree with that. That's what she would have said to Pat today if she'd gone to Maryport to see him as she'd planned. She didn't know how he might respond. He had surprised her before with his generous spirit and the depth of his respect for her, and perhaps he would do so again. And after all, it was Lawrence who had sown these doubts; maybe he had a motive too. She was in a muddle and unhappy about it all.

As she reached for the bread to make some toast, the envelope that had arrived for Lawrence the previous day escaped from its hiding place and fell to the floor, the address face up, a dumb accusation. She picked it up, aware of an overwhelming desire to know what lay inside. It was from Rebecca, she was sure of that – the handwriting, educated and confident, flowing and beautiful. The writer was sure of herself, or at least knew how to impress others. Jessie felt the envelope, trying to gauge how many sheets of paper were inside. It was more than one sheet, she could tell that from the weight, more than just a thank you note. What would Rebecca be saying to her husband? He would have to see it. She couldn't hide it from him forever.

When she could distract herself no longer with domestic activity she put the letter on a tray alongside a hot drink and a slice of toast and carried it up the stairs to the top floor, balancing it on the banister while she leaned forward with an ear to the door. He must have heard her.

'Jessie?' His voice was very quiet.

'Can I come in?' she asked. 'I've brought you a drink and some toast.'

'What time is it?' he was saying as she pushed open the door. He struggled to sit up in bed and she put down the tray to open the curtains. A seagull's cry close by was loud and harsh. When she turned back towards the bed he had pushed a pillow behind him and had settled himself. She put the drink on his bedside table and then placed the tray carefully on the bed before standing back, looking down at him.

'How are you feeling today?'

'Better, I think,' he said, wiping a hand across his mouth. His hair was standing out from his head like a halo, and he asked again, 'What time is it?'

'Nearly noon,' she said. 'Have you been asleep all this time?'

'Must have been. I was very tired.'

'And ill,' she said. 'If it's the same 'flu that everyone else has, you'll feel bad for a while yet. There's tea, and some toast. Plenty more downstairs, or I could do you a proper breakfast.'

He smiled at her. 'You must have been a nurse in a former life,' he said. 'Excellent bedside manner, sister. I feel better already.'

'Don't mock, or I'll take the tray away again. There's a letter for you, too. It came yesterday, but you were so exhausted last night I forgot about it.'

Lawrence picked up the letter.

'From your wife?' Jessie asked.

He nodded. 'Yesterday, you said?'

'Mm. I hope it isn't something urgent.'

He looked at the letter, turning it over in his hands. 'I couldn't have done much yesterday, even if it was.'

'Well I'll leave you to it anyway. Call me if you want anything, or come down if you can manage it.'

He looked at her standing by the door. 'It's Wednesday, isn't it? I thought you were going out today.'

'I decided not to go. I said I had a sick friend who needed looking after.' She pointed at him. 'That's you, and you do,' she added, before she left the room and closed the door behind her.

Half an hour later Lawrence appeared in the kitchen in his long tartan dressing gown.

'Everything alright?' Jessie asked. They both knew what she was referring to.

He shrugged. 'Just a thank you note for the weekend,' he said, but the letter in his pocket stayed there, invisible and silent.

'Do you want some food?' she said.

'No, thanks. Has anyone phoned from the plant?'

Jessie remembered about the phone being off the hook. She shook her head.

'Must be OK then,' he said. 'I'll take a few more hours in bed while I have the chance. Thanks for the tea and toast, it's all I need for now.'

As soon as he had gone back upstairs she went into the hall and looked at the telephone. Thank heaven he hadn't noticed it. She picked up the receiver, but then decided to leave it alone. Lawrence was not fit for work anyway, it was best to let him recover.

The rest of the day passed uneventfully. Lawrence hardly stirred out of his room. Jessie wondered if she could have gone to Maryport after all. Lawrence didn't really need nursing, he just needed time to rest. But she knew too that she really didn't want to face Pat's questions, however kindly they were meant. For a while she listened in case Lawrence showed signs of stirring, but then turned the radio on and whiled away the evening listening to a play and doing some ironing.

Thursday morning was similarly quiet; Jesse was engrossed in measuring and cutting material for a pair of curtains that proved to be unexpectedly awkward. The time passed quickly, with no interruptions to disturb either her concentration or Lawrence's rest. She took him tea and a sandwich at noon, but he didn't stir and she crept away again.

Just before four in the afternoon, with still no sign of movement from upstairs, the front doorbell rang, long and insistent. Jessie hurried to answer it before the sound might wake Lawrence. Kath was on the doorstep.

'Oh, you are here,' she said. 'I knew you might be going to Maryport sometime this week.'

'I should have gone yesterday,' said Jessie, closing the door as Kath walked towards the kitchen. 'But Lawrence is so sick I felt I had to stay and look after him.'

'So he's not at the plant?'

'No, he's asleep upstairs. Not moved much since yesterday afternoon. Why?'

'Something's going on,' said Kath. 'There's stuff coming out of one of the big stacks at the plant, and a Windscale van is just down the road, taking air samples by the look of it.'

'That could be just routine, couldn't it?'

'Maybe, but I have a feeling something's happening. Could be wrong. I rang you to see if Lawrence had said anything, but I couldn't get through. Is something the matter with the phone?'

'Oh, Lord,' said Jessie, remembering, 'I took it off the hook yesterday. They rang here for him and he went in when he shouldn't have done. Came back looking wretched. Quite a few of the managers are off apparently, but what's the point of him going in when he's too sick to do anything?'

She went into the hall and put the phone receiver back on its cradle.

'There,' she said, returning to the kitchen, 'the phone's back on now. If he has to go in, at least he's had a really good rest today. He might be over the worst by now.'

'Has John said anything about the plant?' asked Kath. 'Ah, but he couldn't have talked to you either, not on the phone.'

'I'm not sure he would want to,' said Jessie. 'We've had another falling out.'

'Again? Same problem?'

158

'It's between me and Maggie again, if that's what you mean. We're trying to keep out of each other's way until it calms down a bit.'

'Bad?' said Kath.

'Bad enough for Maggie to say she wanted to move away.'

'Just to get away from you? That's a bit drastic isn't it?'

'I know, but it's been niggling away for so long, and she was really angry.'

'I don't want to hear any more,' said Kath.

Just then the phone rang. Jessie's heart jumped. She hurried to pick it up.

'This is Tom Tuohy at the plant. Is Dr Finer there?'

'He's sick, Mr Tuohy,' said Jessie, 'Been in bed all day.'

'Tell him we need him at the plant, immediately. Meeting in the reactor control room in thirty minutes. Tell him it's urgent.'

Before she could respond the phone went dead.

'Was that for me?' Lawrence called from upstairs.

'It was Tom Tuohy,' she called back.

'Tuohy?'

'He said it was urgent. Meeting in the control room in half an hour.'

'Damn!' said Lawrence. 'I'll be down in a minute.'

He didn't register Kath's presence as he rushed through the kitchen to the backyard a few minutes later. He was unshaven and his hair was still sticking up all round his head. He brushed aside the toast that Jessie held out to him without a word and they heard the bike roar once, twice before he steered it into the alley behind the house and was gone.

'There is something happening,' said Kath. 'I knew it. Let me see if the Windscale van is still there.'

She ran out into the front street where a steady drizzle had started to fall.

'No sign of it,' she said, coming back into the house. 'Leave the phone on, Jessie. I'm going home. I'll ring you if I hear any more, and you do the same.'

Jessie heard the front door slam, and was alone again in the quiet house. She went back into the kitchen and sat down. Then she took her coat from its hook by the back door and went out, walking round onto the front street and down the hill and up again towards the golf course, to where the tops of the plant chimneys came into view to the north. There was the faintest trail of something coming out of one of the chimneys with the big square filters on the top, which Jessie knew were the reactor stacks. But that's what the filters were put there for, she told herself. Nothing much can escape into the air, whatever's going on in the reactor. What could be happening? Why was Mr Tuohy, the Deputy Works Manager, calling an urgent meeting? As she retraced her steps to the house, the village looked the same as ever, nobody on the street or standing in doorways, no more traffic than usual at the end of the working day.

In the hall, she looked again at the telephone. If something was happening, surely John would know. She dialled the number, hoping against hope that John would pick up the phone at his house, but it was Maggie's voice that answered.

'Maggie, it's Jessie.'

Silence. 'What do you want?'

'Is John in?'

'He's only just got in from work. Thursday is wages day – you know he's always busy. He's tired. Do you have to speak to him?'

Jessie hesitated. 'Yes,' she said, 'I'll only be a minute.'

Silence again, then whispers and a rattle on the phone and John's voice.

'What is it?'

'Is there something happening, at the plant?'

160

'What sort of something?'

'I don't know. Lawrence, Dr Finer, has been called in urgently. I just thought you might know…'

'Nothing urgent that I know of, and I wouldn't tell you anyway,' he added, 'unless I had to.'

She swallowed. He distrusted her more than ever.

'I see,' she said. 'Sorry to have bothered you.'

She put the phone down wishing she'd not made the call. She had hoped that the animosity would have faded a little in the few weeks since they had last spoken, but it seemed as bad as ever. Maggie would have been listening, she told herself. John would have to be brusque, just to show his loyalty.

She went up to Lawrence's room to tidy up and bring down the tray. The room was stuffy and smelled of sleep, and she opened the window just a little, feeling the sharp rush of cool damp air. The draught caught a page of the letter that had been left on the bed, and it beckoned to her. She knew it was wrong, but she could not resist.

My dear, the letter began. Jessie peered at the script in the half-light, but didn't dare pick up the page. If I don't touch it, she reasoned, it's not so bad. She read on, moving the counterpane a little to uncover the bottom of the page.

I hoped that coming to see you last weekend would make it all clear to me, but I am still unsure. If there had been any sign from you that you still love me, but there was nothing. You have withdrawn from me before. I told myself then that it was to protect you when we had to live apart, far apart, not just a long train journey as it is now. If it would save our marriage I could come and stay with you until you are sent back here. But I don't think it would, and you know how much I need to be here, in my own home, near our family.

There is nothing for me in that miserable place so far from anywhere. You have no choice, as it's all about your precious work, but I can choose, and I am choosing…'

Jessie looked for the second page, but could not see it. Maybe it was underneath. In any case, she didn't want or need to read any more. She sat on the little chair by the window and looked out at the slate grey blur of moving sea and sky.

Chapter 17

LOOKING BACK LATER ON THE AWFUL DAY, Lawrence could remember very little about what happened before he arrived at the plant. He had woken up feeling thick-headed, he'd drunk the tea Jessie had left, and at some point he had read a letter from Rebecca. All he could remember was something about choices. Then he'd heard the phone ring. After that he could recall nothing until he opened the door of the Windscale control room. Inside the air was blue with cigarette smoke and unspoken anxiety. Everyone was standing, hands in pockets or holding cigarettes, looking at their feet or at the dials and controls that surrounded them. There was not much conversation. Like waiting for the coffin at a funeral, Lawrence thought.

It looked like everyone was there: some he hadn't seen for days who'd been off sick, others from different shifts that he didn't recognise at all, even some of the young ones from Greengarth, looking more serious than the last time he'd seen them. Gethin Davey, the Works Manager, was at the far end of the room. Lawrence had heard the man was ill, really sick, not just the 'flu, and he looked it. They were obviously waiting for something.

'Tuohy's gone down to the charge face to see what's happening,' said an older man standing next to him who turned and held out his hand. 'Ross,' said the man, 'from Risley. Came up for a routine visit yesterday. Bad timing. Bit of a mess, eh? Not met you before, have I?

'Lawrence Finer, from Harwell. I'm a visitor too, "offcomers" I think they call us. They seconded me here for a while to check the Wigner release process. Started the anneal on Monday, you probably know that. Looked as if it was going by the book for a while and then all sorts of odd things were happening. I was feeling so deadly I might have missed something. Flu, I suppose, like everyone else. I was in bed when I got the call to come in. I wasn't here yesterday at all. Do you know what's been happening?'

'When I got in this morning there was a flap on,' said Ross, keeping his voice down. 'Second release, the one they authorised on Tuesday, should have been just about finished but the temperatures had kept on rising apparently. Next thing we know there's radioactive material sending the monitors on top of the stacks off the scale, kicked off a site emergency. I'm surprised they didn't get you back in then. Tuohy was at home with his wife and kids, 'flu as well. They couldn't get the remote scanners to work to see what was happening, so Tom Hughes got suited up and went to have a look. They took out an inspection plug and the damn thing was bright red, glowing like a cherry, Tom said. Balloon went up after that. Cigarette?'

'No, thanks,' said Lawrence. His mind was racing. The pile was on fire. What the hell would they do now? He went back over the events on Tuesday when they'd decided on the second release. He could hardly remember anything except feeling ill. So what had happened, and what was happening now?

The control room door opened and Tom Tuohy came in. Everyone knew him: tall, energetic, lots of auburn hair. A handsome man, thought Lawrence. Looks pretty healthy compared to the rest of us, especially standing next to his boss, Mr Davey, as he was now. The two had a brief conversation before Tuohy stood up and faced them all. The room went very quiet.

'Sorry to keep you, everyone,' he said. 'Had to go down to see for myself.' He hesitated. 'Not sure where to start.'

Gethin Davey looked up at his deputy. 'Tell them what we know, Tom,' he said wearily.

As Lawrence listened to the catalogue of the day's events he began to feel sick. They'd found the hotspot in the pile and a team of men had been suited up and sent down to get rid of the overheating fuel rods by pushing them through and out into the pool on the other side. When the rods came out they were red hot. That was the seat of the fire. So all the neighbouring channels had to be cleared to make a fire break.

'What about the fans?' someone asked.

'Fans were left on to try and cool the pile, and then when the men were working at the charge face we kept them on, to keep heat down for them,' said Tom. 'No other way to get temperature down.'

Lawrence put his hand to his face. He knew what everyone was thinking; if the bloody pile's on fire, the fans will just spread it.

'We've had eight men working down there for two hours,' Tom was saying. 'They need steel poles.'

Ross leaned in to whisper to Lawrence. 'Aluminium poles were melting onto the floor, and the channels were so distorted the men were exhausted trying to push them through. Fire chief said he'd never seen anything like it. Bloody heroic, he said.'

Tom carried on. 'Have to get more men at the charge face. Can't leave them there for long, too much exposure, even suited up. There's some steel scaffolding poles on t'other side, at the power plant. Heavier, but they won't melt so quick. We'll need as many as we can get. And the temperatures in the pile are still going up.'

Lawrence looked in horror at the dials he could see. Nothing like this was recorded in any of the previous history of the reactor. This was uncharted territory and they were lost.

'What's next?' said a voice. Tom Tuohy looked out into the crowd in front of him. 'Gausden, Finer, what will this heat do?'

Heads turned towards Lawrence, but he was rescued by Ron Gausden's voice from the other side of the room, speaking quietly, deliberately.

'If the temperatures keep rising we could have a release that ignites the whole core. Burning radioactive material is already getting up and through the filters, and they might get blown away altogether. Then there's nothing to stop the stuff shooting out. Radioactive material would be spread over the whole area, beyond the plant.' He paused. There was absolute silence for a moment while every man's mind worked on the horrific implications, thinking of their families.

'That's what we have to stop,' said Tom, taking control of the room once again, forcing people back to action. 'We'll shift as many rods out as we can, but it's getting harder because of the heat distortion. When the fire break is as big as we can get it, then we go for the seat of the fire and get it out, whatever it takes. As soon as the men are withdrawn finally we can cut off the fans. Then we try carbon dioxide, or argon. Last resort is water.'

Lawrence caught his breath. Ross felt the reaction and turned toward him. They looked at each other. Both of them knew what could happen.

'*Shtup*,' said Lawrence. 'You know Yiddish?' Ross shook his head. 'Just as well,' said Lawrence. 'It means a bit more than "oh, dear".'

Davey had struggled to his feet. 'Tom will stay here. I need Ron Gausden, Dr Finer, Mr Ross, in my office now please. Police and fire chiefs are here, and we need your expertise. Carry on everybody.'

Carry on with what, thought Lawrence. The room began to empty. Where were they all going? Why was no one shouting or asking more questions?

'Come on,' said Ross.

In Gethin Davey's office there were no easy answers. The emergency plan had been in place for years but seem to be limited to a predictable radioactive release through the stacks, with the assumption that most of the fallout would be caught by the filters. People in the area would be warned to stay indoors with the windows closed, but who could predict the speed or direction of the wind that would carry a plume of radioactive material? It seemed to be a case of first things first, and no precipitate decisions. These men were used to dealing with emergencies, thought Lawrence. That must be why they all seemed so calm.

'Finer,' said Gethin Davey. 'We need you to explain what we have to consider if the carbon dioxide and argon options don't work. We already know we probably don't have enough carbon dioxide on site, and the argon method's never been used in these circumstances. Is that right, Mr Ross? So water may be the only chance. Keep it simple, if you can. The practical implications, please.'

Ron Gausden looked across at Lawrence, as if to say 'Get on with it.'

Lawrence took a deep breath,

'I can give you the basic science,' he began, 'what could happen, but these are exceptional circumstances...'

'Yes, we know that,' Davey interrupted him. 'Just spell it out, man.'

'Let's say that several tons of uranium are on fire,' said Lawrence. 'The heat is going to weaken the structure that contains the pile, and the metal parts will already be melting, unless we can contain the fire by other means. Contact with water oxidises the molten

167

metal, strips the oxygen from the water molecules and leaves free hydrogen. This could combine with the incoming air and cause an explosion.' The faces he could see around him registered frozen fear. No one spoke, and Lawrence continued. 'The containment structure housing the pile would probably be torn apart by the explosion, and possibly the stacks and the filters too. Nothing to stop burning material being blown for long distances. There could be blast damage across the plant where we are and severe irradiation across the whole area.'

The silence persisted.

'This is what could happen, but if we can get the right volume and direction of water, then the flames could be swamped and the reaction not take place. And if there is a reaction we can't predict its strength. We just don't know, won't know until it happens.'

'Christ,' said the fire chief at last.

'What about the fans if we have to use water?' Ross asked.

'I've been thinking about that,' said Lawrence. 'Seems to me there are three considerations. First, we have to keep the core as cool as possible to avoid a high temperature release; second, on the other hand, the fans will be helping the existing fire to spread. Third, and this is really imponderable, if and when hydrogen is released, having the fans on could disperse it and reduce the impact of any reaction.'

All the men considered these implications, then Ross spoke again. 'What's your advice?'

Lawrence thought about it again. 'On balance,' he said finally, 'If we're using water, I'd leave the fans on until we're sure that any hydrogen has dispersed, then turn them off.'

'Good,' said Davey. 'Agreed, gentlemen?'

They nodded.

Gethin Davey moved on. 'What about evacuation? Take us through that, Superintendent.'

'First step is to declare a full alert, get an incident centre set up here at the plant, arrange transport, evacuation centres, all that. It'll take a few hours, and it's always a risk, especially in the dark. Can't make people stay in their houses under cover and then have them standing around outside waiting for transport. They could be worse off being evacuated than they are now, depending on what happens with the fire.'

'So we're back to the first priority, getting the fire out,' said Davey. He may be sick, thought Lawrence, but his mind's OK. He wondered what the illness was.

Davey turned towards Lawrence. 'You stay here, Finer, with the fire chief and Tom, and we'll get the firefighting organised. You stay too, Ross, if you will. You've worked in oil haven't you, all that experience of fighting fires?'

'Well...' Ross began, but no one was listening and he fell silent.

Davey looked round the room. 'We have representation from Risley here in the person of Mr Ross. I suggest that for the time being we put all our energy into dealing with this situation ourselves. No time to start detailed briefings or wait for a Risley team to get here. Agreed?'

They all looked at Ross. 'Agreed,' he said.

Gethin Davey tried to stand, but grimaced with pain and slumped back into his seat.

'If I have to leave,' he said, 'Tom's in charge. We can talk on the phone if we need to.'

They all nodded. Thank God for Tuohy, thought Lawrence.

For the rest of the evening on that long Thursday, Lawrence was as fully engaged in a problem as he had ever been. He blessed the extra rest he'd been able to get earlier, but still when he heard at midnight that Gethin Davey had gone home, he longed to do the same. While the fire and police teams began their preparations Lawrence was able to escape, go to the toilet, wash his face, and get a drink for the first time in hours. It was then that a heaviness of body and spirit swept over him.

He went back to his dark quiet office and sat for a while, thinking. Even as he'd given the barest details of what might happen, part of his mind had seen images that he could not get out of his head. Burning lumps of toxic metal and brick raining down on the plant, breaking through roofs, shattering windows. Deadly steam and dust blowing through the sleeping village, onto the school playground, gardens, fields, sheep, cattle. In the morning those same cows would be milked, they had to be, and the milk would be collected and bottled and delivered and drunk.

He found a list, checked it and picked up the internal phone. A sleepy voice answered.

'Howells here.'

'It's Lawrence Finer.'

'Yes, Finer, sorry, I was asleep. No point in going home but I had to get a bit of rest before all hell breaks loose. Whatever happens … well you know what I mean. It's started already, fallout all over the place. Filters no bloody use, not for this.'

'I've done what I can for now,' said Lawrence. 'They know all I can tell them about the water option for the fire. Even if it works there's going to be a terrible mess.'

'Terrible,' said Huw.

'You're the health physics man, Howells, but I can help out if you want. Have to do something useful. Nothing worse than feeling redundant when things are as bad as this.'

'They are bad, aren't they? Is it just you and me who can see that? Pretty stoical lot up here but you'd think there'd be a bit more weeping and wailing going on. Nobody's even raised a voice.'

'Fear, probably, and knowing we have to get this right. Panic would be a bit of a luxury.'

'Well I'm panicking, I can tell you. Wife and three kids just down the road, all asleep I should hope, and then what? Stuck in the house for days, or bundled off to some godforsaken school hall somewhere. I want to ring, but I'd only wake them up and what could I say?'

'You must be thinking about the milk,' said Lawrence. 'I'm sitting here picturing all those bloody cows munching away, and trotting off into the milking shed in a few hours, udders full of iodine 131, and that's just the start. Whatever happens with the fire, there's more irradiated pasture out there with every minute, and we're sitting here, waiting.'

'And I'll tell you something else,' said Huw, fully awake now. 'I can't find any figures about safe levels of ingestion for anyone except adult males. So even when we get the milk and test it, what are we looking for? How much iodine 131 will harm a baby?'

'There's nothing?'

'No data at all. That's why I need to get some sleep. As soon as it's light and I can get some help I'll start doing the calculations.'

'What about the milk samples?'

'I'll get those organised too. It's the afternoon milk we'll need most urgently, from local places first and then further afield, when we know … when the fire's out and we know more.'

'Right,' said Lawrence, thinking that by the Friday afternoon testing milk might be the least of their problems. 'You go back to sleep. I'm going to do the same. They're going to try the carbon dioxide for the fire. That might work.'

'Right,' said Huw.

Lawrence put down the phone. He was sure there wasn't enough carbon dioxide or argon available to be effective, but there was no point in spreading any more gloom. He looked at his watch. It was just before 1 a.m.

He reached for the phone again, an outside line this time. It rang for a long time before she picked up.

'It's me,' he said. 'I want you to listen really carefully.'

Jessie felt her heart pump. 'I was asleep. What's happening?'

'Can't tell you much. Is there any way you could get out?'

'Out of the house?'

'No, out of Seascale, right away?'

She thought for a moment. 'It's the middle of the night, Lawrence. When are you coming back?'

'God knows. Jessie, listen, if you can't get out, just make sure all the windows are closed tight, and don't go outside. D'you hear me?'

'Yes. Why, what's happening?'

'Don't ask. It's bad here. You may have to be evacuated. Start getting a few things together, essentials, just in case.'

'What about you?' she said.

'I'll have to stay, we all will.' He hesitated. 'Can you ring John?'

'It'll have to wait till morning.'

'Before he goes to work, call him and tell him not to go in. And Maggie should take the children away.'

'Away where?'

'Anywhere. As far as they can get.'

'Whitehaven?'

'No good. Maryport might work. Do they know Pat, the priest?'

'Pat married her and John ten years ago. They haven't seen much of him since he left.'

'Maryport would be good. Tell them that.'

'Lawrence,' she said. 'Take care of yourself. Please.'

'Goodbye, Jessie.'

172

CHAPTER 18

JESSIE PUT THE PHONE DOWN. It was one o'clock on Friday morning. Surely Lawrence was exaggerating. He couldn't expect them all to set off in the middle of the night. And she couldn't ring John again. Lawrence had sounded strange, maybe the news from Rebecca had upset him so much he wasn't thinking straight. He couldn't have been drinking, not at work. She had the number somewhere to call him at the plant if ever there was a need. It took a while to find it, and when she dialled there was no response. Greengarth, she thought, and dialled that number. A sleepy voice answered.

Jessie didn't give her name. 'I'm trying to reach someone who works at the plant, one of the scientists. It's a family emergency. But I can't get through.'

'Can't help you. No one here, they've all been called in.'

'Has something happened?' she asked.

'I can't help, sorry,' said the voice.

She wanted to walk round towards the plant and see for herself, and had got half dressed before she remembered what Lawrence had said about staying inside. But how could they be evacuated if they had to stay inside? None of it made sense. She made herself a cup of tea and went back to bed, setting the alarm for seven o'clock to phone John before he left for the office. He was usually up first in the house, and she might be able to talk to him without Maggie listening in.

* * *

'Hello,' said John's voice. It was just after seven.

'John, it's Jessie. Don't hang up on me, please. I don't want to pester you, but Lawrence Finer rang me late last night and made me promise that I'd speak to you.'

'What about?'

'He said that you shouldn't go in to work today, that you and Maggie should take the boys away, maybe up to Maryport. You'd be safer there.'

'What? Was he at the plant when he rang?'

'Yes. He said there was a problem, he didn't say what it was, and that you should keep away. I'm not making this up, John. That's what he said.'

'I've heard nothing about it, whatever it is,' said John. 'Someone would have told me if the plant was closed.'

'It's not. I phoned Greengarth hostel and someone there said that they'd all been called in.'

'Called in, not sent away. That doesn't make sense. I can't just not turn up. And I'm sorry, Jessie, but the chances of Maggie saying "Right-oh, let's all go to Maryport because Jessie's lodger says so", well, that's not going to happen, is it?'

'I told him that,' said Jessie miserably. 'I said you wouldn't listen.'

'Well, you've done what he asked, so that's all you can do. I'm going to work like I normally do on a Friday. I'll tell Maggie to keep her ears open in case anything has happened, but leave that to me. Now I have to go or I'll be late.'

There was a brief pause as he hesitated. 'Are you still there?'

'I'm here,' she said.

'Let's try and sort this mess out. Maggie's calming down gradually, and I want to persuade her that we can manage, all of us, without anyone having to move house. We're happy here, and you want to stay in Seascale, don't you?'

Jessie didn't respond. She was so confused she didn't know what she wanted any more.

'You have to help me, Jessie,' he was saying. 'Don't do anything for another few weeks and we'll see how it goes. Let's all just concentrate on living our lives.'

'Alright,' she said.

'Goodbye, Jessie. Take care of yourself.'

There was nothing more she could do. For a while she sat by the phone, still only half dressed. Nothing seemed real or certain. She had trusted Lawrence's judgment, but now he was acting so strangely. Something was going on, Jessie was sure of that, but what, and why did nobody else know anything? She needed to eat and made some porridge. There wasn't much food in the house but she wasn't supposed to go out. It was all ridiculous. Just before nine she had a brainwave and called the school. Hearing Kath's familiar voice made her feel a little better.

'There must be something happening,' said her friend. 'Half the children haven't turned up. One or two messages saying they wouldn't be in, but for most of them no word at all. They're just not here.'

'Maybe it's the 'flu,' said Jessie.

'I think something's happened at the plant and the word's got around. The school is like a morgue.'

John saw smoke coming out of one of the Windscale stacks when he arrived for work as usual at eight-fifteen. Nothing was said at the gate, but as soon as he got to the office, a message from the General Manager arrived to say that everyone should assemble in the canteen straight away. No questions, just do it. He wanted to call Maggie, but there was no time. As manager of his own department it was John's job to make sure that everyone did as they had been told. There was some grumbling, and he noticed that a fair number of people were absent, but by ten to nine they were all in the crowded canteen, asking what was happening and would they be sent home early. Some problem at the reactor was all they were told, which might explain the smoke he'd seen. No one seemed unduly concerned. Card games were started, newspapers read, cups of tea drunk. It was quite enjoyable, John realised, to have the time to talk to some of the people he worked with every day. Maybe they should do this more often. He looked at his watch: five minutes to nine.

On the other side of the River Calder, a few hundred yards away in the Windscale control room, Lawrence looked at his watch. It was five minutes to nine, the agreed time for starting the flow of water on the burning pile. As expected, using carbon dioxide or argon had proved to be fruitless. In the early hours of the morning he, Tuohy and the fire chief had planned and supervised the setting up of four massive fire hoses and a gantry of scaffolding to take the hoses to about a metre above the pile. The fire was at the base and the water would need to drop down almost vertically to have the greatest effect. Preparations were complete around seven o'clock, but then Tuohy decided they would have to wait until the night shift was safely away and the day shift had arrived and could be confined under cover. Lawrence could see the reasoning, but a delay of two hours was terrifying. Already the fire at the back of the pile was burning blue; Tuohy checked it regularly by climbing onto the pile roof to look down through the inspection window. 'It's an inferno,' he said.

When the operation started, only Tuohy and the fire chief would remain in the reactor building; everyone else was ordered out for their own protection. Lawrence had decided that he would stay in the control room to see it through. He'd expected others to find a more distant spot or an urgent reason to go home but when he opened the heavy door it was even more crowded than before, quiet and tense. There was little conversation. The men stood in small groups or alone, watching, waiting. For many hours none of them had slept, and the air was thick with smoke, sweat and silent fear.

Tuohy was hidden from sight, but they could hear his voice over a loudspeaker, and the dull roar of the fans. If it blows, we'll hear him die, thought Lawrence. He held onto the back of a chair, his knuckles white. Tuohy's voice was clear and steady. One last check with the fire chief and then the instruction.

'OK, water on.'

They heard the crash as hundreds of gallons of water hit the burning pile. In the control room, no one moved. Nothing. No explosion. A young man standing next to him turned his face to the wall. A long moment. They held their breath. Still nothing. Lawrence relaxed his grip on the chair. He breathed out. 'Thank God,' the young man whispered. Lawrence put a hand on his shoulder.

'Tuohy?' said the man with the intercom microphone.

'Less pressure,' Tom's voice came back. 'Turn the pressure down, not much. Water has to drop, not getting close enough… Better, better, keep it coming.'

One thousand gallons of water per minute was cascading down onto the scorching pile. Irradiated steam and smouldering toxic fragments propelled by heat and pressure from the fans were swept up the stack and out into the morning air, caught by the wind and blown away, over the village and the fields and the fells and the east coast and the North Sea, on and on.

'Fans off?' yelled Tuohy.

Lawrence pushed through to the microphone. 'Not yet,' he yelled back. He could see the reaction in his mind's eye, the hydrogen waiting to catch and blow the reactor apart. 'Keep the water coming, drown it.'

For another hour while the water poured down, the fans stayed on, until the hydrogen danger had passed. When they were turned off, almost immediately Tuohy saw the flames begin to subside. Up and back he went to the inspection window, checking, checking, for two more exhausting dangerous hours. When he was certain that the fire was out he climbed down, took off his soaking protection suit and helmet, showered and scrubbed the poison from his body and emerged to report to his boss that the job was done and that Pile No. 1 was a tangled wreck.

* * *

The water was kept running for many hours, contaminated puddles forming outside the reactor building. Men in protective suits brushed and channelled the water back into the ponds and buses arrived to take home all the day shift workers who had been confined under cover throughout the morning. The unusual convoy, several hours earlier than normal, was the first clear and public indication that something important had happened at the plant.

Lawrence took the first opportunity to get away and drove his motorbike unsteadily back to the house. Hearing the engine throb and fade, Jessie held out her hand to him as he almost fell in to the kitchen. She asked no questions, helped him out of his coat, sat him in the best chair by the range and made tea for them both before anything was said. He held the mug in both hands and sipped slowly.

'Lots of sugar in it,' she said, watching his hands. 'You look pretty shaky.'

He nodded, and looked up at her, his eyes red-rimmed behind his glasses.

'Are you alright?' he asked. 'Did you stay inside?'

'I called John like you said, but he insisted on going to work. I don't know what happened with Maggie and the boys. Kath says half the children didn't turn up at school.'

He nodded. 'Good. Now we have to deal with the milk.'

'What milk?' she said, glancing at the jug on the table.

'The milk that's not been produced yet,' he said.

She stared at him. 'What happened, Lawrence? Tell me.'

He looked at her again. 'We're still alive,' he said, 'that's the good news. For a while I thought…' He looked away. 'I thought I might never see you again.'

She helped him up the stairs and into bed. Before she left him, he gripped her hand. 'Don't let me sleep too long. Four o'clock latest. I have to be back by the time the samples arrive.'

'What samples?' She wondered if shock had affected his mind.

'Milk,' he said. 'Before I came back, I had to get that organised. Have to get them to Harwell tonight.'

She wanted to ask more, but he was gone, curled up with his knees towards his chest, like a foetus.

She got to the village shop just in time before they ran out of bread. Outside the Scawfell Hotel two men were getting out of a car. One of them called across to her. 'Do you live here, madam? May we ask you some questions?'

'Too busy,' she called back, quickening her step up the hill to avoid them. Newspapermen, already? What had they heard, she wondered, and how did they get here so fast?

She made lunch for herself. It was too early to wake Lawrence. She turned on the radio and listened to the news, but there was nothing. As she turned it off, he was standing at the kitchen door.

'Can you tell me now?' she said. 'Sit down, I'll make us a drink and you tell me what's been going on.'

Lawrence told her what he knew, about the fire and the water. 'I thought there might be an explosion,' he said. 'We all did. None of us knew for sure what would happen when they turned on the water.'

Jessie listened, her hand over her mouth.

'Is the fire out now?'

'Yes, just about, and the reactor is finished. Tuohy says it's just a mess, irreparable.'

'Who called the press?' she asked.

He groaned. 'Somebody will've done. There are thousands of people at the plant. Someone will have made a call, pocketed a fiver.'

'There were two men, strangers, outside the hotel when I went to the shop,' she said. 'They tried to ask me questions.'

'What did you tell them?'

'Nothing. I didn't know anything.'

'That won't stop some people talking,' he said. 'They'll make up all sorts of stuff and the papers will love it.'

She made some lunch for Lawrence and he ate as if he'd been starving for days.

'I'm going to Harwell tonight,' he said.

'Tonight? How? You're not fit to drive.'

'They're giving us a driver, me and the health physics man. We'll take the first milk samples down for analysis. I can sleep in the car. We can't do all the milk testing here.'

Jessie looked again at the jug on the table.

180

'Throw the milk away,' said Lawrence. 'We'll have to do without for a while. The grass has probably been contaminated since the fire started, but the filters will have caught some of it. It's from this morning that it really matters. We still don't know what we're looking for, but my guess is that all the local milk will have to be destroyed. After that, it depends on the wind.'

'That's terrible,' said Jessie, appalled. 'What about children, babies? And the farmers?'

He shook his head.

'Maggie needs to know,' he said. 'Should I call her?'

'I can't do it,' said Jessie. 'If you speak to them at least they'll know I've not been making a fuss over nothing.'

Later in the afternoon, Lawrence was ready to leave. It was only when she saw the overnight bag that she knew what he was going to do.

'You'll stay at your house, won't you?'

'Of course,' he said. 'Rebecca's expecting me.'

'How long will you be away?'

He looked at her. 'I'll be back tomorrow, late probably. All hell will break loose in the next few days. I need to be here.'

A car horn sounded outside in the street. He glanced at his watch. 'That'll be for me,' he said. 'Don't talk to anyone about what I've told you, please, Jessie. The less people know about what actually happened over there, the better.'

'Lawrence,' she said, reaching out to him. He took her hand and squeezed it.

'I know,' he said. 'We need to talk. We will.'

He left the front door open and she watched him climb into the back of a large black car. The car pulled away down the hill towards the main road. She watched until it turned the corner, but he didn't look back.

She'd been back in the house only a few minutes when the

phone rang again. She hated the thing but it was proving useful today.

'Jessie?'

'Pat, it's you.' She did not want to speak to him.

'I've just heard. Something's going on down there isn't it, at the plant. Mrs Foster's daughter rang. Her husband works at Windscale and they were all taken home early by bus. That lodger of yours works there, doesn't he? What's he said?'

'He's not here,' said Jessie. It was true; he wasn't there, not now. 'He's had to go to Harwell.'

'Do you know what happened?'

She thought quickly. 'Gossip round here is about a fire in one of the piles. It's out now, apparently.'

'But what about you?' he asked. 'Are you OK?'

'Yes, I'm fine. Can't see the plant from here, so it's hard to tell what's happening. I know they sent everyone home.'

'I'll come down myself tomorrow,' he said, his voice raised with the excitement of it all. 'We need to find out as much as we can. This could be it, Jessie, just what we've been waiting for, to show how reckless the whole business is. The place will be crawling with press. Just what we need. I'll get the first train in the morning, be there about eight. Don't meet me, I'll come straight up to the house.'

'Pat,' she began, but the line went dead.

CHAPTER 19

JESSIE WAS SURPRISED to see Pat O'Toole so animated. 'Never seen the place this busy!' he said, striding through to the kitchen. 'Lots of people milling around near the station. You'd know better than me, but they don't look like locals. There's a van outside the hotel with some kind of aerial on top. Could be television. They didn't take long to get here.'

'Like vultures finding a corpse,' said Jessie.

Pat seemed not to hear her. 'You should feel vindicated, Jessie, after all you've said about safety and everything. Now it's happened. A fire! You can smell it out there. Think what's been coming out of the stack! Now we can hammer them.'

Jessie turned from the sink where she was washing her break-fast pots, looking for her favourite mug for more tea.

'Hammer who?' she asked.

'The government, of course,' said Pat. 'You made me see how the rush for bombs was putting the plant under pressure. And here we are. We can blame the fire on the bomb programme, and people will have to listen. What a gift, and the timing! Couldn't be better.'

She stared at him. 'Is that what you think? Really?'

'Of course. Don't you? Can't you see it?'

She looked at his gleeful face. 'Listen, Pat,' she said. 'I live

183

here. Most of my neighbours work at the plant, their children go to school just down the road. Right now we're all worried about how much radioactive rubbish is settling on us. I haven't given much thought to anything else.'

'Of course, of course,' he said, only mildly deflated. 'What have they told you about all that. What's the risk?'

'We've heard nothing,' she said, 'except someone on the radio this morning saying everything is under control, no danger to life and so on.'

'But they would say that, wouldn't they?' He spoke over her, shaking his head. 'They'll want to play the whole thing down, stands to reason.'

Jessie sat down opposite her old friend and leaned forward, trying to get through to him. 'You're still not listening to me, Pat,' she said. 'This is serious, not just some stunt you can make a meal out of. God knows what happened there yesterday, but we saw the smoke pouring out, at least it looked like smoke. All the day shift were sent home in buses yesterday afternoon. And now the Windscale vans are scuttling around taking samples. Those press people you're so excited about, they'll be having a field day, but they can go home later and forget all about it. We have to live here. Here, in Seascale, not in Maryport.'

'Yes, I was thinking about that,' he said, impervious. 'If that lodger of yours is away, I wondered if I could use his room for a day or two while it's all going on. Need to be on the spot really, to get all the information I can.'

She slammed her hand down on the table between them. 'Stop it, Pat' she said. 'Just for a minute, stop prattling on like a schoolkid.'

She waited. Pat's face lost its gleam.

'Of course I can see what you're so excited about,' she said quietly. 'With all the national anti-bomb campaigners getting together, I know how much they could make out of this. But don't expect me to feel the same about it. We know what it could mean for this village. Half the children weren't at school yesterday. Mothers have gathered up their children and gone, anywhere, just to get away. There must have been plenty of phone calls flying around yesterday. But no one's making a big fuss about it, not yet. Half the plant's shut down, and heaven knows what a mess the fire has made. How long will it take to get it running again, and what happens to the workers in the meantime?'

'There's always been a risk...' he began.

'What?' She was furious now. 'Are you actually saying that people who work at the plant have got what they deserved, that they shouldn't be working there at all? What are they supposed to do? Stay down the pits? Go on the dole?'

He leaned away from her and held up his hands. 'Whoa,' he said. 'Let's calm down a bit. That's not what I'm saying. It just seems as if something like this was bound to happen, sometime, and now it has. It's an accident. No one got hurt, as far as we know. Ten years ago an accident in a pit killed a hundred men, You remember that.'

'Of course I do,' she said. 'An old friend was one of the few who survived. And John was involved too. It was a dreadful time.'

'Well then, compared with that, this is just property damage.'

'That's not true. We have no idea what the fallout will be. They're worrying about the milk already.'

Pat thought about that for a moment. Jessie got up from the table, wishing she hadn't mentioned it.

'The milk, yes,' he said suddenly. 'Radioactive stuff falls on the grass, cows eat the grass, cows get milked, people drink the milk. Children drink more milk than the rest of us. Oh my God.'

'You see?' she said, turning back to him. 'You see why we're worried about that rather than some blip in the bomb programme?'

'No wonder those press people looked so pleased,' he said. 'That's what they're going to write about, most of them anyway, not about bombs.'

'Do you want tea, or are you too excited for that?' she asked, filling the kettle. Her anger was beginning to subside. Having someone in the house with her, someone to talk to, was better than fretting alone in the big empty space. She wanted to call John but couldn't take the risk of upsetting Maggie again. Kath had the school to worry about. What would happen there?

Pat had taken a little notebook out of his bag and was scribbling in it.

'What are you writing?'

'Just a few notes, things I'll probably forget. There are bound to be questions at the next meeting about this. They'll want to know the real story, not just the versions the press and the government put out.' He looked up. 'What about that lodger of yours?'

'You know he's not here. I don't know when he'll be back.'

'Pity,' said Pat. 'Would have been useful to see what he's up to.' He waited a moment before asking his question again. 'So can I stay a few days? Just while it's all going on. I'll keep out of your way.'

Jessie was surprised how quickly she decided. 'Not a good idea,' she said. 'I'm in enough trouble round here for speaking out against the plant since I retired. I honestly don't want you using my house as a base while you join the feeding frenzy. Anyway, I'm not sure what I want to do. Getting right away for a few days feels like a good idea, and – before you ask – that doesn't mean you can move in.'

For a moment Pat was tempted to argue, but knew Jessie too well to bother.

'That's a pity,' he said again.

'I'm making tea anyway,' she said. 'If you want some, before

186

you go out again. Have to be without milk, I've not got any.'

She smiled as she busied herself with the comfortably routine task. She disliked being taken for granted and took perverse pleasure in contradicting his assumptions.

They drank their tea without further conversation. When Pat left 'for a walkabout' as he put it, Jessie closed the door behind him with some relief, picturing him rehearsing his lines for the journalists. She took her mug of tea into the front room and looked out at the sea. The tide just carries on, she thought, creeping in and out, undeterred by anything we may be doing. She loved its predictable movement, the inexorable motion of water below and sun above that changed the light and the colours of her world hour by hour, minute by minute. The sun was still rising and the room was in shadow, but soon the light would move around towards the south, threading through her window. As the afternoon wore on, the light would broaden and move from wall to floor until it filled the whole space, bouncing off the sea and sand into her eyes, warming the room.

Lawrence loved the sea too, she remembered. He would pull the chair in his top floor room over to the window and sit there when he could, looking out, watching, just as she did. They seemed to take pleasure in similar things; maybe that was why she enjoyed his company even when there were disagreements. At first she'd found him strange, exotic almost, with his science and his Jewishness. And after all those years in universities and labs and in Canada he'd ended up here, in her flat in Seascale. She remembered the way he danced with his wife. He was a physical man, she thought, but not in the same way as Andrew. An image of Andrew naked swam into her mind, unbidden – in her bed in the schoolhouse, the light from the fire glinting on his hair, the curve of his shoulder. She hung her head. The memory of passion was as strong as ever and for a moment it overwhelmed her. That was twenty years ago. Now she was almost sixty, but the yearning was still there. Did Lawrence still love his wife? Did they make love? She struggled with the thought and put it out of her mind. He was married, that was all that mattered. Why should he be interested in her anyway, a middle-aged provincial woman with grey hair and a temper?

And why was she interested in him, for heaven's sake? Another unsuitable man. Matthew Dawson had been suitable, but she hadn't loved him and knew in the end that it would never have worked. She liked him, and he would have been kind and generous, but that wasn't enough to give away her freedom. 'How pompous that sounds.' she said to herself. 'No wonder people don't like me sometimes. I don't much like myself. Maggie thinks I'm too self-centred, and she may be right.' And there was Pat, who said he loved her, but that didn't feel the same any more. They had been close for years, but lately he seemed to have changed, and now she was less sure about him. When the crisis was over and he'd calmed down she would talk to him properly. There were things they needed to sort out.

Jessie's tea cooled unheeded on the table while she stared out of the window, thinking. She wondered if she'd ever really loved anyone, and whether she ever could. Not a child, like Judith, but an adult, an equal. She knew that real love was more than passion, the desire of the moment. She might love Pat, but she was not attracted to him. She was attracted to Lawrence, but love was different, in a way that she couldn't disentangle. What did it feel like to trust someone so deeply, to take that risk? She might die before she ever found out. The thought upset her and she got up, took the mug back to the kitchen and decided to get busy. She'd noticed dust hanging in the morning air, and a thin film along the window sill. Dust didn't seem benign any more, its innocence was gone. She looked in the cupboard under the sink and took out all the cleaning materials she could find.

An hour later she was upstairs scrubbing the bathroom floor when the phone rang. She managed to reach it just before it stopped.

'Jessie?' It was John. She was very glad to hear his voice.

'I thought you were exaggerating yesterday,' he said, 'I wanted to say I was sorry for sounding so sceptical. Looks like it's pretty serious.'

'I was in a bit of a state,' she admitted. 'And it was too early, but I wanted to catch you before you went to work.'

'I should have stayed at home, as it turned out. Spent the whole morning sitting in the canteen. It was strange in there, we all knew something was going on but no one talked about it much. All the bosses would say was that we had to stay put, couldn't go out. I was waiting for something to happen but I didn't know what. It was like a shared fear that couldn't be spoken. And then we all got sent home. Still don't know what really happened.' He was quiet for a moment, waiting for her to answer, but she said nothing.

'What does Lawrence say?' he asked. She was getting tired of being asked that.

'He's not here,' she said. 'Went off to Harwell last night.' She hesitated, making up her mind. 'John, I think you should throw away the milk, and don't give any to the children.'

'The milk? What…'

'Just throw it away, John, and don't buy any more. That's what Lawrence would say.'

'Oh, Christ,' he said. 'Whatever came out of the stacks yesterday could be in the milk by now. But what about those massive filters? That's what they're there for isn't it?'

'Maybe they worked,' she said. 'But it's not worth the risk. Milk's only as healthy as the grass that goes into it. Who knows what fell onto that grass yesterday, or before that?'

'Is that what Lawrence said?'

'You don't have to be a physicist to work that one out. I managed it all on my own.' It was a lie, but who cared?

'Of course, sorry,' said John. 'I just hadn't thought about it.'

'Doesn't matter. I'm sure Maggie will understand. But don't say it was me who suggested it or she'll probably drink a pint of it straight away.'

He laughed. 'Oh dear. How did I manage to get in the middle of you two? We'll deal with the milk, but what about everybody else? Who's going to pass that advice along, and when?'

'I'm sure they won't want to say much about what happened,' said Jessie carefully, 'but they'll have to say something about the milk before too much of it gets drunk. Not everyone will put two and two together like we have. I had Pat O'Toole knocking on my door first thing this morning. He was putting two and two together and making a hundred. The press are all over the place already, local probably but the nationals won't be far behind. They'll find someone to give them a story, and Pat was falling over himself to talk to them.'

'What's got into him?'

'Any kind of nuclear accident, if that's what it was, plays right into the anti-nuclear hands.'

'Is he anti-nuclear? I thought he was just against the bombs.'

'That's the interesting thing, how thin the line is between the two,' said Jessie. 'I think he can see the difference, but many of the people I met at those meetings couldn't see it. They're bound to use all this as a stick to beat the whole idea of nuclear energy.'

'Where's Pat now?'

'Gone out, sniffing around,' she said. 'I was pretty upset with him, to tell the truth. He was practically salivating about it. Didn't seem to understand what the fallout might be, I mean the people fallout, not the just the radioactive stuff.'

'I thought you liked him,' John ventured.

'I respect him,' she said. 'I admire what he did for those men in the camp at the end of the war. He's a man of principle, but he doesn't see all the ramifications.' She paused. 'I didn't like him very much this morning.'

'It's always easier when you see one side of things,' said John. 'I know everybody thinks I'm too cautious, but I can't help seeing the ups and downs of everything, if you know what I mean.' John paused before he spoke again. 'Talking of ups and downs, Judith will be home from school in a couple of weeks. Would you like to see her while she's here?'

Jessie felt a sudden burst of relief. The offer had been made. John wouldn't have dared say it if he knew Maggie would never agree.

'I'd love to see her. Are you sure it would be alright?'

'I'll make sure it is,' he said. 'It's too painful to have you and Maggie falling out over a child who loves you both. And it's not fair to Judith.'

'That would be grand, John. Thank you so much.'

'No need for thanks,' he said, 'Oh, and Jessie?'

'Yes?'

'You haven't said much to Pat, have you?'

'No,' she said, regretting again that she'd mentioned the milk.

'Don't,' he said. 'I know he's a friend, but if he wants to make mischief I think you'd better keep out of his way for a while.'

Her instinct was to argue but she stopped herself.

'Let me know about Judith,' she said. 'And thanks for ringing.'

Just one phone call, she thought as she put the receiver down, and I'm feeling better. The fear of being kept away from Judith and the rest of the family had haunted her, nagging at the edge of her mind for weeks. She couldn't insist on anything where John's family were concerned, but she had so hoped they would relent.

She and Judith would talk again, she would hear all about school, and see how she'd changed, and laugh with her, even if Maggie was still frosty. It would work out.

She'd gone back upstairs to finish the bathroom when the phone rang again. He's changed his mind, she thought. Maggie has said no. She snatched up the receiver, breathless from running down the stairs, dreading what she might hear.

'Miss Whelan?' said a woman's voice. 'It's Mrs Finer.'

For a moment Jessie couldn't place the voice or the name.

'Mrs Finer? Oh, Mrs Lawrence Finer.'

'Mrs Rebecca Finer,' said the voice firmly.

'Is Lawrence alright?'

'He's exhausted and not well at all, actually,' said his wife, making it sound like Jessie's fault. 'He won't be coming back this weekend, no matter how much he wants to do so. Far too unwell to go anywhere at present. He will stay here with me.'

'When he does comes back, will he be wanting his room?' said Jessie, realising as she did so what a stupid question it was. The woman was making her nervous.

'His room in your house, you mean? Of course he'll be needing his room. Where else would he stay?'

'Well, er, if you were coming with him, you'd be staying in the hotel, I suppose.'

'Me?' Rebecca's tone was incredulous. 'Nothing would induce me to go back there again, especially not now when the place is so dangerous. I can't imagine why anyone would choose to stay there if they didn't have to.'

Jessie was taken aback and stumbled on. 'When will Lawrence be back? His room…'

'We'll let you know. Goodbye, Miss Whelan.'

'And goodbye to you, too,' said Jessie as the line went dead.

She took out her irritation on cleaning the bath. 'That's it,' she said to herself, 'If the weather's half way decent tomorrow I'm getting away to fresh air and sanity and people who won't patronise me.'

Pat called briefly at the end of the afternoon, still excited and rushing for the train. They didn't have time to talk about what he'd been up to, which was just as well, and she was tired after hours of unaccustomed housework.

* * *

The following morning Jessie put a jar of the summer's jam in her bag, caught the early train down to Newton and got a ride up to Boot with George Steele, the postman. How useful it was to be so well remembered in a place; as they drove up the sunny valley in his van, George told her all about his children whom Jessie had taught in the school many years before. The day was bright, with a breeze from the sea. Jessie thought about the milk again and the invisible poisoned dust being carried on the wind wherever it chose to blow. She didn't mention her thoughts to George: she'd said quite enough for one day. When he asked about what had happened at the plant she just repeated what she'd heard on the radio: it was the easiest thing to do. At the end of the lane down to the mill she thanked him for the ride and walked down to the cottage, enjoying the feel of wind in her hair and autumnal sun on her back. On the fells at the head of the valley the bracken had already turned, adding more colours to the view she loved so well.

The cottage door was closed, which surprised her. Hannah usually had the door open unless wind or rain made it impossible. She and Fred wore their coats in the house on all but the warmest days. Jessie knocked on the door and stepped back, waiting. The door opened and Hannah peered out, her lopsided face squinting into the sunlight. Jessie noticed how much older she looked.

'Why Miss Whelan,' said Hannah, smiling broadly. 'Reet grand to see you. Come away in. 'Ave you come to stay? Parkinson's lad says there's all sorts of muck and smoke around in Seascale. Fire at the plant or summat.'

'That was Friday, Hannah,' said Jessie stepping into the dark of the cottage. 'Now the place is full of newspapermen and people taking samples of the air we breath. I needed to get away for a few hours and I thought of you.'

'Well, I'm reet glad you did,' said Hannah. 'It's Miss Whelan, Fred,' she shouted. 'All the way from Seascale to see us.'

'Who is it?' a voice responded. Jessie's eyes were still adjusting to the light. She could make out a figure in the big chair, sitting low and leaning to one side. Hannah took hold of the man's shoulders and pulled him upright.

'Miss Whelan,' Hannah repeated. 'John's mam.'

'John who?' said the voice.

Hannah took Jessie's arm and pulled her away before Jessie had the chance to speak to Fred herself.

'You can see how it is,' she said. 'Just this past month or so, his mind's started to go. Cannut remember owt, people especially. And 'e struggles to find words. Poor man. Nearly drives me mad, and 'im too, I don't wonder.'

'Has he been ill?' Jessie asked.

'Bad 'eart, same as ever,' said Hannah. 'And 'e would never see a doctor, of course. Can't get it into 'is 'ead that it wouldn't cost anything. But this memory problem, that's just recent.'

'How old is he now?'

'Sixty-five or so,' said Hannah. 'No age at all. Me dad went the same way afore he died, but 'e were eighty odd. Fred sounds that old sometimes, you know, like an old man. Don't know what to do with 'im.'

'I'm so sorry, Hannah,' said Jessie. 'I had no idea.'

'Well, 'ow would you miss?' said Hannah, falling back into the old way she'd addressed Jessie when they first met. 'Not the kind of thing you'd put in a letter, if I wrote letters, which I dinnut.'

'I suppose not,' said Jessie. 'And what about the doctor?'

'Aye, what about 'im? No way Fred would agree to see 'im. And I couldn't get 'im down there, not on me own.'

'Would you like me to ask Dr Whittaker to call? I have his phone number at home. I could forewarn him, so he knows how Fred might react.'

'Aye, could you? I need some 'elp, I reckon. Not that's 'e's going anywhere, mind. Fred's home is 'ere, allus will be. But I need some 'elp, getting 'im out of the chair, you know. Neighbours are grand, but this is 'ard to deal with. I wondered about district nurse, but doctor would 'ave to set that up.'

'I'm so sorry, Hannah,' Jessie said again. She was thinking of Fred as she'd seen him a year or so before, at Eskdale Show, getting around on his stick as he always did, as attentive to Hannah as ever, the two of them still so happy together. And now this.

On the bus back to Seascale later in the day, Jessie was very sad. She felt that Fred would not recover, and how hard that would be for Hannah, to watch the man she'd waited so long for dying slowly before her eyes. Hopefully Fred would not realise what was happening to him; it would be have been too hard to bear if he did. Life is so short, she reminded herself. Just five years older than she was, and Fred's life was as good as over. None of us could know what lay around the next corner, unseen, unexpected, that would change our lives forever.

She walked on the beach before going home, standing to watch as the sun sank below the level of the cloud bank on the horizon, golden light flooding across the sands, burnishing the rock pools, lighting up the sea-facing walls of the houses behind her. Lawrence would have to come back soon. When he did, she would ask John to take him up one of the mountains that he knew so well from his climbing days. Rebecca might hate this place, but Jessie wanted Lawrence to love it as much she did. Maybe he would want to stay a little longer.

Chapter 20

The queue at the shop spilled out onto the pavement.

'What's happening?' Jessie asked the woman in front of her. 'Looks like we're all here for the same things,' said the woman. 'My house feels dirty, but all the cleaning stuff has gone apparently. Feels like the war, queuing up for things. Do you remember?'

'I do indeed,' said Jessie. She waited patiently as the queue shuffled forward, but in vain. 'It's all gone,' said Mr Tomlinson, shrugging his shoulders. 'I rationed it this morning, that's what all the argument was about. Folk panicking about cleaning everything. I were raised in Barrow, never worried about all the stuff in the air there, soot and smuts on everything.'

Jessie remembered that too. It seemed like a century ago.

Back at the house, she gathered up all the soap she could find and set about the rest of the cleaning, and as much laundry as she could manage. There was a snapping wind and sheets would dry quickly if she could get them out before the sun went round to the other side of the house. By mid-morning her hands were raw and her arm exhausted from turning the heavy mangle. She did her own bedding first; Lawrence's could wait until she knew when he was coming back. The thought of him with his wife lurked in her mind, the cultured voice that he'd lived with all these years. What must he think of us here? What must he think of me?

When the washing was on the line and she couldn't do any more without making her hands unbearably sore, she walked down to the school. Kath was busy in a classroom and beckoned to Jessie to go in. The children were used to seeing her and got on with what they were doing while Kath and Jessie whispered to each other talked in low tones at the door.

'Some of them came back over after the weekend,' Kath told her, 'but quite a few are still away. Once they started pouring milk down the drain, that started the panic all over again.'

'Is that what they're doing?' said Jessie.

'Didn't you see it, in all the papers?'

'Didn't get one yesterday, and this morning I've been cleaning like a mad thing. Look at my hands. I had to stop.'

'Funny, isn't it?' said Kath. 'I looked at the dust in my house and wondered what to do about it. Then I had to come to work, thank God. Otherwise I'd be as worn out as you are.'

Jessie laughed. 'It's hard work,' she said. 'Almost made me want one of those washing machines they keep telling us to buy.'

'Well, you're a landlady now, so that makes it alright,' said Kath.

'Not for much longer maybe,' said Jessie, wondering again about Lawrence coming back. 'My lodger went off on some secret mission on Friday night and I've not seen him since. His wife rang, said he was too poorly to come back.'

'That's the dark woman we saw at the dance. She looked pretty posh.'

'She is,' said Jessie. 'Very sharp with me on the phone. Said she couldn't imagine why anyone would want to live here.'

'Well, sod her,' whispered Kath.

'My thought exactly,' said Jessie.

Kath looked at her friend closely. 'You like him, don't you?'

Jessie looked away. 'I didn't at first. But now I can't stop thinking about him.'

Kath squeezed her arm. 'Trust your instincts, Jess,' she said, 'and don't frighten him away.'

* * *

There was a letter on the mat when she got home. It was Lawrence's writing on the envelope. Jessie tore it open.

Dear Jessie
    I'll be coming back on Wednesday, on the train, arriving quite late. Hope that's OK.
    Yours,
    Lawrence.

Is that all, she thought? No polite enquiry about her health and welfare, just a couple of lines. She turned the paper over in case there was more, but there was nothing. Being at home with Mrs Rebecca Finer hadn't cheered him up much by the sound of it. So now she had to get his room sorted out. No rubber gloves in the shop. Maybe she could borrow a pair. What a way to spend another day. But the day after that he would be back. She felt a flutter in her stomach.

Just before seven on the Wednesday evening she heard his key in the front door. She wanted to meet him with a smile but then thought better of it, so she waited until he knocked on the kitchen door and pretended to be surprised when he walked in.

'Here you are,' she said, keeping on with the ironing. 'Good journey?'

'Long,' he said. 'I'll put my bag upstairs and then I'm going out again. I hope you haven't made anything for me.'

'You said it would be late, so I didn't bother,' she said, thinking of the pie in the larder and how long it would keep.

'Fine,' he said. 'I'll be going out early tomorrow. Enquiry team arrive on Friday and there's a lot to do before they get here.'

'What enquiry team?'

'About the accident.'

She waited, but Lawrence just smiled, and turned around. She heard him on the stairs, up and then down again, and the front door slammed. He'd been in the house no more than five minutes.

For some reason she felt both angry and disappointed. Why had she bothered fussing over his room and worrying about his meals if he was going to treat the house and her like this? Even so, she made sure that she was up the following morning when he emerged from his room. He was going to speak to her for a few minutes even if she had to physically stop him leaving the house until he'd done so.

'You're very quiet,' she said as he ate his porridge in silence. 'Is everything alright?'

'Not really.' He put down his spoon and looked up at her. 'Sorry, Jessie,' he said. 'It's all a bit tense, with the enquiry starting. Half the key people at the plant are off, apparently, and everyone's worried about it.'

'Can you talk about it?'

'Not really,' he said. 'And not now.'

'But will you, tonight maybe? I don't want to know all the details. Just the things you're allowed to tell me. I've been worried...' She didn't know what else to say.

He looked at his watch and got up from the table.

'OK,' he said. 'Tonight, I promise. Now I've got to go.'

'Shall I make supper, or are you going out again?'

He smiled at her. 'Greengarth dinner's are good, but I'd rather eat here, if that's alright with you.'

'Good,' she said, relieved that the pie would find a good home. 'Dinner on the table at seven.'

By six-thirty there was still no sign of him, but she felt sure he would be there. He wouldn't make a promise and then break it.

She changed into a fresh blouse, combed a semblance of shape into her hair and even dabbed some rarely-used scent behind her ears before she laid the table for two, feeling unaccountably excited. Maybe this was how it felt to be married, at least for a week or two before the novelty wore off. This time she did go into the hall when she heard him come in, and he seemed pleased to see her.

'What a day,' he said. 'I need a wash. Down in a minute.'

She took off her apron and put the warm pie in the middle of the table like a trophy at a horse race. It smelled good.

He was clearly hungry and it wasn't until Jessie had served them both and sat down at the table that she felt ready to speak to him. There was no rush, and she knew he might be unsure how much to tell her.

'Can you tell me anything about the enquiry, or whatever it is?' she began.

'Whatever it is,' he repeated. 'That's half the problem.'

'Why?'

'We were expecting something quite official, after what happened. Not public, they couldn't do that, but bigger than what they're planning. Feels as if they're rushing it through.'

'Who's in charge of it?'

'That's another funny thing,' he said. 'Look, Jessie, this is between us, right? All of it. People at the plant don't know much about it, but I want to see what you think.'

She was pleased and said nothing, to encourage him to say more.

'It's as if the Authority is investigating itself,' he said. 'The chairman is Bill Penney. He's up to his ears in the bomb programme, doesn't really know much about reactors. He says he wants it all over by next week, report written, everything done and dusted, so he can go off somewhere. We don't know what to expect. If they do a proper job it's bound to take longer than that. It should take longer than that, to do justice to what happened.'

'Low key is better, though, isn't it?'

'Only if people respect the conclusions. We can't get on with things until the truth comes out. Then we can act on what it says, put things right.

'Sounds as if you think things are going to brushed over.'

'That's part of the worry. If it's not thorough enough the government can turn round and blame the Authority. Pass it all off as a minor hitch so the Americans won't get cold feet about us.'

Jessie thought about this. There was always a bigger picture.

'It's all politics,' he said, as he carried on eating. 'The anti-bomb people are going make a meal out of it. Well, you'll know all about that.'

She looked at him. Was that what he was worried about? 'Pat O'Toole was here,' she said, responding to the implication. 'Early on Saturday morning. He was very excited. Said the timing was perfect.'

Lawrence looked up at her. 'There, you see? The fire's a gift for politically-motivated people.'

'People like me, you mean?'

'I'm not sure what you might think about it. Did you tell him anything?'

'You think I would help him use this for his own purposes?'

'Possibly. Did you?'

Jessie looked at him, irritated by the assumptions he seemed to be making. 'That's unfair, Lawrence. Yes, I've been concerned about what's been happening at Windscale. You have, too. But that doesn't mean I'd help some outsiders undermine the plant or the village.'

'I thought Pat was an old friend of yours, from way back.'

'He is, but we don't always see things the same way.'

'So what did you tell him?'

'Nothing! Why do you assume I'm careless or stupid enough to tell him things that matter? Telling Pat would be like telling the journalists.'

'Exactly,' said Lawrence. 'I just wondered if he might try to push you around.'

She pushed back her chair and stood up, feeling the flush on her face. 'How could you say that? I let myself be pushed around once in my life and vowed it wouldn't happen again, and it never has. I am who I am and I make my own decisions. If you can't trust me, just say so. And if you can't stay here, tell me soon so I can find another lodger. But don't assume I'm being pushed around.'

He stared at her.

'If you've finished with that plate,' she said, reaching over to pick it up, 'I'll start the washing up. No doubt you'll be going out again.'

'Jessie,' he began. She was pouring water into the sink. He got up from the table, said 'Thanks for the supper,' and walked out of the kitchen.

When he had gone, she leaned forward over the sink. Her eyes were pricking. 'What's the matter with me?' she thought. 'Why am I such an idiot?'

Lawrence crept upstairs to his room as quietly as he could. Where did all that come from, he wondered, going back over what he had said that had made her so angry? Most of the time she was a rational, measured person, like him, but sometimes she just boiled over. Energy, anger, passion. He wanted to take her in his arms and hold her close, to feel the heat of her. He shut the door of his room and sat on the bed. What was he going to do? On the long drive down to Harwell he'd told himself he needed to get away, to get his feelings about Jessie into perspective and under control. For a few days he'd been his usual calm self, too tired for anything else. Rebecca had looked after him dutifully but they hadn't really talked. Sitting on the train back north, he'd assured himself that things would be back to their steady normality from now on. He and Rebecca would settle their differences, or not, but he would not complicate things by falling in love with his landlady. And now, within a few hours of his return he was back in the same turmoil, and Jessie was threatening to throw him out.

He sat quietly for a while, gathering his thoughts, trying to make sense of it all. He'd never loved anyone except his wife, and they had been together since their student days forty years before. He'd looked at other women, nothing wrong with that: he could be forgiven a bit of sexual desire now and then. But this wasn't about lust. Jessie was different. She was complicated: independent, protective of herself, strong-willed. But she cared deeply about things, too, and let it show. She hadn't been schooled and trained to control herself, to be polite all the time, to be 'ladylike'. 'I am who I am,' she'd said. That's what he was falling for, despite all his resolution and rationality.

Lawrence still didn't know what to do. He'd upset Jessie. She felt he didn't trust or respect her, which wasn't true, and he had to put that right no matter what else happened. He should probably move out, but everywhere was crawling with journalists and there wasn't a room to be had. They would have to find a way to co-exist in this house, and he needed time to think. If he and Rebecca were to part, properly and legally, there would be all the paperwork to deal with. He was sure she didn't want to carry on as they were: they hadn't been happy together for years and the longer he stayed in Cumberland the worse it got. And if he wanted to be closer to Jessie he would have to be a friend, not just a lover. She'd had lovers before, he was sure of that, but nothing had lasted. They could have an affair, but she would be more compromised by that than him. She was known here, and he was not.

The first essential was to try and undo the damage of the past hour. They needed to spend some time together, away from the pressures of the village and the plant. The enquiry. He groaned. Anxiety about the coming few days flooded back into his mind. Was the enquiry about understanding what had happened, or was it a search for fault? He went over the decisions he'd made yet again, looking for mistakes. He was still sure that they had all done the best they could, given the information available. And once the fire was discovered, he'd been astonished at the resourcefulness and courage he'd seen among the men who'd tackled it, and the risks they had taken to avert a worse catastrophe. He buried in himself in his notes for a while, just as Jessie had thrown herself into cleaning the house, to occupy his mind and his body.

Downstairs in the kitchen, Jessie was drying dishes and putting things away. She too was trying to work out what had happened, why she suddenly felt so angry with Lawrence. It's because I like him, she thought. If I didn't like him, I wouldn't care so much what he thinks of me. It would be easier if we weren't in this house together, but the village is full and he'll have to stay here, unless he just can't put up with me any more. I shouldn't have blown up like that. He looked stunned. Is he still upstairs, hiding? I'll leave it a while, and then I'll apologise. We need to get along. Maybe we could go for a walk together, away from the house and the village and the enquiry, just for a few hours, just the two of us. She let her mind run on, imagining, and then forced herself to think about something else.

In the middle of the night, Jessie woke suddenly. She'd been dreaming about yellow choking clouds that she couldn't find her way through. Sitting up in bed she breathed slowly, in and out, to clear her head and her lungs. When she felt better she pummelled the pillow and lay down again, but sleep seemed to have melted away. She looked at the little clock by her bedside with its small fluorescent hands. Twenty past three. A nothing time: too early, and too late. She lay on her back and stared at the invisible ceiling. Lawrence was in the room right above her. She wondered if he was awake. Suddenly a thought jumped into her mind, something that Kath had said earlier in the day: 'Don't frighten him away.'

Was that what she was trying to do? If he went away she wouldn't have to worry about it any more. There would be no dilemma, no choices to make. She could keep her precious independence, and blame him. All these years she'd clung to the only person she felt she could trust – herself. It was lonely, but it was safe. And now? Was that still what she wanted? A miserable confusion settled over her and daylight was beginning to silver the sea before she was able to sleep again.

Chapter 21

THERE WAS NO SOUND FROM JESSIE'S ROOM when Lawrence crept down the stairs early on Friday, and no evidence of her presence in the kitchen; the kettle was cold. He would have loved a coffee, but the little coffee pot he'd brought with him was in the back room upstairs, so he made himself tea instead. The bread was stale, but it was enough to keep him going before he got to the canteen later.

Outside, it was another bright October morning, with wind off the sea. He drove his motorbike along the cinder track by the shore to the plant, a bit bumpy but a great way to start the day, looking out over the receding tide, with the gulls overhead. When he got to his desk, there was a typewritten note, informing him that the enquiry would be grateful if he could make himself available at 11.30 a.m. He had three hours to go over his notes yet again, but first he needed a proper breakfast.

The canteen was busy, and he took his coffee and toast over to the tables at one end where the unspoken stratification of the room dictated that he should sit, alongside the other 'scientists' while the 'technicians' sat together elsewhere. Lawrence was so used to these arrangements that he hardly noticed them any more. He sat with Tim Fahey and they shared what they knew about the members of the enquiry team. Lawrence had worked with one of them, Basil Schonland, at Harwell, and most of the others were names that he recognised, experts in the relevant areas.

'That's reassuring,' said Tim. 'What were they saying about all this at Harwell when you were down there?'

'I was in bed most of the time I was away,' said Lawrence. 'It all caught up with me.'

'Same for all of us, I think,' said Tim. 'My wife says I've been tossing and turning and mumbling half the night since the fire. It all feels a bit rushed, but I don't think I'll be able to settle until the enquiry is behind us.'

'Nor me,' said Lawrence. He hesitated and lowered his voice. 'Actually, Tim, I was a bit bothered about some of the rumours at Harwell. Not about the fire; people seemed to understand how it might have happened, and were amazed we managed to get it under control. It was the politics of it that they were talking about.'

Tim looked around. 'Anything you can tell me?' he asked, leaning forward.

'Just that Macmillan is in the middle of talks with the Yanks about sharing nuclear secrets and this puts him in a tricky position. The fire makes it look as if our nuclear programme isn't as safe as it should be.'

'He gets on well with Eisenhower, doesn't he?' said Tim.

'Yes, "Mac 'n Ike" are good buddies apparently, but Congress is suspicious. They've been pretty paranoid since that spying case a few years ago. Some of them think Britain is full of Commies.'

'So what could Macmillan do?' asked Tim, turning over the implications in his mind.

'Blame us, basically,' said Lawrence. 'He could say that the fire was just local carelessness or something to that effect, and no reflection on the British nuclear programme as a whole.'

'But it wasn't local carelessness, was it?'

'Not sure that'll make any difference, not with the stakes as high as this.'

Tim sat back. 'Shit,' he said.

'Exactly,' said Lawrence.

At eleven-thirty precisely the door of the enquiry room opened and Lawrence was invited inside. It looked like any other committee meeting, with people sitting at tables placed round the room. The air was already blue with tobacco smoke and the chairman, Bill Penney, was asking for a window to be opened, which gave Lawrence the chance to look around. He saw Basil Schonland and nodded to him. Propped up against the far wall was a large blackboard, with scribbled notes and diagrams on it. When things settled down, Bill Penney introduced himself with the slow drawl that Lawrence knew so well, and then asked the other members to do the same. It was all very civilised, and Lawrence felt himself relax a little.

As expected, most of the questions he faced were about the Wigner release process, by which the pile was heated up deliberately to allow excess energy to be discharged. Lawrence had all the facts at his fingertips. He talked about their experience with both the Windscale piles and how there had never been time or opportunity to develop a written manual about Wigner release. 'The release has varied from one event to the next,' he said. 'It's been difficult to find a definitive pattern.'

'With no operation manual, how did the technicians know what to do?' came the inevitable question. Lawrence was ready for it, talking about how the physicists worked closely with the technicians to manage and monitor the process, reacting to the behaviour of the pile as they went along. 'Not ideal,' he said, 'but it seemed to work.' Damn, he thought, as soon as the words were out of his mouth.

'But it didn't work on this occasion, did it, Dr Finer?' someone said, and he had to agree.

From then on, the questions seem to converge around the decision to re-start the heating once the first attempt had faltered. Lawrence wished he'd made more notes at the time. He could remember only snatches of that day, the Tuesday before the fire, when he'd been starting with the 'flu and was feeling wretched. He went through the details, the readings they had taken, the anomaly of one area of the pile that was not cooling down and their doubts about the instrumentation. Someone pointed at the rough diagram of the pile that Lawrence could see on the blackboard, and there was discussion about the exact location of the hot spot. Lawrence was able to say truthfully that he had spent much of the following two days at home in bed, returning when the fire had already taken hold. Before the end of his interview, he also managed to add how impressed he'd been with the resourcefulness, courage and resolve of the Windscale men to get the fire under control.

When he'd finished, Bill Penney nodded slowly, leaned back in his chair, looked round the room, asked if there were any further questions at this stage, and then suggested that they might need to talk to Dr Finer again. Lawrence thanked them all, got up and left the room, realising only as he did so that his legs felt quite weak. Outside in the corridor he sat down next to the man who was waiting to be called.

'How was it?'

'Alright, actually,' said Lawrence. 'They're very focused on that week, how the fire started, how we got it out, and what's happened since then. Nothing before that. I was expecting questions about the early days, the filters business, clipping the aluminium off the cartridges and so on, but there weren't any. They must have quite a limited brief.'

The door opened again. 'Good luck,' Lawrence whispered, before he walked slowly back to his office.

All through the day men went in and out of the enquiry room, They weren't supposed to talk to each other about it, but there were some whispered conversations. By the end of the day Lawrence was feeling more nervous about going back to Jessie's than about dealing with any more questions from the panel. He was getting ready to leave when an idea occurred to him.

Tim Fahey was in his office packing papers into his briefcase when Lawrence found him a few minutes later.

'Tim, you know you said you wouldn't be needing your car this weekend?'

'Yes,' said Tim. 'I'm taking the wife to Edinburgh on the train for the day tomorrow. She says she's hardly seen me for weeks. We'll be back late.'

'Could I borrow your car, just for tomorrow?' Lawrence asked. 'I need to get out of here for a few hours, probably up Wasdale, and the person I'm taking won't go on the bike.'

The obvious question about this mystery companion went unasked.

'Good idea,' said Tim. 'We could all do with getting away from this place. We'll leave the car at the station when we go, around nine. You could pick it up from there. That's quite close to your digs isn't it? Then drop it back at the station and leave the keys on the front wheel. That should work. Don't worry about petrol, Wasdale's not that far from here. Going with somebody local?'

'Yes,' said Lawrence. 'We'll find the way. Thanks, most kind of you.'

'Have a good time,' said Tim, still wondering, knowing that Lawrence had a wife back at Harwell. He smiled, and Lawrence smiled back, and nothing more was asked or said.

Friday night was always busy at the Greengarth bar, and on this Friday it was busier than ever. They had managed to keep most of the journalists out, and hilarious stories were circulating about stupid questions that the press had been asking around the village, and the even sillier answers they'd been given. The scientists didn't trust the press, and locals didn't trust offcomers, especially those from London.

As he ordered his first pint, Lawrence went back over the curious conversation he'd just had with Jessie. After her reaction the previous day he'd been wary and careful with his words. 'I can get hold of a car tomorrow,' he'd said, apropos of nothing, standing at the kitchen door. Jessie had her back to him, busy with something at the sink.

'Oh, yes,' she'd responded, without turning round.

'I'd like to go up Wasdale, if the weather's fine, and wondered if you'd like to come.'

Her hands were still for a moment, and she turned to face him.

'Go to Wasdale, tomorrow?' she repeated.

'Do you have something else to do?'

'No, no,' she said quickly. 'That would be very nice, thank you.' They both waited, as if there was more to be said.

'Right then,' said Lawrence eventually. 'I'm picking up the car around nine. I thought we might do a bit of a walk somewhere and have lunch at that pub at the top of the lake.'

'Oh,' she said. 'That sounds lovely.'

'Right then.'

'Right,' repeated Jessie.

The exchange was over as suddenly as it had started, and he still couldn't work out whether she was pleased, or just surprised. He was thinking about it when a voice interrupted.

'That anti-nuclear chap from Maryport's been hanging around all week,' said the man next to Lawrence at the bar. 'D'you know him, Finer? He used to be a priest apparently.'

'Yes, I know him,' said Lawrence. 'He's making as much as he can out of all this, I expect.'

'Isn't your landlady mixed up with that group as well?''

'Used to be, I think,' said Lawrence. 'We don't talk about it, obviously.'

She's not asked about what was happening at the plant, he said to himself. No argument about that, or about going out to Wasdale. Had something happened, he wondered? Why was she being so agreeable all of a sudden?

* * *

In the corner of the Scawfell Hotel lounge bar Jessie sipped her glass of shandy and wondered the same thing. She and Kath often went out together on Friday evening, and after a week in school Kath was keen to pick up as much of the gossip as she could.

'What has Lawrence said about the enquiry?' she'd asked Jessie when she sat down with their drinks.

'Nothing much. I didn't ask him. I know they're not supposed to talk about it, and we certainly can't talk about it here,' she said, gesturing with her head towards the next table where two young men were swapping notes.

'Press,' Jessie mouthed to Kath, who nodded and strained to hear what they were saying.

'Oh, by the way,' said Jessie, as nonchalantly as she could. 'He asked me to go for a drive up Wasdale with him tomorrow.'

Kath's attention to Jessie was immediate. 'Who did? Not the precious Dr Finer?'

Jessie nodded.

'Well, I never,' said Kath. 'What did he say?'

'As soon as he came in from work, he just said he'd borrowed a car and would I like to go out tomorrow. Lunch at the Wasdale Head. I said I would.'

Kath looked at her closely. 'I can't make you out,' she said. 'One minute you two are arguing about all sorts of stuff and the next minute you're swanning off together for lunch. What's going on? He's still married isn't he?'

'Oh yes, he's still married, as far as I know. He's a friend, Kath, that's all, and I need the rent. His wife thinks we're in the outer darkness up here, but he loves it, I know he does, and I love it too, so why shouldn't we have a day out together? Nothing's going to happen.'

'What if someone sees you?'

'What if they do? We don't have to have a chaperone. We're friends, even though we disagree about things sometimes. He's never been up Wasdale, I haven't been there since I sold the car, and it's supposed to be sunny tomorrow. I'm looking forward to it.'

Kath's interrogation continued. 'Has he ever said anything about his wife, about how they get on?'

'No. But you saw them together at the club that night. What did you think?'

'Actually,' said Kath, thinking about it, 'It looked as if they were bored with each other. She didn't look very happy, considering they hadn't seen each other for weeks.'

'I don't understand much about marriage,' said Jessie, toying with her shandy. 'What happened with you and Ted?'

The question surprised Kath and she looked away. 'It was OK for a while,' she said after a pause. 'But even before he went off to the war things were rocky. We married young, you know, like people do and we both changed a lot. He never liked me training to be a teacher and getting a job. Might have been different if we'd had kids, but we didn't. Just the two of us. Felt like we were stuck together in a cage. Then he found that Maisie woman, and I was quite relieved actually. I worried about being on my own, but it's been better than those last years with him. Nothing lonelier than a bad marriage.'

Jessie had never heard Kath speak like this, and regretted asking the question.

'Sorry,' she said.

Kath looked up. Her eyes were bright. 'Doesn't matter now,' she said. 'Why do people stay together? Loyalty? Friendship? Love? Sometimes it's just a habit you get into and can't break, for fear of the unknown.'

'So I haven't missed much?' said Jessie.

'Who knows?' Kath replied. 'Have you ever found someone you really wanted to marry?'

'I wanted to marry Clive, but we were very young, like you and Ted. We could have made a go of it, but as you say, who knows?'

'And now you're going on a date with the lodger,' said Kath. 'Well, make sure he keeps his hands on the wheel.'

They both needed to laugh, and they did.

The following morning dawned fine and clear, with a whisper of offshore breeze that flattened the sea. Jessie slept late. When she went to make tea she found a note on the kitchen table. It was from Lawrence: *Gone to pick up the car. Back soon. Looks like we'll be lucky with the weather.*

Jessie thought about the day ahead. It's just a day out, she told herself. But she felt the anticipation in her chest, and thought carefully about what she was going to wear.

CHAPTER 22

'WHOSE CAR IS THIS?' said Jessie as she climbed into it. It was quite the fanciest car she'd driven in; Agnes would have loved it, she thought.

'Belongs to Tim Fahey. He's taken his wife to Edinburgh on the train for the day.'

Lawrence steered the unfamiliar car carefully under the railway bridge and round onto the main street. 'But don't let's talk about all that, not today. I'm trying to have a break from it all.'

'Quite right,' said Jessie.

'Shouldn't have gone to Greengarth last night,' he said, ignoring his own advice. 'The place was full of gossip and rumours. Some of those young chaps don't seem to realise how serious it is.'

'Pretty hard to cover up what's happening with the milk,' she said, as a milk tanker passed them on the road.

'It gets worse,' he said. 'They've extended the milk ban to two hundred miles now. Hundreds of farms involved. Still no idea how long it's going to last.'

'But we're not talking about that today are we?' said Jessie.

'No, of course,' he said, smiling. 'Absolutely not. Let's talk about the weather. What a lovely day! And which way are we going, by the way? You're the local. Advise me.'

'Straight across the coast road, through Gosforth and then – what a surprise! – the Wasdale Road. We'll be there in no time.'

And they were. The steep rock screes on the far side of Wastwater came into view, hundreds of feet high, dropping down into the lake that was out of sight at first and then gradually revealed itself as they drew closer. Near the lake's edge, Lawrence got out of the car, walked a few steps and stood motionless, staring across the dark water to the wall of rock on the other side. Gulls screeched close by.

'I had no idea,' he said. 'I've lived in England all my life and I never knew there was a place like this. Look at it!'

A breeze from the west ruffled the glossy black surface of the lake into a thousand winking diamonds. Lawrence walked down towards the shore, following a stream that burbled under the road and fanned into a wide delta where it met the lake. A line of flat stepping-stones led to a rocky island and Lawrence embarked on the crossing before stopping midway to see if Jessie was following him. When she hesitated, he came back, holding out his hand to guide her. They scrambled to the top of the outcrop and sat down close to each other in the small space, back to back. Jessie looked south towards the sunlight and the pale clear sky above the invisible sea. Lawrence gazed at the mountains that clustered round the head of the lake.

'This is John's favourite place,' she said, turning to follow his gaze. 'As a young man he came up here every weekend, to go climbing. That's why he moved up here from Ulverston.' She pointed across to the north end of the screes. 'A few miles over there, that's where he used to live, in Boot.'

'There's a little train up Eskdale, isn't there? That must have been fun.'

'It was a nightmare, actually,' said Jessie, remembering. 'He got ill, lost his job. I'll tell you about it sometime, or you could ask him yourself. I thought you and he might go walking together, if you were going to stay here for a while.'

It was a veiled enquiry, and Lawrence didn't respond.

'Where could we walk today?' he asked. 'Nothing too strenuous, just a bit higher, to get a bigger view of it all, up there.' He pointed towards the head of the lake.

Lawrence talked incessantly about what he could see as they drove up the narrow road towards Wasdale Head. It was still quite early, with very little traffic, which was just as well as he pulled up frequently, getting out to look and exclaim about the light and the clarity of the air and the height of the towering screes.

'We should have brought the camera,' said Jessie.

'No point,' he said. 'A camera couldn't capture the scale of it, or the smell of the water and the trees.'

'Might help to remind us,' she said.

'It's all in here,' said Lawrence, tapping his head. 'I'll never forget this.' He turned towards her, the rising sun catching his animated face. 'This is where you live, Jessie. Just minutes from your home. It's wonderful, magical.'

'When you live with this valley on the doorstep, you take it for granted, until you bring someone new, like yourself. Then you see it afresh.'

'And are you seeing it afresh?' he asked.

'I am,' she admitted, smiling, thinking how young he looked.

'Look at these stone walls,' he said, as the valley floor widened out. 'Someone must have built them all. Thousands of stones left by the glaciers, hauled off the ground with bare hands and placed so carefully with nothing but gravity to hold them together. And they're still standing, hundreds of years later.'

She let him talk as they drove the last mile or two from the head of the lake towards the pub.

'Is this where we'll have lunch?' he asked. 'But not yet, surely? I have to walk. Will you come?'

She laughed. 'I've never seen you so excited – like a boy with a toy.'

'Come on,' he said.

Jessie remembered the little rucksack she'd brought with her with a flask of coffee and some shortbread. He was already well ahead of her, striding towards the stand of old yew trees that surrounded a tiny church. She had to run to catch him up, the first time she'd run anywhere for years, and she felt faintly ridiculous, holding the straps of the flimsy bag to stop it bouncing on her back. The church door was open and he was standing just inside the door. 'It's so small,' he said, looking round. 'You could fit ten of this into the synagogue back home.'

'It's been here a long time,' Jessie said. 'Those beams are supposed to be from a Viking longship, but who knows?'

He turned to her. 'Thanks for bringing me here. I love this place, all of it.'

They looked at the gravestones under the yews in the churchyard and then set off down a grassy track between high stone walls towards Great Gable and through a farmyard to join the winding path to Sty Head. It was a gentle climb compared with the steep slopes all around them, but the gradient and the uneven stony ground slowed them down. Lawrence stopped and turned regularly as they walked, checking on the changing view down the lake and beyond it to the flanks of Yewbarrow and Pillar. Ahead of them, across the steep gully and its splashing stream, Scafell reared into the sky.

'Next time we'll go up there,' said Lawrence, pointing, 'Or up this one on the left. What's it called?'

'Great Gable,' she said. 'Once we reach the shoulder and the tarn you'll see the path going up.'

'Shall we keep going, all the way up?' he asked.

'Not today, Lawrence,' she laughed. 'You promised me lunch at the pub.'

'I did,' he said, 'and you shall have it, even if it's a little late.'

By the dark tarn they found a spot to sit and drink their coffee, dwarfed by the surrounding slopes. A large bird soared on its broad wings above the gully below them.

'Is that an eagle?' Lawrence asked.

'A buzzard,' Jessie said, smiling. 'Quite common on these fells. There's a bird book at home, and binoculars too. From your window at my house you'll see all sorts of different birds on the beach.'

'How long have you lived in that house?' he asked.

'Not long,' she said. 'My friend Agnes died last New Year. She left me her house in Newton, and I sold it and bought the new house with the money.'

'Didn't you want to live in her house?'

'It is a lovely place,' said Jessie remembering, 'but filled with memories, and too far from work. I lived there with Agnes for a while, before I got the job at Windscale, but it didn't work out. Before that I had the schoolhouse in Newton, when I was head-mistress there.'

'You were headmistress of a school? I had no idea.'

'Why would you? I was there for many years. It was long enough, I suppose, and in the end I didn't have much choice about leaving.'

'What happened?'

She smiled and shook her head. 'It seems so long ago now.

After the war, things changed. It was a church school and the new vicar was, well, difficult. Very fixed views. He didn't think it was right for me to have the schoolhouse all to myself. When the other teacher came back from the navy, he wanted the house and my job too, and the new vicar thought he was right. They didn't exactly force me out, but it was so difficult that I gave up. Moved in with Agnes, then got the job at Windscale ten years ago, right at the start.'

'You must have seen a lot, being there so long.'

'Oh, yes,' she said. 'That's one of the reasons I was – I am – worried about safety, and what the place is really for. I ended up thinking that the power station was just a side issue. What they really wanted were bombs. You know that, we've talked about it before.'

'I remember it well,' he said, 'That day we were arguing and here we are now, enjoying each other's company. How does that work?'

'I'm not sure,' she said. They looked at each other.

She saw a lively, curious man with a sharp-featured face and round glasses that caught the light as he moved. Despite the white hair there was something endearingly boyish about him as he sat comfortably on a flat rock by the water, at ease with himself and with her. Lawrence saw a woman about the same age as his wife, but different from Rebecca in almost every respect. Jessie had carved her own way through life, unprotected by marriage. She must have had offers, he thought. Her face, those eyes, the shape of her, the energy. Other men must have seen what he could see, and felt the way he did. Jessie defied the conventional notions he'd been brought up with about women and their place in the world. He was falling in love with her; there was no other way to explain what he was feeling, and he had no idea what to do. He looked away. 'Shall we go back?' he said.

By the time they arrived back at the pub it was well after one. 'Only sandwiches in the bar,' said the landlord, 'but if you care to step round to the hotel, there's a bigger lunch on offer there. Not many people around, with it being such a good day.'

They went through the hall where the climbers would pile up their boots later in the day, into the quiet dining room.

'It's more expensive,' whispered Jessie as they sat down by the window looking across to the path they'd been on.

'Made of money,' Lawrence whispered back. 'This is my treat to you, and to myself. All work and no play makes Lawrence a very dull boy.'

She smiled. Anything but dull, she thought.

A little later when their plates were almost empty Jessie dared to ask the question that had been on her mind.

'Do you think your wife would ever come here?' she said. 'When we spoke on the phone, while you were away, she said she would never come north again.'

Lawrence looked up. 'You spoke on the phone?'

'She rang me, to say that you weren't coming back for a while.' 'When?'

'On the Sunday, I think.'

'What did she say?'

'I asked if she would be coming back with you, and she said something about never wishing to do so again.' She paused. 'She was quite sharp about it.'

Lawrence looked at the ceiling. 'I gave her your number, just in case, but I had no idea she'd phoned you. I'm sorry…'

Jessie shrugged, 'It doesn't matter.'

'Rebecca,' Lawrence began. 'She… Oh, it doesn't matter, you're right. Her world is different, very different. She's not like you, Jessie, not a bit.'

Jessie waited, but there was nothing more. They finished their meal and walked slowly back to the car.

'I don't want to go back yet,' he said as he started the engine. 'Where else can we go, to make the most of the day?'

'The other end of the lake is lovely,' said Jessie. 'Beyond the Gosforth road junction. We could go there. See the afternoon light on the screes.'

'Sounds grand,' he said. 'Take me there.'

Lying in bed early that morning, Jessie had planned for this moment. She had pictured in her mind where they should park the car, and the narrow bridge over the river. In May the woods between the river and the lake were full of bluebells. Today in the crisp cool of October the leaves were drying on the trees, some already carpeting the ground, others fluttering like brown and yellow moths, waiting for the wind to release them into the rushing air. She wanted to take this path, to surprise him with the best view of the lake as they rounded the last bend. On rare still days the reflection of the sloping screes created an improbable symmetry, a chevron of grey, green and brown. Today the water's surface was fractured by the wind, breaking reflections into fragments. At the far end of the lake rose the pyramid of Great Gable and above their heads, through the lattice of thinning branches, the sky shone blue, deepening towards the end of the day.

There was an old wooden seat, green with moss, at exactly the right spot, and they say down, side by side, looking.

'Do you get lonely?' he asked, without turning his head. 'I've never lived alone. Rebecca and I met at university, and we've been together ever since. I went straight from my parents to my wife, and then the children came. Even when I was living in Canada there were always people around me. You've lived alone for most of your life, haven't you?'

'At first, I had no choice,' she said. 'My mother didn't want me to stay.'

'Because of the baby?'

She nodded. 'Yes, because of John. And when he was born,' she hesitated, 'they took him away, and I was alone from then on, even though I shared a house for a while, during the war, the first war.'

'What did you do?'

'I worked in a munitions factory. Then after the war, I lied about what had happened and went back to teacher training. Worked in Liverpool for a while and then got the job in Newton. I was lucky.'

In the shelter of the water's edge, a pair of mallards floated past, looking up at them.

'Did you never want to marry?' he asked.

'I had the chance to a few years ago,' she replied, watching the ducks, 'and for a while I thought I would. But, well, in the end I decided against it.'

'Why?'

'He was a kind man, but it felt as if he was doing me a favour. I couldn't bear the thought of being beholden to him. So I turned him down, and he married someone else pretty quickly afterwards. His name is Matthew Dawson. He's a doctor. I saw him at Agnes's funeral.'

'Do you still love him?'

'I'm not sure I ever did,' she said. 'I'm not sure I've ever loved a man, not really, not like you read about.' She turned towards him. 'You love Rebecca. What's it like?'

Lawrence looked at her. 'Love? Do I love Rebecca?'

He turned away and stared ahead of him, at the water and the mountains. 'I did love her,' he said. 'I loved her because she was calm and quiet and beautiful in a grave kind of way, and she loved me, and our parents liked each other. Getting married was the logical step for us. Everyone said we were the perfect couple, made for each other.'

'And were you? Are you still?'

'We were very young, and over the years we got interested in different things. She enjoyed being at home; I had my work. And then the children came, and we loved them, doted on them actually. Didn't have to focus so much on each other any more. When I was asked to go to Ottawa I wanted Rebecca to come with me, but the children were quite small and she didn't want to uproot them, so she stayed. While I was away, I think I knew even then.'

'Knew what?'

'That we weren't in love with each other any more.'

'You can't be "in love" with someone forever.'

'But I wanted that,' he said. 'I wanted to feel strongly about her, passionately, like I had at the beginning, but I didn't.'

'And what about her?'

'I don't know. We never talked about it. I came back, and the children grew up and we went on in the same way...' He tailed off, then, 'You may say it shouldn't matter, but the physical side, that changed too.'

Jessie stayed very quiet.

'It's as if she's doing her duty,' he went on, 'like making a meal for me, or mending something. I still want it, but it makes me feel wretched.' He hung his head.

She looked across at him. His eyes were wet. She put her hand on his shoulder, and he crumpled towards her. They sat awkwardly together, saying nothing.

'And now I don't know what to do,' he said, his voice muffled against her shoulder.

'Nothing,' she said. 'Don't do anything. You're exhausted by what's happened at the plant. Not a good time for knowing what to do.'

'It's not just that,' he said, pulling himself upright, away from her. He took off his glasses and wiped his eyes. 'You know, don't you?'

Jessie looked at him, but said nothing.

'You must know I'm in love with you, Jessie. Don't – just let me say this. I'm sure of it, and I'm afraid.'

'Afraid? Of me?'

'No, not of you. I'm afraid of what might happen. More than anything else right now, I want to live with you in your house, talk to you, hold you, sleep in your bed, make love in the morning.'

Jessie listened. His words overwhelmed her.

'But I can't,' he said. 'Not yet, anyway. I have to talk to her, tell her, before I can even ask you about what you want.'

Jessie couldn't speak. Things were happening too fast. Lawrence went on, as if talking to himself. 'How long will it be before someone notices us? She's probably guessed already. She asked me all sorts of questions when I was there. And that phone call. Why did she ring you? I can't have you dragged into this.'

'So what will you do?'

'I have to move out,' he said. 'For a while at least. There's no other way. I have to keep things separate if I can.'

Jessie felt suddenly angry with him. 'Do I get a say in this? Whatever I may feel about you, Lawrence I'm fighting it, because you're married. I've met your wife. She's real and she's part of your life and your family, and I feel like a poacher, a thief, however much I might want the thing I'm stealing. I don't know what to do either. If you need to move out, do it, but please Lawrence, don't just go away and leave me, not now, not yet.'

Lawrence put both hands behind her head and kissed her. She kissed him back, and then pulled away from him.

'No,' she said. 'I can't. We'd better go, before it gets dark.'

She got up, holding the back of the seat for a moment before walking away from him, back towards the car and home.

CHAPTER 23

THEY DROVE HOME IN THE GATHERING GLOOM, saying nothing to each other. Each of them was struggling with the uncertainties that the end of the day had brought. Lawrence didn't regret kissing Jessie. He'd been wanting to do so for weeks and part of him was relieved that the tension of anticipation was over. For a few moments she had been as responsive as he had hoped, but then, too soon, she'd pulled away. Had he frightened her? Or was she so outraged that she could not speak? Without stopping the car and looking into her face, he didn't know what she was thinking or how he could respond. Any of the things he wanted to say, the questions he wanted to ask – all of them sounded crass and insensitive. Better to say nothing than to say the wrong thing, but the silence between them was palpable.

Sitting beside him, staring ahead at the familiar road and at the tunnel of light under dark trees, Jessie felt sick. It was a long time since she'd been kissed, and she was shocked by its effect on her. Her stomach was churning and her head felt light, as if she'd been drinking. She suddenly remembered another time she had felt the physical symptoms of desire: her bedroom at the schoolhouse, the glowing fire, the light on the young man's skin. She had to hide her face and turned away, closing her eyes against the images. She was sixty, sixty for heaven's sake, twenty years older than that other Jessie in that other place. And Lawrence was older too, much older than Andrew Leadbetter. What were they thinking of? This wasn't supposed to happen. She'd not expected a kiss but now she wanted more and felt ashamed. What must he think of her? She wanted to ask, but no words came.

Lawrence stopped the car outside the house. 'I'll drop you off,' he said, as if nothing had happened, 'and take the car to the station, so it's there when they get back.'

'Right,' said Jessie. As she was turning her key in the front door lock he drove away, leaving her staring after him. Confused and upset, she put the kettle on, hung up her coat, emptied and washed the coffee flask, made a pot of tea and sat down at the table, unaware of what she was doing. She touched her mouth with her fingers. He had kissed her. They had clung to each other, sitting there on the old seat by the water, and now she was at home again, alone, unsure of when he might come back and what they could possibly say to each other.

An hour passed, and Lawrence did not return. Jessie listened to the radio for a while, hearing nothing, and then went slowly, reluctantly, up to bed. She'd undressed and had just got into bed when she heard his key and his step on the stairs. Then she heard the tap on her door.

'Jessie?' came his voice. 'Are you awake?' The twist in her stomach hit her again.

'Lawrence?'

'May I come in?'

'Wait.'

She sat up, pulling her red dressing gown from the end of the bed and round her shoulders. 'Yes,' she said.

The bedroom door opened slowly and Lawrence put his head round.

'Were you asleep? Did I wake you?'

She shook her head. 'Come in.'

He stood awkwardly, looking down at her. 'May I sit down?'

She nodded and he perched on the end of the bed.

'Where have you been?' she asked.

'I dropped the car off, and then I walked a while. Wanted to clear my head.' He paused. 'And then I went down to that guest house near the golf club and booked myself a room there from tomorrow.'

'How long for?' she asked.

'For as long as it takes me to sort this out.'

'With me?'

'No, with Rebecca. I can't go on like this, it's tearing me up… Can I talk to you? Is it too late?'

'What time is it?'

'Nearly midnight.'

'That's alright,' she said. He looked sad and anxious in the dim light.

'I'm sorry about what happened,' he said. 'I just couldn't help myself. That place, having you so near me.'

'No harm done,' she said.

He looked up at her. 'Are you angry with me?'

'No, just confused. I didn't expect…'

'I'd been wanting to do that all day,' he said. 'No actually, longer than that, much longer. And now I don't know what you're thinking. You were so quiet.'

'So were you. When we got back, you just drove away.'

'I know. It seemed the easiest thing to do.'

'And now you're going to move out. Are you disgusted with me?'

'Disgusted? Of course not. How could I be? That passion of yours. I knew it was there, and I felt it.'

'What are we going to do?' she said.

'I have to tell Rebecca that it's over. I think she knows that too, but one of us has to say it. I can't pretend any more, not now.'

'Will you tell her about me?'

He shook his head. 'That's why I have to move out for a while, to keep things as simple as we can. I don't want her to drag you into anything. This is between her and me, regardless of my feeling for you.'

Jessie was curiously disappointed, but said nothing.

'You haven't asked what I want,' she said.

'I'm asking now.'

'I told you, I'm confused. This is stirring all sorts of things for me, things I've never told you about.'

'Do you want to tell me now?'

She looked across at his face, wanting to trust him.

'Not sitting here like this. Can you make us both a drink? We can stay here, but I don't want to be in bed.'

'Alright,' he said, and he left the room.

Jessie got out of bed and put the dressing gown on properly, tying the belt at her waist. She went to the bathroom and combed her hair. The mirror showed the slack skin round her neck and under her eyes, like her mother. How could he love me, she thought, and turned the mirror face down. There were two chairs in her bedroom and she took the larger one for herself, leaving the little wooden one for Lawrence. When he came back, he put the tray of tea on the little chair and sat on the bed, closer to her than she wanted, but she said nothing. It didn't matter.

He poured tea for them both and waited. Jessie put her mug on the floor and looked at the far wall of the room. She did not want to look at him. Before she could speak, he raised his hand, as if anticipating what she was about to say.

'This is about Pat, isn't it?' he said.

She looked at him, astonished.

'Pat? No, why should it be?'

He was confused. 'I thought – I thought you wanted to tell me about him.'

'There's nothing to tell.'

'You're not, you know, involved with him?'

'With Pat?' She shook her head. 'Pat's an old friend,' she said slowly, 'and that's all. We've never … I've never thought of him like that.'

'Oh,' said Lawrence. He'd been sure that was what Jessie wanted to tell him. 'Well then, what?'

This time it was Jessie who raised her hand slightly, trying to decide how much to say.

'Twenty years ago,' she began, 'I had…' struggling for the right word, '… an affair, with a young man, younger than me. I couldn't believe that he would want me, but he did. I was still working at the school. If anyone had known about it, I would have lost my job.'

Lawrence was taken aback. Questions jumped into his mind, but he could not interrupt.

'This man sometimes drank too much, and he had a temper. One night he – he forced me, after I'd told him to leave. He was too strong for me. I had been so, so involved with him, and it shocked me, hurt me.'

Lawrence stared at her, trying to imagine. 'Did you tell anyone?' he asked.

'I didn't dare,' she said. 'I was afraid of what might happen.'

'What did happen?'

'Nothing. When I was angry with him, he claimed he couldn't remember it. Things got complicated and he went to Canada, started a new life. He was with the Canadian air force over here during the war.'

'Did you see him?'

She nodded, remembering. 'He came to see me. He'd been in an accident, his hands and face were burned. He wanted me to go back to Canada with him.'

'After what he'd done?'

'He said he'd changed. I believed him.

Lawrence sat quietly. 'Was that the last time?'

'That's why I wanted to tell you,' she said. 'So you would understand…'

'Why you pulled away from me?'

'Not just that – why I like to feel more in charge of things.'

Lawrence was picturing what Jessie had said and finding it painful. He didn't want to think of her having sex with a much younger man. He hated the man and was jealous of him, both, and all at once.

'Did he hurt you?'

She nodded.

'I could never hurt you.'

She didn't look at him. 'I know that,' she said. 'But it's hard now, to let myself go.'

She looked up at him, her eyes glistening in the low light. 'And I feel old, Lawrence. My body feels old. I don't like my body really, not any more.'

'I love your body,' he said.

'You don't know it like I do. It's an old woman's body.'

Lawrence wanted to get up and take her in his arms straight away, to show her how much he wanted this old woman's body, but he stayed where he was.

'What do you want to do?' he asked.

She shook her head again. 'I don't know. You say it's all over with your marriage, but it can't be as easy as that. Being married matters.'

'You want to be married?'

She smiled. 'No, not me, you. You're the one who's married, with children and grandchildren and obligations. You have to decide what to do next.'

'I will. She and I started to talk while I was back there earlier.'

'And you'll have to talk some more. What happens in Jewish marriages, is it the same?'

He shook his head. 'Bit different.'

'Well, you must do whatever you think fit. And for now, we do nothing.'

'I have somewhere else to live. I have to move out, or it'll be too complicated. Can I leave some of my things here, or do you want to rent out the rooms?'

'I don't know,' she said. 'I can't think that far ahead. One step at a time. Promise me you'll talk to Rebecca, soon. It's too hard to leave things like this.'

'I promise. I may have to go down there. We can't talk about this over the phone.'

'You do whatever you need to. I'll be alright.'

While Lawrence was out, taking some of his things down to the guest house, Jessie made the phone call she knew she had to make.

'Can we meet?' she said. 'I need to talk to you… No, not here. In Whitehaven, maybe. Yes. Wednesday at eleven o'clock? … That'll be fine, thanks… No, nothing about the enquiry… I don't know what's happening. It's about something else… See you on Wednesday then.'

At least some things were becoming clearer in her mind.

* * *

'Over here,' she called, when Pat's familiar figure appeared in the door of the Market Café a little after eleven. He was muffled against the sharp wind that swirled into the café whenever the

233

door opened.

'Cold out there,' he said, unbuttoning his long coat. His glasses had steamed up and he sat blinking at her for a moment while he wiped them.

'That's better,' he said, 'now I can see you. Always good to see you, Jessie.'

She smiled, unsure how to start what she wanted to say.

'Have you ordered?' he asked. 'I'll do it, what would you like? Tea?' He pushed back his chair, and she gave up. She would have to wait until he was settled and ready to listen. Ten minutes later, when the teapot sat on the table between them and Pat was spreading jam on his toasted teacake, Jessie tried again.

'I think I'm going to drop out of the group for a while,' she said. 'With everything that's happened, I just want to step away from it for now.'

He stopped with the first slice of teacake half way to his mouth.

'Drop out? But it's just beginning to take off. The Windscale accident has pushed things forward, galvanised everybody.'

'I know you feel that,' she said, 'but it's different for me, living where I do.'

'That should make you even more keen, not less,' he said. He chewed the teacake for a moment, looking carefully at her. 'That's not it, is it? It's that man, that scientist, he's changed your mind.' He sat back suddenly, emboldened by certainty. 'He's been pushing you, hasn't he? He wants to break us up. What did he say to you?'

Jessie glanced around the crowded café. This was not going as she had planned. Pat's voice had risen and she worried what he might say, what others might hear.

'No, Pat, that's not it,' she began. 'Listen, could we finish our tea and then go somewhere else, somewhere not so crowded? We need to talk about things, but not here.'

234

'Right,' he said. 'Of course, not here.'

A little while later, in the sheltered porch of St Nicholas church, he held her hand confidently and spoke with unstoppable conviction.

'He wants you for himself, that's why he wants you to give up working with me.' He nodded at her and smiled. 'I'm not surprised, Jessie. You're a very desirable woman. He thinks if he can winkle you away from me, he can have you all to himself.'

He looked at Jessie, his eyes gleaming, sure of himself and expecting her to agree.

Jessie took a deep breath. 'No, Pat,' she said. 'You've got it all wrong. This has nothing to do with him.' The lie came to her easily. 'It's me. I've decided for myself. I don't want to carry on with the meetings and all that, either at my place or with you. I'm not sure enough about it any more. Lawrence has said nothing about it. I've hardly seen him, what with the enquiry and everything. And anyway,' she continued, 'he's moved out. Gone to a guest house.'

'Hah!' said Pat. 'That's just a blind. He's after you Jessie. I'm surprised you can't see it yourself.'

It took her a moment to decide what to say. 'Actually, Pat,' she began eventually, 'you couldn't be more wrong. It has nothing to do with Lawrence. He hasn't pushed me into it, as you call it. I didn't know you felt that way, and I'm sorry for any confusion.'

Pat looked surprised and hurt. 'Sorry if I've spoken out of turn, Jessie. I'm disappointed, that's all.'

'Yes, I'm disappointed, too. We've been such good friends all these years. You can make my apologies at the next meeting, no need to give a reason.'

'Jessie,' he began, but she put her fingers to her mouth.

'No more,' she said. 'Thanks for the tea, and the information. I'll get the bus back. Too cold to stay here.'

She turned round and walked quickly away from him.

* * *

Back at home, driven by a surprising urgency, Jessie found writing paper and her best pen and sat down in the draughty front room, determined to find the words that had had eluded her earlier. The room was too cold for comfort, but she did not want to be comfortable: she wanted to punish herself.

Dear Pat, she wrote, and stopped, the pen poised but motionless over the empty white space.

We've been good friends over the years. I've never forgotten your kindness and care when I was so low, after that poor Polish boy was drowned and I made such a mess of things with John. You pulled me through then and I'm grateful to you. Maybe that's why I've stayed close since then, and tried not to see that you and I have been wanting different things. You've been honest with me about your feelings recently, but I fear I have not been honest with you.

Since I was a very young woman I've felt the need to protect myself to survive. Sometimes that makes me very self-centred. Does this sound like a confession? Well in a way it is. I've let you carry on believing things about me that aren't true.

You said something today about Lawrence… She stopped, and thought, screwed up the paper and started again, copying out what she had written but changing 'Lawrence' to 'Dr Finer.' Then she carried on.

… Dr Finer wanting to 'break us up', I think those were your words. I realised that's what you must have thought all this time, that you and I have been 'together'. That's why you introduced me to Mrs Foster, as if we are a couple. But that's not right, and I should have said so before. I have lived alone for many years, and sometimes I have been intensely lonely. You have been a good friend at those times, but no more than that. There, she'd said it. That

was enough. She stopped herself from saying any more, adding only: *It will be better for both of us if we do not see or contact each other for a while.*

    Yours,

    Jessie

    She folded the letter, slid it into the envelope, addressed, sealed, stamped and posted it before she could change her mind.

CHAPTER 24

IT HAD BEEN OVER A WEEK since her letter to Pat, with no response, and Jessie blamed herself. She had questioned Pat's friendship after many years, and watched Lawrence move out, leaving her alone in this big house with empty airy rooms, exposed to the gales and driving rain of late October. There was nothing green and growing to be seen from the house, just the constantly changing patterns and colours of light, cloud and water. She wondered how she would survive the winter here. She longed to see Lawrence, to soak up some of his strength, but heard nothing from him. One evening, restless in the early darkness, she pulled a hat over her face and walked round towards his lodgings at the time he normally left work, just to catch a glimpse of him, but there was no sign and she felt too foolish to wait.

The next day, Jessie was awake early and still anxious when a letter arrived with the first post. The writing on the envelope was large and ill-formed: it must be Hannah, she thought, tearing the envelope open, fearing the worst. It was the worst. Poor Fred was dead. The doctor had seen him and arranged for an ambulance to the hospital the following day, but then she'd found Fred in the morning, dead and cold in his chair.

Just like he was asleep, Hannah wrote. *He mebbe knew, and it was time for him to go. He didn't want to go to hospital. Funeral's on Friday, ten o'clock. Please come, and tell John. Fred would want him to be here.*

Jessie checked the time and decided to call John right away. Mercifully it was he who picked up the phone.

'It's about Fred Porter,' she said. 'You know how ill he's been. Well, he died, at home, in his chair. Hannah said he must have known they were going to take him to hospital.'

'He would have hated that,' said John. 'Maybe it's as well, but he was too young.'

'Not much older than me,' said Jessie. 'Hannah's asked if you and I can come to the funeral, on Friday morning, at St Catherine's.'

'Of course, I'll come,' said John. 'Fred was almost like a father to me. Both of them, they were so good, when I was lonely and low, before…'

'I remember,' said his mother.

'It was them I talked to, about you,' said John, quietly.

'Yes, I know,' she said.

'I'll take Friday morning off. I can still get back to work for the afternoon, to pick up on anything I've missed. I'll bring the car, what time?'

'Make it nine o'clock. Funeral's not till ten, but I'd like to be there to support Hannah any way we can.'

John was punctual as always, and they drove up to Boot together, talking about Hannah and Fred in happier times. 'He had such energy,' said John, 'even with the wooden leg and his sticks.'

'And those wonderful rugs he made,' Jessie added. 'Such simple designs. Works of art, Agnes called them.'

'She should have been here,' said John. 'She loved them both. Fred gave a rug to Maggie, you know, the first time I took her to Mill Cottage. It's still in the house at West Row. Violet was fond of it. They use it as a draught-stopper at the front door.'

John parked the car at the Boot Inn where the funeral breakfast was to be held, and they walked up to the cottage. Hannah was already surrounded by friends and neighbours from all around the valley where she had lived all her life. She looked strong and cheerful. 'Fred never wanted to leave this house,' she whispered to Jessie as they greeted each other. 'Said we'd 'ave to carry 'im out feet first, and we will.'

When the hearse arrived, they followed it on foot slowly down the track to the church, dozens of people shuffling quietly along in unaccustomed clothes and shoes. The air was calm after days of wind and rain, the sky clear and pale over their heads. A blackbird sang in the holly tree as they passed by.

Hannah had asked John, as the son they had never had, to say a few words, and Jessie was deeply proud of him as he spoke about his love and respect for Fred, who had helped him, he said, to come to terms with himself as a young man. Jessie understood what that meant. Despite all her fears and anxieties about John when he had found and claimed her as his mother, she would be eternally grateful to Fred and Hannah for encouraging him to do so. This was her son, she thought, Clive's son, so like him in some ways, so unlike in others. A good man, a wonderful husband and father, capable and respected at work, and now, at last, they could be comfortable together as mother and son, after all the years of deception. She cried, as much for that as for the memory of Fred. When John returned to his seat beside her, he squeezed her arm, and her tears continued.

Hannah walked slowly to stand beside her husband's coffin in front of the altar.

'As soon as I saw him, I knew,' she said, making everyone smile. The story of the love affair between the two of them, thwarted for years by Hannah's father, was well known. 'We were as 'appy as any two people can be,' Hannah went on. ''E were a stubborn old bugger, and he knew 'e were ill, but 'e wouldn't 've wanted to die anywhere else. So we should be glad that 'e's found 'is peace as 'e would 've wanted. And 'e'd be reet glad to see you all 'ere,' she added. 'There's summat to eat at the Boot after. Come along, all of ye, and 'elp us send 'im off.'

Breakfast was a splendid affair. 'Miss Plane paid for this lot,' Hannah whispered to Jessie. 'We didn't know what to do with that money she left us, so it's paying for all this. Fred would've loved to see everybody 'ere. Allus loved a party.'

When the bar opened and the singing started, John and his mother decided it was time to leave, and they drove back down the valley, still talking.

'You know what you said about Fred helping you, when you first lived with them? Were you very unhappy?'

'More confused, I would say. Angry about being lied to at home, and not knowing how to deal with things. I didn't like women much, I remember that. The day I found Hannah and Fred, there were two women I spoke to at Hill House. They laughed at me, made me want to hit them. Hannah and Fred talked me round.'

'You were angry with me too, weren't you?'

'I was, to be honest. I felt you'd abandoned me. I understand all that better now though. I was very young then.'

'Did Maggie ever tell you that she was very angry with me too? She came to see me at the school.'

John turned to her and smiled. 'I was furious about that at the time. Now I wish I could have been there.'

She laughed. 'It was a long time ago.'

'Maybe that's why I loved Maggie almost from the first. She has such spirit. And she'd been married before, she wasn't shy and coy like other girls.'

'Do you think she's changed?' Jessie asked.

John paused before answering, 'Maggie's got more to lose now than she had before. And she's always wanted the best for the children.'

'And for you, too,' said Jessie. 'That's why she's been so worried about, you know, how you were born.'

'Our dad's a bastid,' John said in his son's childish voice, and they both laughed.

'Has she got over that now?' Jessie asked.

'I think so, although she'd probably say not. She knew it had to come out sometime, but perhaps not that way.' He smiled, and they both laughed again.

'What did Lawrence make of all that?' John asked.

'He hasn't said much about it. Doesn't seem to worry much about social niceties.'

'You're fond of him, aren't you?'

Jessie blushed. 'I am,' she admitted, 'But he's married.'

John turned something over in his mind. 'Why don't you come to lunch on Sunday?' he said. 'It's time we started being a family.'

'Will Maggie be alright about that?'

'I'll use my fatal charm,' he said. 'She knows it's the right thing to do. We'd already agreed that you should see Judith when she comes home and she's due back today. Family's important to Maggie,' he added. 'And our family includes you.'

Jessie was delighted. She knew how upset Maggie had been. This was a chance to heal the rift and she never expected it to arrive so soon.

'Thank you, John,' she said. 'And thank Maggie for me, too.'

242

They were quiet for a while before John broke the companionable silence.

'Tell me more about him,' he said.

'Lawrence? He's moved out, to the guest house near the golf club. Haven't seen him for a few days.'

'What made him do that?' asked John, surprised, after what Jessie had just told him.

'There was some gossip, I think,' said Jessie. 'He and his wife are not on good terms, but he didn't want me to get mixed up in anything. So he left.'

'Do you miss him?'

'I miss having someone in the house. It's a big space for one person. And we get on well, very well considering what different lives we've had. He's a clever man, and he doesn't patronise me, and I like that.'

'So are you going to rent the rooms to someone else now?'

'Not just yet, until we see how things turn out,' she said.

'You mean he might move back in?'

'I don't know, John, to be honest. I think he wants to stay up here and his wife wants him to go back south. That's one of the problems they have.' She thought for a minute. 'I think you and he would get on,' she said. 'And he wants to see more of the hills. We went up Wasdale last week and walked as far as Sty Head. I could tell he wanted to do more.'

'Haven't had a good walk for ages,' said John, realising what his mother was trying to say. 'We could do High Stile ridge, before the days shorten too much. Do you think he'd like that? I know I would.'

Jessie beamed at him. 'I know he would,' she said. 'Ask him.'

* * *

'Is that all she said?' Maggie asked when John reported their conversation later that evening. 'He's having trouble with his wife? Nothing about how she feels about him?'

'I couldn't ask her straight out,' he chided. 'It's none of our business.'

'But it could be,' said Maggie. 'She's your mother, John, but I find her hard to deal with.'

'I know that. Maybe if she and this man were friends she might be happier, calm down a bit.'

'Or not. God knows she's embarrassed us enough in the past. This could be something else we have to put up with.'

John put his arm round his wife and pulled her towards him. 'You worry too much,' he said. 'I'll get him out on the hills and ask him if his intentions are honorable, OK? But right now, Mrs Pharaoh, you and I are going to bed.'

On Sunday morning Jessie arrived at the Pharaohs' house in St Bees at exactly the specified time. She knew she would need to behave really well and watch her words, to avoid giving offence yet again. She had dressed with care, and carried a bunch of flowers that she'd kept in the back porch overnight to make sure they didn't droop in the warmth of the kitchen.

Maggie was obviously trying hard, too. No reference was made by any of them, including the children, to the unfortunate incident at Gosforth Show. Children's memories are short, Jessie reminded herself, but she also wondered whether special inducements or threats had been necessary to avoid any sensitive topics of conversation. She offered to help in the kitchen, but Maggie and Judith were clearly in charge there. Jessie sat with John and the children in the sunny front room as they waited for the call to the table. Jessie heard both boys read, while John looked on, pleased that his mother's professional eye appreciated how well they were both doing.

'Any news from Lawrence?' he asked.

She shook her head.

'When I'm back at work tomorrow, I'll invite him for a walk next weekend,' he said. He had already told Maggie of his plan, and had clear instructions to find out as much as he could.

During lunch Jessie realised that Judith wasn't really looking at her. As they cleared the table together at the end of the meal, Jessie took advantage of the relative privacy.

'Will you walk down to the beach me?' she asked.

Judith looked up. 'Me? Just me?'

'Yes, please, if you would. I'd like to talk to you.'

'What about?' said Judith suspiciously.

'You know, school and things. I've not seen you for weeks.'

'OK,' said Judith, without enthusiasm.

As they headed down the road, heads down against the breeze, Judith took her granddaughter's arm.

'I'm sorry about what happened,' she said.

Judith said nothing.

'I told you more than I should, about your father and me. It wasn't fair.'

'I'm old enough to know things like that,' Judith protested, stopping and turning towards her.

'But the boys aren't, are they?' said Jessie.

'You can't blame me for that,' Judith said, looking away. 'Frank's so silly, and Vince is just a baby.'

'I'm not blaming you, dear,' said Jessie quickly, 'I'm blaming myself. I talk too much sometimes, and at the wrong times.'

Judith giggled. 'Mum says I show her up. Maybe I got it from you.'

'Well, we'll both have to watch what we say, won't we?'

They walked on, close together against the wind that had sharpened as they turned towards the beach.

'You're not like a proper granny,' said Judith.

245

'Oh,' said Jessie, taken aback. 'Is that bad?'

'Actually, I like it, even if Mum doesn't. Other people's grannies are really boring.'

She turned towards Jessie and gave her a hug.

'Thank you, dear,' said Jessie. 'Now, tell me about school.'

Judith chattered as they walked, while beside her Jessie vowed, yet again, to be more careful in the future.

The walk with Judith tired her; she was sitting on a little chair in the hall when Maggie found her there.'Are you alright?' she asked.

Jessie looked up and smiled. 'I'm fine,' she said. 'I'm not as young as I used to be, that's all.' For a moment she wanted to tell Maggie about the lump in her breast, which had been worrying her for a while now. But the moment passed, and she moved on to what she wanted to say, while she had the chance.

'I wanted to tell you how sorry I am about telling Judith more than she was really ready to hear, about John. It was a mistake, and I regret it. It wasn't fair to Judith to burden her with that, and, well, I'm sorry for what happened. I know you were very upset about it.'

'Come in the kitchen. We can talk in there. Yes, I was upset,' said Maggie, tidying the remaining things off the table. 'Judith is just a child still, and telling her brothers put all of us in an awkward position.'

"Yes,' said Jessie, 'and that was all down to me and my big mouth. It gets me into trouble, and it shouldn't, not after all these years.'

'We'll get over it,' said Maggie. 'Are you sure you're alright? You look very tired. Are you sleeping properly?'

'There is something that's making me uncomfortable at night,' said Jessie, but again she backed away from telling Maggie what it was. She knew there would only be a fuss, and that was what she wanted to avoid.

* * *

The following Saturday morning found John and Lawrence braving the thin drizzle on their way up to High Stile. It wasn't the best weather for a long walk, but neither of them seemed to mind. John was very happy to be out and up high, loving the space and air on either side of the ridge. For Lawrence it was the first time in his life that he'd done something so physically challenging. He'd worried whether his legs would be strong enough to keep up with John's longer stride, and he'd had to stop once or twice on the way to pull more breath into his lungs, but once they reached the ridge he could stop looking at his feet and stand, taking in the view all around.

'Better without the low cloud,' said John. 'We could see all the high peaks from up here on a better day.'

'It's wonderful,' said his companion. 'I told Jessie I'd no idea a place like Wasdale existed in England, and this is the same. Unbelievable. I can't thank you enough for suggesting it.'

They found a sheltered spot close to an overhanging rock and sat to eat their lunchtime sandwiches. John knew what Maggie expected him to ask about, but that's not what should happen, he thought, not here, not today. Instead, they talked about the plant and the future.

'How long before the official report comes out?' John asked.

'November 8th is the date they gave us,' said Lawrence. 'End of this coming week.'

'How are people feeling about it?'

Lawrence didn't respond straight away, munching his sandwich, trying to identify what he really believed. 'I'm not sure,' he said finally. 'I think we all feel that once the fire started we did everything we could to control it, and the result could have been far worse than it turned out.'

247

'But?' ventured John. He could see that Lawrence was still thinking.

'Yes, there is a "but", or at least I think there is. I'm concerned how the government may react to the whole thing, put their own take on it.'

'The enquiry team did a good job, didn't they? Most people I spoke to said so.'

'It was what they didn't ask about that worried me,' said Lawrence. 'They didn't ask about all the shortcuts we've had to take with the reactor over the years, to keep up with the needs of the bomb-builders. If any of those shortcuts made a fire more likely, that's not going to come out. So how will the fire be explained?'

'Are you worried about that?' John asked.

'I am,' said Lawrence. 'I could be completely wrong of course.'

'Not long to wait, anyway.'

'True, it's been mercifully quick.'

John pressed on. 'And what about your future here?'

'Well, I'm seconded from Harwell, as you probably know. How long that continues might depend on what the report says. Part of the underlying problem with the reactor was what I was sent up here to investigate. Number One pile will never work again now, but there will be lessons we need to learn.'

'Do you want to stay?'

Lawrence wondered whether Jessie had already said something. 'It's a bit complicated at home right now,' he said carefully. 'I may have to go back for a few days to sort some things out, but no decision yet on the longer term. Are you bothered about Jessie renting the rooms out? I'm worried about her losing money if things go on much longer.'

'She's not without a bob or two,' said John. 'Her friend Agnes left a very valuable house, and I think there was enough left over after the Seascale house was paid for.'

'Even so,' said Lawrence. 'I need to make up my mind pretty soon, I know that.'

John knew he should ask more, but he did not. He liked Lawrence, and didn't want to poke around in his private life and ruin a good day on the hills.

'He's a thoughtful man,' he said later, in answer to Maggie's questions. 'Hinted that things at home weren't good, but nothing more than that. Whatever's going on, we need to leave them alone.'

'I hope she knows what she's doing,' said Maggie. 'I never understood why she broke up with that nice Dr Dawson. And she doesn't look very well, John. I asked her if anything was the matter, but she said not.'

'She's hardly had a day's illness in her life,' said John. 'I'm sure she's just fine.'

Chapter 25

Lawrence stared at his plate, on which a pale lump of something lay in a thick orange sauce. 'What is this?' he asked the young woman who had put the plate in front him and seemed to be waiting for something. The young woman looked down, her head at a slight angle, wondering.

'Chicken in mush,' she said. 'Cook says it's very nice.' She turned and walked away across the empty room. Evening meals were on offer at the Fairway Guest House, but Lawrence was beginning to understand why he was the only diner this evening. The problem was that everywhere else in the village, and the hostel too, would be full of talk about the imminent official report on the fire, which he was trying to avoid. So, here he was, alone in the depressing dining room with 'chicken in mush' on his plate and no particular desire to eat it. He pushed his chair away from the table and looked out of the window. The sun had set earlier with a glorious flourish of pink and gold, and the moon would be bright later in a cloudless sky. A freshening breeze seeped through the ill-fitting windowpane. He couldn't stay in this place all evening, not again. He had to get out, and he had to think.

Moving out of Jessie's relatively comfortable home had seemed sensible at the time. Suddenly his life had seemed too complicated, he'd felt an urgent need to be alone, to take stock, to make some decisions for himself. Being close to Jessie Whelan was too distracting when the priority was to break away from his wife of thirty years. Reduce the variables, his science mind had whispered, but it had been in vain; Jessie was on his mind as much as ever, and Rebecca's failure to respond to his letters left him in a limbo of longing. He hadn't seen Jessie for over a week, and now he wanted to, desperately.

Another long lonely evening yawned ahead. Lawrence made a decision: he would go for a walk. The night was clear and the tide far enough out to make the smooth sand of the beach accessible. Down to Drigg and back along the lane, over the railway bridge. He'd lunched well in the canteen at noon. If he was hungry a pint or two at the pub would probably suffice. A few minutes later, coated and booted, he turned up his collar and set off.

At the same time, a few hundred yards away, Jessie cleared her supper things and thought about her evening. A walk might help to pass the time, and give her a better night's sleep than the past week had provided. Reading for an hour two in the very early hours of every day had left a legacy of tired eyes and headaches. As always, it was anxieties about things beyond her control that had been keeping her awake.

Lawrence's departure from the house had seemed very sudden. Was he trying to reconcile with Rebecca now, regretting his lapse by the lake? She'd tried so hard not to let her feelings for him show, to reduce the tension between them, but he had removed himself. In the past week she'd heard nothing, not even a phone call. She'd cut herself off from Pat, and Kath was rarely available during the week. John and Maggie had their own life together. Of all Jessie's wide acquaintance, there was no one she could turn to; she was part of so many lives and at the centre of none. If she died here tonight, quietly, would anyone truly care, as Hannah grieved for Fred? The question was ridiculously maudlin, but she had asked it many times over the years, and the answer was never reassuring. Agnes had cared, but Agnes was gone. And now there was Lawrence: clever, successful, lovely Lawrence with a wife and children and a home far away. It was just loneliness for him too, she surmised, that had driven him to tears and into her arms. He's gone, she told herself firmly. Stop feeling sorry for yourself. If it's fine and dry, get some exercise and clear your head. She walked through to the front room to check the weather.

Lawrence began his walk striding purposefully ahead, watching the flattened disc of the rising moon, breathing the cool air. But glancing up at the houses standing tall at the edge of the village made him falter and stop. He knew which was her house. It was in darkness. He stared at the house, imagining, as water pooled under his boots. Was she there? Was she with that priest, or out enjoying herself, relieved to have the house to herself again? Or was she missing him as much as he was missing her? The image of her filled his mind: the curve of her waist, her bright eyes. If he just arrived at the door, unannounced, would she send him away, or invite him in? Might he kiss her again? Oh, how he wanted to. Desire curled through his body like smoke.

From the darkened window of her house, Jessie was watching him, hardly daring to breathe. She had seen the figure walking along, and knew immediately who it was. She had seen him stop and turn towards the shore, and she stepped away from the window, although she knew he could not see her. Then he began to move again, not along the beach but up towards the house. A sudden blur of panic overwhelmed her. She ran back to the kitchen, turning on lights, creating normality, pretending that she had not been watching and did not know that soon he would knock on her door. When the knock came she steadied herself before she walking slowly to open the back door. No time to decide what to say, or what to do. Lawrence stood in the pool of light from the kitchen, looking at her.

'Hello,' he said. 'May I come in?'

Pretence slipped from her like an abandoned shawl, falling to the floor.

'I saw you on the beach. You were walking and then you stopped.'

'I was looking up here,' he said. 'The house was dark. I wondered if you were at home. I wanted to see you. If you don't want to see me, just tell me to go away.'

For a long moment they stood motionless, before Lawrence stepped forward and took her in his arms.

'Jessie, Jessie,' he said, burying his face in her hair. 'I've missed you. Lying in bed every night, thinking about you, wondering about you, wishing I could be here.'

'I know,' she said. She stroked the back of his head, passively, finding no more words. He raised his head and looked into her face.

'I love you,' he said. 'I'm sure of it, even more than before. I've never felt like this before, not even when I was young.' He pulled her to him again, one hand round her shoulders, the other low on her back. She could feel the warmth, the urgency. All her caution, her concern for his wife, for her son and his family, for her reputation, all flowed away as they stood together.

'Please,' he said. 'Take me to bed, Jessie. Let me lie with you, hold you.'

Without a word she turned, reached for his hand and led him up the dark stairs to her moonlit room.

They left the curtains open. He took off his clothes and then helped her to do the same. She had no time to think about her body as he pulled her down onto the bed and covered them both with the counterpane, holding her close, stroking the skin on her back and buttocks, murmuring her name. She was aware of nothing save his body, his mouth, his long fingers. He was slow, gentle, warm and loving, everything she had hoped he would be in those dark hours when she had let herself imagine. When he could hold back no longer and entered her she was ready for him but still she gasped, and he held back for an instant. 'Don't stop,' she said. 'Go on.'

She felt his strength inside her and held him close until he relaxed. 'Don't go,' she said. 'Stay inside me.'

'I can't,' he mumbled into her shoulder. 'All done.'

He rolled off her and lay on his back, breathing hard. Neither of them spoke. She heard a patter of rain on the window. He turned towards her, laying his arm over her. 'Are you alright?' he said. 'Did I hurt you?'

She smiled. 'You were very gentle, until right at the last.'

'I'm sorry, couldn't hold back any longer. I've wanted you for so long. But I wasn't sure, after all that's happened… And that man, the one who really hurt you.'

She lay still, her arms around him, remembering. 'That was long ago, and this is different. We're friends. He and I were never friends.'

'I didn't mean this to happen,' he said. 'I've been trying to clear my mind, but I couldn't stop myself in the end. As soon as I saw the house, and thought of you here, I was lost.' He turned towards her. 'Did I rush you?'

She shook her head, and traced his mouth with her fingers. 'You didn't rush me. I thought I'd given up hope, but when I saw you start to walk towards the house, I knew you would knock on the door. And I knew what I wanted to do. You didn't rush me. It was wonderful, I'd forgotten.'

He smiled. 'It's been a long time,' he said, 'for us both.'

'I couldn't help myself,' said Jessie. 'I know I should, but I couldn't.'

He pulled the counterpane over them both again and they curled into each other like two cats in a basket.

When they woke, the moon had moved around, shining directly onto the end of Jessie's bed. Lawrence craned his head, looking at the moon and the silver sea,

'There's no one out there who can see us,' she said, 'unless they're hanging onto a balloon or something.'

'Or on a boat with a big telescope,' he said, cuddling into her again. 'Anyway, what's to see? Two old people loving each other.'

'Not so old,' she said. 'We're healthy and fit and have all our faculties, thank God.'

'Thank God,' he said. 'Now all we have to do is work out what to do next.'

'Does this really change anything?' she asked.

He stared up at the ceiling. 'Officially, of course,' he said. 'For us, it's just what was going to happen, and I love that we're here like this. But I moved out so people wouldn't talk, and that still bothers me.'

'Does Rebecca know, how you feel about me?'

'I'm not sure,' he said.

'Are you going to tell her, about this?'

He thought about it. 'No,' he said. 'Not yet. We have to work something out, a proper separation, or whatever she will agree to. After that you and I will have to decide what to do. But I've told her I'm living at the guest house and see you only occasionally, both of which are true. I don't want to share this with anyone but you. It's our secret.'

He pushed himself up on his elbow and looked down at her. 'Is that alright with you?'

She stroked his face, feeling the evening stubble on his chin. 'It would be easier for me here if people didn't know,' she said. 'But I don't like the idea of you lying to Rebecca. If you feel you must, that's up to you. But you have to be clear with her, if this is really the end of your marriage. We can't go on for long, deceiving everybody.'

He pushed himself out of the bed, bent down and kissed her forehead.

'Bring me a towel or something,' she said. 'I'd forgotten how sticky it is.'

He laughed. 'So much for romance,' he said. 'Thank God for you, Jessie.'

He washed, dressed and sat on the edge of her bed. 'I'll go out the back door,' he said, 'and make sure no one sees me. Life is complicated enough. When the report comes out, I'll talk to Harwell about the implications. I'll tell them I want to stay here, either as a longer secondment or else permanently. Rebecca and I will have to discuss that and I'll tell her then that I don't want to go back. From what we've already said to each other, I don't think she'll be surprised.'

'Will she divorce you?'

'It's not as easy as that when you're Jewish. The rabbi will have things to say, no doubt, and Rebecca will probably listen. But that's all down the road. For now, you and I are here, loving each other and happy to be so. Aren't we?'

She smiled. Right now, right here, she could think of nothing else she would want. 'I'm more happy than I thought possible,' she said. 'But come the daylight, who knows.'

'We'll see each other, just as we have done before,' he said. 'Go for a walk, have supper together here. We're not doing any harm, and people can say what they like.'

'Can we go to bed again?'

'Not right now,' he said, smiling. 'I'm an old man don't forget.'

She laughed. 'Sometime,' she said. 'Come for supper tomorrow.'

'Are you sure?'

'Yes. We'll have sausage.'

He laughed. 'You're wicked,' he said. 'I'm going. Give me a kiss.'

The following evening Lawrence arrived at the front door, carrying two bottles of beer, and they ate their supper at the kitchen table like an old married couple. The only difference was that after supper they made love like newlyweds.

* * *

'You're looking well, Finer,' said Tim Fahey. 'That walk with John Pharaoh obviously did you good.'

'It was a revelation,' said Lawrence. 'I'm fitter than I thought I was, which feels good at my age.'

'Planning to do it again?' asked Tim.

'Hope so,' said Lawrence.

Like everyone else on the reactor team, they were waiting anxiously for the report to be issued. Lawrence had heard that the Atomic Energy Authority bosses had seen it, but security was tight, and he couldn't be sure whether his anxieties had any foundation. Late on the Friday afternoon, the day when the report was due out, they were summoned to Gethin Davey's office. He looked pale. Tom Tuohy was there too, with an odd expression on his face. Lawrence suddenly feared what was to come.

There wasn't room to sit down, so they stood awkwardly.

'Gentlemen,' said Gethin Davey. 'The final report of the enquiry is out, and we've had our first look at it. You'll read it for yourselves, no doubt. There is plenty to be pleased about. Many people are commended for the actions and their bravery in getting the fire under control…' But, thought Lawrence. He could hear it before it was spoken.

'…But,' said Davey, 'there are some phrases in here that we're not happy about.'

Tom Tuohy interrupted, speaking quite quietly. 'Mr Davey's being polite,' he said. 'There's talk in this report about "faults of judgement" here at the plant. Nothing like that was said before, but here it is in the report. "Faults of judgement"– that means mistakes, made by us, here. I have to say, I'm shocked. Nay, worse than that.' Lawrence could see it in his face, hear it in his voice. Tuohy was having trouble controlling his anger.

Gethin Davey held up his hand. 'Tuohy's not happy as you can see, and nor am I. We will write to whoever we need to register our dissatisfaction, although I'm not sure what good that will do. The report's already gone to the press.'

There was an audible groan round the room.

'I know,' Davey went on. 'They'll be back with more bloody daft questions, accusing us of God knows what. We'll just have to ride it out. It goes without saying that as far as Tuohy and I are concerned, we couldn't be more proud of what we achieved that awful week, but that's not what others may say. We can debate here, and in private, but nothing is to be said out there, please. We'll do what needs doing officially, and some of you might want to consult your professional associations. As far as the next steps go, we will start a detailed examination of the report's recommendations. Too late for No. 1 Pile, but that was almost dead anyway. We need to salvage all the information we can get from what happened. I know the teams at Harwell and Risley will be doing the same. You'll need to check with Harwell, Finer, about where they want you to be. If you want to stay here, we could certainly do with your help.'

Lawrence nodded. Things had turned out as he had feared, but at least he wasn't too surprised. He looked around the room. Some of them men here would feel that their careers and their futures might never be the same. Those bastards in London, he thought bitterly, they have to placate the bloody Yanks, so we'll throw a few scientists and engineers to the wolves. They're so far away, in the frozen north after all, so who cares?

They shuffled out of the room. 'You were right, Finer,' Tim Fahey whispered to him as they walked slowly back to their office. 'That's what you said might happen. Blame the locals, that's exactly what they've done.'

'And we know why,' said Lawrence.

* * *

Lawrence had only just got back to his office, when his phone rang again. He listened carefully to the familiar voice.

'Risley?' he said. 'How long for?'

After a further pause, his mind racing, Lawrence coughed to give himself time to think.

'Can I get back to you on Monday about this? One or two things I need to check, you know, family matters… Yes, Monday morning, first thing.'

Chapter 26

'You look pretty glum,' said Jessie, 'Bad day?'

'The report came out,' said Lawrence, putting both hands round his mug of tea, warming his fingers. 'It's not good. They said they found "faults of judgement" at the plant. Virtually blamed us for making the fire start, and then praised us for putting it out. Everyone's pretty upset about it.'

'Are they surprised?'

'It's what the Harwell people were saying might happen. But up here we never expected it would be the in the actual report. Can't believe Penney agreed to it. At the enquiry they told us they weren't there to find fault, but now here it is.'

'What will you do?'

'Nothing we can do, except complain. Don't expect anyone will take much notice.'

He sipped his tea. 'There was someone in the canteen at lunch-time talking about "them and us". "They think we're all lazy or stupid or raving Reds," he was saying. I'm sure a lot of the locals would agree with him.'

'That's what people said in Barrow during the first war,' said Jessie, 'that London didn't trust them.'

'Well nothing's changed much then,' said Lawrence. He hesitated, looking into his mug. 'Actually something else came up today as well, and I need to talk to you about it.'

'Rebecca?'

He looked at her enquiringly. 'No, not Rebecca. Nothing to do with Rebecca. They want me to go to Risley.'

'Risley, why there? Why now?'

'Some new Health and Safety group they've been setting up. Plan's been around for a while but all of a sudden it's more urgent, of course. They need someone from up here to fill them in on what happened, how to prevent it happening again, all that. I'm the obvious person to go.'

'When?' she asked.

'Straight away by the sound of it. I said I'd think about it and tell them next week.'

'Do you have any choice?'

'Not much. If Harwell objected it could only be because they want me back there.'

Jessie turned away towards the sink. 'Did they say how long for?' she asked, her back still towards him.

'No. They're all running around like headless chickens.' He watched her. 'What do you think?'

She turned to face him. 'I don't know what to think.'

'You know I don't want to go, don't you? I want to stay here.'

She hung her head. 'So you say.'

He got up and put his arms round her. Jessie's arms stayed at her side.

'Of course I want to stay,' he said, looking into her face.

She pulled away from him. 'Something was going to happen, I knew it. It was all too much of a fluke.'

'A fluke?'

She shook her head. 'You know what I mean, unpredictable. The classic landlady and lodger cliché. I knew it couldn't last.'

'It's not like that,' he protested. 'This isn't a passing fancy, not

261

for me anyway. You must know that by now. I want to be here with you.'

'But you can't,' she said. 'So everything has to change.'

'Not everything. They won't need me there at weekends, I can come back.'

She shook her head. 'I wasn't expecting this.'

'I know, neither was I.'

'When do you have to decide?'

'By Monday. We've got the whole weekend.'

Jessie took a deep breath. '*You've* got the whole weekend. This is your decision.'

'But we can spend the weekend together, can't we?'

'I'm not sure,' she said. 'I need time to think.'

'About us?'

'About me. Too much is happening.'

'Can I stay now?'

She looked at him, knowing what he meant. She shook her head again. 'No, not now. Kath and I are going out.' The lie dropped from her mind to her mouth and out, smoothly and without hesitation.

'Oh,' he said. 'Tomorrow?'

'Not sure about tomorrow. We thought we might go to Carlisle shopping, on the train. I'll call you when we've decided.'

'Jessie,' he began, but she had already walked over to the back door.

'Kath'll be here soon,' she said. 'I have to get ready. Thanks for telling me your news, Lawrence. We'll talk about it tomorrow, alright?'

The back door stood open. Jessie stood by it, looking at her feet. Lawrence picked up his coat and hat and went out into the night.

Jessie closed the door and leaned against it, hating herself.

Speculation and regret tumbled round in her head like leaves in a swirling wind. All she could think of was that he was trying to get away from her, using work to make a difficult decision easier. He'd gone to bed with her because he was lonely and now he regretted it. He could even have asked them to send him to Risley, well out of the way of her and Rebecca, running away from both of them. She wasn't surprised. Why would he want a woman older than himself, with a sagging body and a suspicious mind? She was not a loveable person, so why should she expect to be loved? He would be better off with someone else, and she could go back to the safety of her old life. If he went away she wouldn't have to worry about him, or Rebecca, or what anyone would think. It would be a relief.

She noticed his scarf hanging on the back of the chair and the tears came. It was over. She'd known it couldn't last. She sat down at the table and put her head in her hands, sad but relieved that the dream had ended. She was suddenly cold and reached over to pull the scarf around her neck. Then she poked the fire back into life and sat for a while until the shivering stopped. For an hour or two she let instincts carry her, making a drink, preparing food, eating it, washing up. Still cold, she ran a bath as hot as she could bear it and went to bed, hoping to wake up to her old familiar reality.

When the morning came, she lay for a while, staring at the ceiling. The house was quiet. She was alone. She remembered what had happened in this bed and turned her face into the pillow. That was all he had wanted. She had loved it too, every moment of it, talking and laughing as well as the sex. But none of it was real. He'd not found the lump in her breast, but it was still there, mocking her, waiting to be discovered. Now she was alone again she had to confront it, without having to deal with anyone else's reactions. Everything was simpler on her own.

Lawrence lay in bed in his small back room at the guest house. It was quiet; most of the other residents went home at the weekend. He didn't understand what had happened. He'd said he might have to go away for a while and she'd turned her back on him, literally. 'A fluke' that was the word she used. Is that all their love-making had meant to her? And then she'd practically thrown him out with some story about Kath, which he didn't believe for a minute. He knew she could react to things pretty quickly some-times. Was it something he he'd said? He went back over the conversation but there was nothing, unless she thought he was just using work to run away. And now he was stuck, waiting for her to contact him. Shopping in Carlisle – very convenient.

Eating his breakfast in the deserted dining room he tried to put himself in her shoes. She'd lived alone almost all her life, and here was this man, living in her house, and then in her bed. Maybe it was all too fast and she just wanted time to think. Or maybe he really didn't know her at all, and she had decided to get rid of him before he took up any more of her space. Anger and sadness mix like oil and water; however much you shake them, one always rises to the top.

Jessie stayed in bed until midday, using sleep to blot out the turmoil in her head. Then she used work to the same end, washing her sheets and pillowcases, reclaiming her bed. She went to the shop, talked normally, did the usual weekend things. The routines reassured and settled her. She didn't ring Lawrence because she didn't know what to say to him, and he didn't ring her. Kath asked if she wanted to go the club, but she declined, saying she didn't feel well. That at least was true; she couldn't settle, distracted by a vague headache above her eyes. On Sunday morning she went to church, where there was no chance of seeing Lawrence. She didn't believe any of it any more, but it passed the time.

The rest of the weekend slipped away. On Monday morning

Lawrence told Mr Davey that he would be ready to go to Risley within hours and could stay for as long as they needed him, provided he could come back at the weekends. When the details were agreed he called Jessie and was surprised when she picked up the phone.

'Did you have a good weekend?' he asked. 'How was Carlisle?' The question caught Jessie by surprise. 'Oh, we didn't go,' she said, 'I must be coming down with something. Spent a lot of time in bed.'

There was a slight pause before Lawrence continued. 'I'm going down to Risley first thing tomorrow.' he said, 'Home on Friday. Then down there again next week.'

'Home, which home?'

'Here. This is home now.' There was a brief silence. 'Jessie –'

She interrupted him. 'See you next weekend then, maybe. Good luck, Lawrence. Bye now.'

She put down the phone and leaned forward, breathing slowly to steady herself. It was done, and she knew what she had to do next. Instead of making an appointment with the doctor, she put on her coat and walked to the surgery.

* * *

Dr Pickersgill's hands were cold and he apologised as he felt the lump with surprisingly delicate fingers. Then he angled the lamp and used a magnifying glass. Jessie stared at the wall.

'Definitely something there,' he said. 'When did you first notice it?'

She knew he would ask that. 'September,' she said. 'Maybe a little earlier.'

'Well it's high time we knew what's going on here. Could be nothing serious, but the tests will tell us. Get dressed now.'

He was scribbling notes when she sat down again on the little chair by his desk.

'The appointment should come through pretty quickly. You'll need to be there for a while, to get everything done. Is there anyone who could go with you? Might feel a bit sore, better to have someone to take you home.'

'What will the tests show?'

Dr Pickersgill looked at her over his glasses. 'You're an educated woman, Miss Whelan. I'm surprised you waited so long to see me, and you must know what this could mean. If it's malignant it will mean surgery as soon as possible. I don't want to alarm you, but you need to prepare for the possibility.'

'Cancer,' she said.

'Not a death sentence these days, but a serious business. It helps that you're otherwise a pretty healthy specimen.' He patted her arm. 'I'll see you again when the results come back and we'll take it one step at a time.'

'Yes,' she said. 'Thank you.'

He pointed towards the door. The consultation was over.

Jessie didn't remember much about her walk back to the house. 'Cancer,' the word bounced in her brain. 'But I'm not ill,' she said to herself. 'Surely I would be ill, losing weight or tired all the time. It can't be cancer.' By the time she was back in the safety of her own kitchen all she could think about was her body without breasts. Her hands were shaking and she sat still for a while.

Who could she tell? Who would go with her to the hospital? It had to be a woman. Maggie would be free during the day, but she couldn't tell Maggie; she would tell John and then there would be two of them looking at her differently, sympathising, trying to cheer her up. She couldn't bear the thought. It would have to be Kath. They were friends but not so close, more detached, and that was better. Would she be able to get away during the daytime? Deal with that later, Jessie. For now, you need to tell someone or you'll go mad, thinking, imagining.

As she picked up the phone in the hall, Jessie thought of Lawrence. He would still be at work, then at the guest house, and tomorrow he would be gone. She stood, unable to move. She couldn't say anything to him, not yet. There was nothing to say and nothing he could do. She dialled the number for the school and left a message. 'Could Mrs Attwood call Jessie Whelan please, at her convenience?' The phone rang almost immediately.

'Here I am,' said Kath's cheerful voice.

'Can you come round on your way home?' Jessie asked, as nonchalantly as she could.

'OK,' said Kath. 'Be a bit late, got a parent coming. Have to go, see you later.'

Thank God for uncomplicated friends, thought Jessie.

The afternoon dragged; it was well after four when Kath bustled past Jessie and down the hall. 'Get that kettle on,' she was saying. 'Couldn't get the bloody woman to stop talking.' It took a while for Kath to stop talking, too. 'That's enough about school,' she said finally. 'Now is there something? Half expected to hear from you at the weekend, but I expect you were busy?'

It was a question, accompanied by a knowing smile.

Jessie looked away. 'I have to ask you something,' she said. 'I need to go to the hospital for some tests, could be next week, and Dr P. says someone should be with me.'

Kath's smile had faded. 'What tests?'

'I have a lump in my breast,' said Jessie. 'They need to see what it is.'

Kath put her hand to her mouth. 'Oh, my God. How long…?'

'Since September.'

'Two months? Why Jessie, why not till now?' Her eyes widened. 'Because of Lawrence? Does he know?'

Jessie shook her head. 'Nothing to do with Lawrence. I just

267

thought it would go away. I'm not ill, am I? And there was so much else going on, you know, you just put it out of your mind.'

'And now you're worried, you must be,' said Kath. She got up and pulled Jessie towards her, and the two women stood together for a few minutes. When they stood back Kath gave Jessie her hankerchief and pushed her gently into a chair.

'Sit there,' she said. 'It's a shock. Heaven knows what must be going through your head.'

'I can't think about it, not yet,' said Jessie wiping her eyes. 'Just have to wait for the tests and then the results. Hope it doesn't take too long. Do you think you could come with me, Kath?'

'Nothing that can't be shifted around if you tell me a day or two ahead. You can't go alone. You don't want to ask Maggie?'

'Not really. Things are better, but that would mean involving John. Too much, Kath. I couldn't cope with that, not yet.'

'Will you be OK? What about Lawrence?'

'Lawrence has gone away.'

'What do you mean, he's gone away? Away where?'

'To Risley. It's a work thing. He'll be back next weekend. I don't want to talk about it, so don't ask me.'

Kath was desperate to know what was going on, but she did as she was asked. For a while they sat together, the two of them, talking about inconsequential things, passing the time, recovering themselves. By the time they had drunk all the tea they could manage it was nearly six. Kath kissed her friend goodbye, told her to call as soon as the appointment date arrived, and was gone.

Only a few minutes later the front doorbell rang again. Kath's forgotten something, Jessie thought. Smiling, she opened the door. A woman stood in the porch, but it was not Kath. It was Rebecca Finer.

Chapter 27

Jessie's smile froze. Rebecca stood, waiting. Behind her a car throbbed at the curb, its engine running.

'I'm Rebecca Finer,' she said. 'Dr Finer's wife.'

'I know who you are,' said Jessie.

'May I come in? It's cold out here.'

Jessie stood back. 'Go through to the kitchen,' she said. 'It's the warmest place.' She followed Rebecca's elegant figure and the faint smell of face powder down the dark hall. 'Lawrence isn't here,' Jessie said, as calmly as she could. 'He's gone to Risley.'

'He's going tomorrow morning. Maybe he told you something different.' Rebecca was pulling off her gloves, one finger at a time, looking round the room. She wore a long blue coat and her dark hair was pulled into a tight pleat at the back. Like something out of a magazine for the older woman, Jessie thought, regretting her own dowdy clothes and unkempt hair.

'Lawrence said we would come and see this place last time I visited,' she said, 'but we didn't come, for some reason.'

'No,' said Jessie. 'I was expecting you.'

'And you're not now, I would guess. Well, when Lawrence told me about his plans, I decided to kill two birds with one stone, as it were. I want to talk to both of you, but definitely not together.'

Jessie wished she'd had the chance to tidy up a little but it was

269

too late now. 'We have met before,' she said, 'at the club.'

'Yes, I remember,' said Rebecca. 'It was ghastly wasn't it? And then we spoke on the phone, a little while ago.'

'Just after the fire,' said Jessie.

'So it was. Lawrence was in no fit state to go anywhere.'

'He doesn't live here now,' Jessie continued, trying to make sure Rebecca knew exactly what she needed to know, and no more.

'I know where he is. I've asked the taxi to wait outside. I'm going to the guest house next. This won't take very long I'm sure.'

'Is there something I can help you with?' Jessie asked. She had not invited her guest to sit down, and they both stood, facing each other like actors in a play.

'I doubt it,' said Rebecca. 'I just wanted to be very clear with you about something, not have the message come through second-hand, as it were.'

'Not from Lawrence, you mean?'

'You're very direct, aren't you? Yes, not through Lawrence. Sometimes he only tells people what they want to hear, not what needs to be said.'

'And what is that?' Jessie asked. She had fallen immediately into Rebecca's pattern of speech, polite, sarcastic and deter-minedly cool.

'I need to tell you that there is no prospect of a divorce. We value marriage highly in our faith, especially where children are involved.'

'You assume this information will be of interest to me?'

'From what I've heard, yes.'

'And may I ask what you've heard and from whom?'

'People talk, especially in a place like this, and it didn't take long to reach me. Never mind how I know, I know.'

Jessie wondered, remembering Angela Meadow at the club that night. She smiled faintly at Rebecca.

'Well, whatever the truth of what you may have been told, you've made your position very clear, Mrs Finer,' said Jessie, warming to the occasion. 'I won't detain you any longer.'

'I felt you needed to know,' said Rebecca. She seemed disappointed.

'Thank you,' said Jessie, waving her hand towards the door. 'We can't keep your taxi waiting.'

Rebecca turned on her high-heeled shoes and walked back down the hall, her gloves in her hand. She opened the front door herself.

'Goodbye, Mrs Finer,' said Jessie. 'Lawrence will be so pleased to see you, I'm sure. You know where he is, of course?'

'Of course,' said Rebecca. 'Goodbye.'

She got into the back of the waiting car, and they drove away down the hill.

Jessie closed the front door with relief and breathed out, feeling curiously exhilarated. She'd faced the woman down – patronising madam. And within minutes Lawrence would have to deal with her. Did he know she was coming? For a moment she thought of phoning to warn him, but stopped herself. This was between them now, and at least it might bring things to a head, unless... Again she doubted him. She wanted to trust him, but was fearful of doing so. Most of the men in her life had lied to her, or backed down when she needed them to stand up for her. Even gentle Matthew Dawson had let his awful daughter Anne browbeat her, or try to. Now Rebecca might make Lawrence choose, 'Your children or that woman!' Compared to them, she had been in Lawrence's life for only the twinkling of an eye, a few months. She had no right to assume his loyalty or his love, no matter how much he assured her of both.

* * *

Lawrence did know Rebecca was coming, but only minutes beforehand; at ten minutes to six when he arrived back at the guest house from work the message for him read: *I need to talk to you. This situation is impossible. Expect me around six. I have booked in at the Scawfell Hotel.*

He glanced at the clock in the gloomy hallway, cursed and crumpled the note into a ball. Before he had time to go up to his room, Rebecca's taxi drew up outside. He watched her get out of the car and walk up the steps towards the front door. Habit told him to open the door for her, but he resisted and stood awkwardly, trying to think where they could find some privacy and what he would say to her when they did.

The bleak residents' lounge was empty.

'You've come a long way,' he said. 'What do you want to say?'

'I wanted to find you, see where you are.'

'Well, now you have. Surprised?'

'I can't trust you any more, Lawrence.'

'What did you expect to find?'

'Is it over?'

'Is what over?'

'You know. Our marriage, our thirty years together, two children, all that?'

'It's been over for a while,' he said. 'You don't love me, and I don't love you, not any more. I wish I did, but I don't.'

'I won't divorce you. If you insist on leaving, that's what you must do. But you won't be free.'

'I can be free in here,' he said, tapping the side of his head, 'whether you divorce me or not.'

'Have you talked to the children?'

'David and Helen? They're hardly children.'

'Have you talked to them?'

'You know I have.'

'They wouldn't tell me anything.'

'I'm still their father, no matter what. It's between us, them and me.'

She looked away, across the empty space towards the window that faced east towards the hills.

'When people ask, I say you're working up here. That's true, at least.'

'You tell people whatever you like. I have my life here now.'

'With her?'

'You don't want to know.'

She was silent for a moment. 'Is that all you have to say?'

Lawrence's voice sounded loud in the empty space and he lowered it to a whisper. 'I didn't ask you to come,' he said. 'I wrote and I phoned but you didn't respond. I'm not going to beg.' He looked at her. She had not met his eye, not once. He went on. 'I'm sorry you wasted your time. Have you talked to the rabbi?'

'None of your business. Your faith means nothing to you. I hope I've made myself clear?'

'Quite clear. Will you go back tomorrow?'

'First thing. Good night, Lawrence.'

Rebecca Finer pulled on her leather gloves, stood up and walked out of the room. Lawrence sat for a while, listening for the car to pull away before he got up and went to his room.

* * *

Jessie knew how to occupy her time, although doing so took an unusual effort of will in the days that followed. When she asked to spend more time at the school, Kath understood immediately and was happy to agree. She could watch over her friend and benefit the children at the same time. The children's innocent company lifted Jessie's spirits and exhausted her, both of which she needed to get through the days leading up to the hospital visit. The procedures were attenuated and uncomfortable and Jessie was glad to have an undemanding rational companion during those hours. When Kath suggested a taxi home rather than the bus she agreed immediately, and was relieved too when Kath offered to stay. 'Not often I have a good reason for missing the staff meeting,' said Kath, before making Jessie laugh with stories of previous staff meetings where the stances and scripts appeared to be preordained.

The phone call from Dr Pickersgill called her to the surgery in the middle of the following Monday morning, and Jessie felt she could not ask Kath, or Maggie, to go with her. Jessie had convinced herself that the tests had been a wise precaution but that she couldn't possibly be seriously ill. She was too young, too healthy, and had too much to live for. When the scare was behind her and the annoying, benign cause of it all was removed she would get on with her life as planned. Lawrence might be with her, or not, either way they needed time to get to know each other properly if he had avoided being sucked back into Rebecca's world.

She sat looking at Dr Pickersgill, feeling better than on the previous occasion. His expression was hard to read.

'I'm afraid I have bad news for you, Miss Whelan,' he said, still looking down at his notes. 'The tests showed that the lump is indeed malignant and will have to be removed. If surgery reveals further growths, they will need to be dealt with, too. Time is of the essence.'

He looked up. Jessie was staring at him, hearing but not absorbing what he was saying. 'Miss Whelan? Do you understand?'

'Yes,' she said. 'Cancerous. Surgery.'

'I'm afraid so,' he said. 'We'll make it happen as soon as we can.'

'What?'

'The surgery,' he said, with a tinge of impatience. 'It'll be at

Whitehaven, which will suit you I'm sure. Close to family and so forth. Is there anyone at home…?' He left the question hanging in the air. Jessie took a moment to know that he wanted an answer.

'At home? No, just me. I live alone.'

'Ah,' said Dr Pickersgill. 'Well, you'll need support for a while. They'll send you home pretty quickly, and you won't want to be in hospital too long, I'm sure. Noisy and so on. So you'll need to make arrangements.'

'What kind of arrangements?'

'Someone to look after you, or maybe going to stay with family. Anyone local?'

'Yes, yes,' said Jessie, picturing herself lying in the Pharaohs' house like an unwanted burden.

'Sister Davies will tell you everything else you need to know. She's here this morning, so see her before you go. Nothing to worry about. You'll have the best of care.'

'Yes,' said Jessie, still trying to digest what he had been saying. 'Shall I go now?'

'Off you go,' he said cheerfully. 'See Sister Davies on your way out, don't forget.'

Jessie walked slowly out of the surgery, past the reception window, and out into the breezy November morning. The wind was cold off the sea and she pulled up her coat collar. This is a dream, she thought. Soon I'll wake up and I'll be the same person I was yesterday, not a sick person waiting to be operated on. A woman with two breasts not one. Someone waved from across the road, but Jessie didn't see or acknowledge it. In the quiet of her kitchen she took off her coat, laid it over the back of a chair and sat down. Then she stood up again, walked upstairs to her bed and lay down fully clothed. Outside the wind and tide crashed onto the beach leaving brown foam that broke into small frothy balls as it rolled and skipped up towards the village.

The doorbell woke her late in the afternoon. Before she could rouse herself she heard Kath's voice calling through the letterbox.

'Jessie, it's me. Are you there? Is the back door open?'

A minute later Jessie heard footsteps on the stairs before the bedroom door was pushed open and Kath's anxious face peered down at her.

'Jessie? Are you OK? What happened?'

Jessie reached up and pulled Kath down towards her. She couldn't speak. Kath disentangled herself and looked again at her friend.

'You've had the results, haven't you? I should have been with you. You poor dear. Look, you're still dressed. Let me bring you a drink, or do you want to get up?'

Jessie lay back for a moment, gathering herself. 'Getting up,' she said. 'What time is it?'

'About four,' said Kath. 'I came as soon as I could get away. Come on, let me help you.'

Slowly, awkwardly, they went downstairs together. Jessie's legs felt weak to start with but stronger as she moved. She sat quietly at the kitchen table while Kath made them both a hot drink and put three teaspoons of sugar into Jessie's cup. The unexpected sweetness made Jessie screw up her eyes.

Kath nodded to her. 'Drink it up, you need it. It must have been a terrible shock. What did he say?'

'Cancerous. Surgery.' Jessie repeated the only two words she could remember. She hung her head.

'Oh, pet, I'm so sorry. You shouldn't have had to deal with that on your own. Is that all you can remember?'

Jessie nodded. 'I think he said I had to see the nurse, Sister something. But I just wanted to get home.'

'Of course you did. And now we have to look after you for a while. You don't know when the surgery will be?'

Jessie shook her head.

'Who else knows about all this, apart from me?'

'No one,' Jessie whispered.

Kath looked at her friend. 'Well, that has to change now. John and Maggie have to know. They'd never forgive themselves if they weren't there to help you when you need it.' Jessie nodded. 'And then there's Lawrence,' Kath continued.

Jessie looked up. 'Lawrence?'

'Of course,' said Kath, taking her hand. 'You can't pretend with me, not now. Lawrence needs to know. He deserves to know, Jessie. It's only fair. But John and Maggie first. I'm going to ring them right now, just to ask them to come and see you. You must decide what to tell them. Can you do that?'

Jessie nodded. 'I'm feeling a bit better.'

'Good. Even strong people need help from time to time. What about that man in Maryport, the one who used to be a priest? You said he was kind when you needed someone to cheer you up.'

Jessie shook her head. 'Pat O'Toole. But he and I – no I don't want to see him, not now.'

Kath wondered, but didn't respond. 'That's fine. Family first. Is John's number by the phone?'

'In the little book,' said Jessie. 'Under P.'

Kath left her alone in the kitchen. Jessie heard her voice, and then she was back.

'I spoke to John. He was just back from work. He said he'd be over here in a few minutes. I'll stay with you till he comes, OK?'

'Yes, thanks,' said Jessie. She was beginning to feel a little foolish.

'You'll have to let us help you, dear,' Kath was saying. 'I know you're used to dealing with things yourself, but not this. Promise me you'll let us in?'

Jessie managed a smile. 'Hard to keep you out,' she said.

'That's the way,' said Kath. 'That's the Jessie I know.'

John came in the back way. 'Hello, Kath,' he said, his face full of questions. They both looked at Jessie. Kath nodded towards her friend.

'Jessie's had a bit of a shock. She'll need your help, John, but I'll let you tell her about it herself.' She put her hand on Jessie's shoulder and squeezed. 'I'll leave you with John now, dear. Call me if you need anything. And you too, John,' she said, raising her eyebrows to him. 'Don't hesitate. Anything.'

'Thanks, Kath,' said John. 'Jessie and I'll be fine now. I'll call you later, OK?'

The back door opened and closed. John pulled up a chair to sit as close to Jessie as he could and took his mother's cold hand in his. 'Tell me what's happened,' he said. 'Kath just said it was something serious.'

Jessie took a deep breath. 'I went to see Dr Pickersgill, about some tests.'

'Tests for what?' John asked, his heart sinking.

'I've got a lump, in my breast. The left breast,' said Jessie. 'I went for tests, and he says it's cancer.'

John squeezed her hand, silent while he took in what she had said.

'And you'll need surgery?' Jessie nodded. 'Did he say when, or where?'

'Whitehaven, don't know when. Soon.'

'Does anyone else know, apart from Kath?' She shook her head. 'I thought it would be fine,' she said. 'I feel so well, or at least I did. I was sure it was nothing.'

'How long have you had it, the lump?'

'Two months, maybe longer.'

John hung his head. 'And you didn't tell anyone?' Jessie shook her head again.

John put his arm round his mother's shoulders. 'You're not staying here on your own tonight,' he said. 'Judith's room is always ready for you. Shall I get a few things for you, or do you want to do it?'

Jessie got up. 'I'll do it,' she said. 'I won't be a minute.'

When she left the kitchen, John put his hand over his eyes. Jessie, invincible, difficult Jessie, who was never ill. She'd sat and heard that news on her own, and it had knocked everything out of her. He couldn't bear to think of it. Now she was like his child, doing as he told her, compliant, not the woman he'd known all these years who battled with everyone, and herself. She would have to fight now, he thought, against this sickness. She would need all her strength, and theirs too. And Lawrence. Where was he? He wanted to know but he dared not ask, not yet. First things first.

Chapter 28

'She has breast cancer,' John whispered to his wife in the hall after he'd ushered his mother gently into the front room and closed the door. Maggie stared at him. 'She got the test results today. Knocked her for six. Kath found her in bed fully dressed and couldn't leave her there alone. That's when she called me.'

'Oh, God,' said Maggie. 'Jessie. And she didn't tell us.'

'Didn't tell anyone apparently. She had the lump for two months before she even got it checked.'

'That bloody pride, or whatever it is,' said Maggie.

'Don't,' said John. 'No good blaming her for being the way she is. Now we know, we can't go on about feeling left out. That's over with. OK?'

Maggie nodded.

'She's brought a few things, just for overnight. Is Judith's bed ready?'

'Of course. I'll put a hottie in it, air it off.'

'Is it alright for her to stay? I couldn't leave her there in that empty house.'

'Where's Lawrence?'

'I daren't ask. I know he's down at Risley most of the time. She won't have told him anything, either. I'll check at work tomorrow. Then we'll see what we need to do. Don't think she's eaten anything much. Supper will stretch to five won't it?'

'Course it will. You go back to her, let me deal with the bed and food. I'll come and see her in a minute.'

John kissed his wife. 'You're wonderful,' he said.

'Maggie's getting your bed sorted, and making some supper for us,' he said to Jessie, who was sitting by the fire in the front room, her coat on her lap. Like a refugee at a railway station, John thought, passively waiting. He took her coat and hung it up in the hall.

'Are you ready to tell me a little more?' he asked when he came back to her.

She looked up at him and held out her hand. 'You're being very good, John. I must be a real nuisance.'

'Nonsense,' he said, putting her hand between both his own. 'What are families for? Now think back to this morning and see if you can remember a bit more about what the doctor said.'

She sat, looking into the fire. 'I went to see him a couple of weeks ago, just after the report on the fire came out.'

'November 8th,' said John.

'That was when they sent Lawrence to Risley,' she continued, 'and I went to the doctor. He sent me for tests at the hospital. Kath came with me. I couldn't ask her to be with me again yesterday when I went for the results.'

You could have asked me, or Maggie, thought John. Aloud, he said, 'Can you remember what the doctor told you?'

'He said that the lump was cancerous and I would have to have surgery, at Whitehaven. He didn't say when.'

John wanted to ask about the surgery, but couldn't. 'What about after the surgery?'

'He just said I would need support at home, after the hospital.'

'We can sort all that out. You could stay here, or we could get nursing care for you at home.'

Jessie looked away. 'I don't want to be an invalid,' she said.

'You won't be. You'll just need some help when you come out of hospital. Everyone needs care after an operation. Even you.'

'Even me, I know,' said Jessie. 'Now you're going to tell me I have to do as I'm told.'

'It's tempting,' said John, smiling at her. 'That would be a first for you.'

They sat in silence for a moment. John could hear Maggie next door talking to the boys. He hoped they wouldn't come bursting in.

'The boys have been out at a friend's house,' he said. 'Would you like to see them? I think Maggie will have told them you're not very well, nothing more than that.'

Mention of the children brightened Jessie's face. 'I'd love to see them,' she said.

Thank God for the boys, thought John, watching his mother sitting with Vince on her lap and Frank leaning towards her over the arm of the big chair. They were reading a book together, talking about Vince's teacher and the nature walk they'd been on. 'We went down on the beach,' Vince was saying, 'to see the old swimming pool that gets covered by the tide.' 'We went there too,' Frank chimed in, 'and we swam in it.' 'You did not.' 'We did too.' Jessie was laughing when John went back into the kitchen.

'Come through and see her,' he said to Maggie who was taking a casserole out of the oven. 'She's perked up a bit now. I think she's a bit embarrassed about looking so helpless.'

'That's a good sign,' said Maggie, taking off her apron. 'I'll be there in a minute.'

'Jessie,' she said. 'Sorry to leave you with these two ruffians. Have they been behaving?'

'As always,' said Jessie. 'Thank you for taking me in, dear. Everyone insisted on looking after me.'

'Quite right too,' said Maggie. 'And supper's nearly ready. Hungry?'

That's the way, thought John, marvelling at his wife's easy manner. No trace of past arguments and bitter words.

They ate in the big warm kitchen. When supper was over Jessie went mildly back to the front room while Maggie finished off in the kitchen. Before he took the children upstairs, John asked his wife's advice. 'I want to ask her about Lawrence,' he said, 'but I'm not sure what's going on with the two of them. They seemed so close for a while and then this Risley thing came up and off he went.'

Maggie kept her voice very low. 'Someone told me they'd seen his wife at the station, just before he went away.'

'So I have to be careful,' he said. 'Could be very touchy. But if he's around, I think he needs to know what's going on, why she isn't at home.'

'How long can she stay here?'

'As long as she likes, I think, don't you? Judith won't need to the room for a month or so yet.'

'I think she'll want to get back,' said Maggie, not relishing the idea of having her mother-in-law around for weeks.

'What day is it?' Jessie asked, when Maggie came in a little later.

'Thursday today,' said Maggie, wondering about Jessie's state of mind.

'Is John coming back?' Jessie asked.

'He'll be down in a minute.'

'Lawrence will be back from Risley tomorrow for the weekend. He might wonder where I am.'

'Does he know about, you know?'

Jessie looked sharply at her daughter-in-law. 'No,' she said. 'And I don't want him to.'

Maggie sat, trying not to react.

'Don't you think he needs to know?'

'No. He's not family. And he has other things to worry about.'

'But surely –' Maggie began.

'Surely nothing,' said Jessie. 'He doesn't need to know anything yet. I don't want his pity.'

Maggie could hear John upstairs. She had a few minutes to say what she wanted to say before he could stop her.

'Jessie,' she began. Jessie turned to face her.

'Lawrence is very important to you. I think he deserves to know something as serious as this.'

'I think I'm the best judge of that, actually. Things are more complicated than you could know.'

Maggie couldn't stop herself. 'With his wife, you mean?'

'That's between us.'

'Not entirely,' Maggie pressed on. 'His wife came to visit him I understand, not long ago.'

'Who told you that?'

'I heard. She went back to wherever she lives, I suppose, and Lawrence comes back to Seascale every weekend. He's obviously very concerned to stay close to you.'

The old spark was in Jessie's eye. 'That's our business,' she insisted, more loudly than before.

'So is your illness, surely, your business. So he has to know.'

'Maggie, will you stop? This is between me and Lawrence.'

John heard the rising voices and took the stairs as quickly as he could.

'John,' said his mother as soon as he came back into the room. 'Will you tell Maggie, please, that I have every right not to tell Lawrence anything about all this?'

John rolled his eyes. Maggie held up her hands. 'I just said what needed saying.'

'And what was that?'

'That Lawrence deserves to know what's happened.'

'And I say that's my business, no one else's,' Jessie insisted.

John rubbed his long hands down his face. He couldn't leave them alone for a few minutes without them going at each other again, but his mother seemed to be recovering her old spirit.

'Alright. Let's make a decision that we can all agree on.' He turned to his mother.

'For what's it's worth, Jessie, I think she's right. Lawrence is part of your life. Certainly he thinks he is, from my conversation with him on our walk. He thinks of this as his home. Whatever's going on with his wife, he's not going back, as far as I could tell.'

Jessie thought for a moment. 'He said that?'

'Not in so many words, but I think he was pretty sure about it.'

'Well, it's still between us,' she said. 'I have to decide what to tell him, and when.'

Maggie opened her mouth to speak, but John held out his hand towards her and she shut it again.

'That's your choice, of course, but he needs to know something, soon. If he finds your house empty, he's bound to worry.'

'Then I'll go back,' said Jessie, pushing to her feet.

'You're not going anywhere for a day or two,' said John, with a firmness that surprised all of them. 'I'll leave a message at the guest house before he gets back saying that you're staying here with us and would he like to come round on Saturday morning to see you? How does that sound? We'll take the children out somewhere and you and Lawrence can talk. You can tell him whatever you want, but at least he'll know you're alright. OK?' He turned first to Maggie, and then to Jessie. They both nodded. He sat back, amazed at himself.

* * *

Jessie heard the motorbike outside. She was waiting in the

front room in the pale winter sunshine that lit the room without warming it. A fire crackled in the hearth. Maggie had made coffee before she and John took the boys out to Whitehaven and the smell of it lingered in the house. Jessie knew how much Lawrence loved coffee. John had brought a change of clothes for her from the house and she had washed her hair. After the misery of the previous few days she was feeling much more herself, the nagging fear pushed further to the side of her mind. She longed to see Lawrence, but wasn't sure what to say, or how he might respond. She felt slightly sick.

He took off the little leather helmet he wore on the bike, ruffling his white hair with his hand, and looked carefully at her. When he followed her inside the door wasn't even closed before he took her in his arms and held her close. This time she responded, her arms tight around his back, stroking his hair. Unwanted tears filled her eyes.

'I've missed you so,' he said. 'I wanted to call, but you were avoiding me. I didn't know why, I still don't.'

She pulled him into the warm front room. 'They're all out,' she said, answering the unspoken question. 'Won't be back till after lunch.'

'So, we can talk,' he said. 'The note just said you're not well. What is it?'

She shook her head. 'Plenty of time for that,' she said. 'You tell me first. What happened about Rebecca? I know she came to see you.'

'How do you know that?'

'Because she came to see me, too.'

'When?'

'On her way from the station. I opened the door and there she was. I knew her from that night at the club.'

'What did she say?'

'She just told me, "There will be no divorce", something like that.'

He groaned. 'Coming all that way, just for that.'

'It seems a long time ago,' she said. 'Took my mind off things for a while.'

'You look tired,' he said, 'but otherwise just the same. I've missed you.' He held her again, feeling down her back, the shape of her hips.

'Sit down,' she said, when he released her. 'I need to tell you something.'

She pushed him into one of the chairs that stood on either side of the fire and sat down in the other one, out of his reach. She wanted to put some distance between them. He leaned forward, waiting.

'I have a lump in my breast. The tests show it's a cancer. I'll be having surgery.'

His expression didn't change, but she could see the reaction in his eyes. He began to get up.

'No,' she said, holding out her hand to stop him. 'Stay there. I need you to stay there.'

'How long?'

'The lump's been there several weeks, I got the test results on Thursday. Kath called John and he brought me here.'

'You never said anything.'

'Not to anyone,' she said. 'I needed to have someone with me when I went for the tests, so I had to tell Kath. It was easier because we're friends, but not –'

'Not lovers,' he said.

She hung her head. 'I thought you might find it, you know, when we were in bed, but you didn't, and then I decided I didn't want to you to know. I didn't want anything to get in the way of us, to come between us. I still don't.'

He leaned back in the chair, looking up at the ceiling. Questions buzzed in his brain, so many questions.

'What did the doctor actually say?'

'I can't remember much about it. I just wasn't prepared and the whole thing felt like a dream. It still does. I want to wake up and know that none of this is happening.'

This time she couldn't stop him kneeling in front of her, taking both her hands in his. 'Never mind what's past,' he said. 'Now we need to know as much as we can about the future. He definitely said you need surgery?'

'Yes, at Whitehaven. Don't know when.'

'Doctor's name?'

'Pickersgill. He didn't wrap it up. Told me to see the nurse but I just wandered off. I feel such a fool. I went home and up to bed like a child. Kath found me.'

He reached up and held her again.

'And I was away. And Rebecca was being a bitch. No wonder you folded up.'

'That was it,' she said. 'I just folded up, as if someone had pulled the plug out.'

'But I'm here now,' he said. They clung together.

He pulled back and looked at her. 'I know someone,' he said. 'Works at the Christie.'

'What's that?'

'The best cancer hospital outside London, maybe including London, too. It's in Manchester. I was at university with this chap, see him occasionally.' He sat back and looked in the inside pocket of his jacket. 'Damn, my address book must be at the digs. Stay here. I'm just going to make a phone call, they won't mind, will they?'

Before she could answer he had picked up the phone in the hall. She heard his voice, silence, then again, and then another call. It seemed like half an hour before he put the phone down finally. How much will this be costing, she wondered?

* * *

Lawrence was smiling when he came back into the room. 'Done it,' he said. 'We have an appointment to see a breast cancer specialist at the Christie in a week's time and it won't cost a thing.' He beamed at her.

Jessie stared back at him. Was this how it would be?

'Why didn't you ask me first?'

'We have to act, Jessie. You've waited too long. He offered and I said yes.'

'But it's about me, not you.'

The smile faded. 'It's your body. But you're my love.'

Jessie closed her eyes. She could feel things slipping away from her, but she had to think about what to say. So often she'd react and upset people, people she cared about.

She held out her hand to him. 'I just wish you'd asked. It wouldn't have taken a minute. I would have said yes, but I want to be asked.'

He sat down heavily in the chair, rubbing his chin with his hand.

'It's what I do,' he said. 'I have an idea and just go. If it's the rational thing to do I never think about possible objections.'

'There are no rational objections, but I have to feel in charge of myself. That's what I do.'

'We're both as bad as each other,' he said. 'Headstrong, wilful, making assumptions.'

'I assumed you were going to Risley to get away from me, and Rebecca too. I even wondered if you'd asked to go.'

He sat forward. 'Jessie, how could you think that?'

'It would have been logical,' she said, 'to get you off the hook.'

'What hook?'

'The hook of having an affair with someone and then not knowing how to end it.'

'But I don't want to end it.'

'Not even now? I'm going to lose my breast, Lawrence. I'll be disfigured, literally.'

He knelt in front of her again, his long fingers stroking her face. 'I love you, Jessie. I'm as sure about that as I am about anything. I don't know whether you love me, you've never said, but that's how I feel. And it's not about bits of your body, it's about you. If you care for someone as I care for you, you'll do anything to help them.' He smiled at her. 'Even if they don't want you to.'

'I think I do love you, actually,' she said, 'although I've nothing to compare it with. I know I get a feeling in the pit of my stomach when you're near me, that I lose myself in you when we're together. I just have to learn to trust you. I've never really trusted anyone, not absolutely. It takes practice.'

When the family came back they found the two lovers sitting on the floor by the fire, their heads close together. In fact, it was Frank who found them, stopping in his tracks and being pushed forward by his mother who followed him into the room. Lawrence got to his feet, blushing.

'Sorry,' he said. 'We couldn't both fit into one chair.'

Maggie smiled at them. Jessie's face was pink.

'I hope you don't mind,' Jessie said, as Lawrence helped her to her feet. 'Lawrence used your phone. It took a while to find the person he wanted to talk to.'

'But I did,' said Lawrence. 'And things have moved on a bit. Jessie is due to see a specialist in Manchester next Friday.' Despite everything, he couldn't keep the note of triumph out of his voice.

'John,' called Maggie over her shoulder. 'Can you come here, please.'

When John arrived, Maggie turned to him. Jessie knew the signs, that Maggie was annoyed.

'Lawrence has arranged for Jessie to go to Manchester for treatment,' she said. 'You're her son. Can he do that?' She turned back to Lawrence. 'You are Jessie's friend,' she said. 'Nothing more. We are family. Surely it's for us to decide things like that?'

Jessie held up her hand. 'Stop,' she cried. 'Stop it, before it starts. You're not arguing over me like a parcel. It's for me to decide things about me. I would have preferred Lawrence to ask me first, but he was able to make this arrangement, and I think it's a gift.' She searched for Lawrence's hand and took it in hers.

John looked from one to the other. 'Why Manchester? It's so far away.'

'Christie is the best,' said Lawrence. 'Jessie deserves the best and she'll get it there. I'll take her, stay with her, do all that needs doing until she's had her surgery or whatever happens.'

'What about your work?'

'I've got leave owing and I'll take it. To be honest, I'm in a strong position to bargain right now, if I have to.'

'You've thought of everything, haven't you?' said Maggie. All her resentment of education and influence was simmering just below the surface, and John could feel it. He put his arm round her shoulders.

'Let's all sit down. I'll make us a pot of tea. Then we can sort a few things out. We're all on short fuses, it's not surprising.'

In the kitchen Maggie whispered fiercely to her husband, 'He's acting like they're married already. Next thing he'll be moving into the house in Seascale, bold as brass.'

John put his arms around her, kissed the hair he loved so much. 'Is that's what's bothering you? Nothing Jessie could do would surprise me, not now. If they love each other, what does it matter?'

291

Chapter 29

THE ORANGE GLOW OF STREETLIGHTS SHIMMERED on the rainy
Manchester pavement and seeped through the curtains of the
quiet hotel room. Lawrence lay in bed, watching Jessie taking off
her clothes. He could see the shape and fullness of her. She snuggled close to him. 'I want us to make love,' she said. 'while I'm still
whole.'

Afterwards he fell asleep, sprawled across the bed with one arm
over her. She felt cramped, pressured by his inert body, desperate
to move but not wanting to disturb him. How do people sleep like
this, she wondered. She had never shared a bed with someone
for a whole night, not one night in sixty years, and the prospect
appalled her. Living alone, she'd found ways of dealing with
her restlessness: she would stay up late and read until her eyes
closed, or sleep for a couple of hours and then wake for a while to
confront the loops of dark nonsense in her mind – more reading,
writing lists, talking to herself, anything she wished. But now

she was trapped. She lifted Lawrence's heavy arm and struggled to push him away. Finally he stirred and mumbled and turned over, and the relief made her smile. Even after that, it seemed like hours before sleep finally released her from the claustrophobia of a shared bed.

All the following day she watched him. Lawrence seemed quite at ease with the confident efficiency of the hospital and the white-coated people who surrounded them, one of whom he greeted as an old friend. They shook hands, Jessie was introduced, there were smiles and polite enquiries and lowered voices and she felt like a specimen. Then Lawrence was gone, her clothes were replaced by a shapeless gown, and Jessie sank deeper into herself, isolated, vulnerable, and at the mercy of others. When the endless questions and prodding and waiting were over she let Lawrence guide her gently back to the car through the swirling drizzle.

'All done,' he said cheerfully, before he started the engine. 'I knew they would do all the tests again. You must be tired.' He looked across at her. She nodded, her eyes closed. 'Do you want to stop somewhere, get a bite to eat?'

'No,' she said. 'I just want to go home.'

For a while she sat still, her head turned away from him, conscious of the sound and movement of the car but not wanting to speak. The streets were brightly lit and thronged with late shoppers and traffic. I'm just a speck, she thought, in all this busy-ness. There are thousands like me, but each of us is alone. She wondered how long she would have. None of the men in white coats could tell her that.

A while later her head lolled forward and she woke with a start. 'Where are we?' she asked, looking into the dark space beyond the car. He glanced across and patted her knee.

'Just coming into Chorley,' he said, 'on the A6. Are you alright? Do you want to stop? There's a place just coming up.'

She nodded, and he pulled into a car park. The rain had stopped, but the stars were still invisible. He buttoned her coat and turned up her collar and steered her into the warm café. When she came back from the Ladies, a pot of tea and some sandwiches were being placed onto the red formica table by a waitress who didn't look up.

'Hope this will do for you,' he said, stirring the tea in the pot. 'Sandwiches were the quickest. I know you want to get home.'

'Didn't sleep much last night,' she said, remembering. 'And I've felt like a parcel all day, being passed around and talked about.'

'I know,' he said, 'Horrid.'

She looked at him. Was this how it would be, she wondered? Was she a sick person now, to be looked after? And when they got back to the house, would he stay there with her, in her bed? All she wanted was to be left alone. But she loved him. Why did she dread the thought of living with him?

'What will you do,' she asked, 'when we get home?'

'I'll stay with you, of course.'

'Can you sleep in your own bed, upstairs?'

He looked at her. 'Do you want me to?'

'Last night,' she hesitated, 'I felt trapped. I've never slept with someone.'

He sat back. 'Never?'

She shook her head. 'I didn't really think about it, what it would be like.'

'And was it awful?'

She nodded. 'I'm sorry. Maybe I'd get used to it. But tonight, I just want to sleep.'

He leaned forward and put his hand over hers. 'Of course you do. I'll sleep upstairs.'

'The bed's not made up,' she said, wiping a tear from her cheek.

'I can do that. You don't have to do everything yourself.'

The house was dark and cold when they got back to Seascale. Jessie was desperate for her bed, and only half aware of how she got there. When she woke in the morning Lawrence was standing by the bed looking down at her. She smiled and held out her hand to him.

'Sit with me,' she said, licking her lips. Her mouth was dry. 'Did you find everything, for the bed.'

He nodded. 'Pretty well house-trained,' he said. 'Did you sleep?'

'Don't remember much about it. What time is it?'

'After nine.'

'What about work?'

He smiled. 'It's Saturday, remember? I don't have to go anywhere. I've had the fire on downstairs and the water should be hot by now. Why don't I run you a bath? Or do you want to go back to sleep?'

'A bath,' she said. 'That would be lovely.'

'Do you need help?'

'No, Lawrence. I can bath myself.'

'I'll see you downstairs, then,' he said, 'in a little while.'

Jessie lay in the water, feeling its warmth creeping into her body. She soaped her hands and found the lump that had changed her life. Things were slipping away from her. Lawrence expected to move into the house, that was obvious. He wanted to look after her. And what else could they do? What if I weren't ill, she thought to herself. Would I want him to live here, with me? She blessed Rebecca for not allowing them to marry; at least that decision was made. And for a while Lawrence would be away at Risley during the week, and she could have the house to herself. But that routine would change, too. She would have surgery, and radiation treatment, and they would drive to Manchester and back, time after time. That would be her life now, and would he

295

help with all of it? What about his job? She wet the flannel and put it over her face.

Clean and dressed in her own familiar clothes she found Lawrence sitting by the fire in the kitchen, reading the paper.

'There you are,' he said, smiling at her. 'You look more your old self.'

'Old self,' she repeated. 'That's for sure. But the bath was a good idea. I feel much better.'

'Hungry?' he asked.

A little while later, poached eggs expertly made and gratefully consumed, she sat watching him clear the table.

'Sit down a minute,' she said. He wiped his hands and did so, on the other side of the kitchen table, looking across at her.

'We need to talk. Everything's changed. I've been thinking about what happens next.'

'Go on,' he said.

'I'm going to be very honest with you, Lawrence. I don't want you to take it the wrong way.'

'I expect you to be honest with me. That's what I want.'

'My being ill changes things,' she said. 'Before that, I hadn't really thought about you moving in here, or of us living together. I need time. I've never really been in love before, not like this. I just want us to get to know each other more. It's all been so quick.'

'Not for me,' he said. 'I've known for ages, almost since the start.'

'How could you?'

He shrugged. 'It just hit me. And I've never doubted it since.'

'What do you want to do?' she asked him, amazed at his certainty.

'I want to live the rest of my life with you,' he said.

'In the same house?'

'Yes.'

'In this house?'

'I was thinking about that on the way home,' he said. 'This house is so big, takes a lot of looking after, and so exposed to the weather. Maybe we should look for somewhere smaller, on one level perhaps, a bit more sheltered.'

She thought about it, and pictured herself in a wheelchair.

'What do you want?' he asked.

Jessie looked away and shook her head. 'I don't know,' she said. 'I know it makes sense, for us to live together. Where else would you go now? Your work is here, and you can't stay in that ghastly guest house, or the hostel. It makes sense for you to be here.'

'Even if we can't be married?'

'I don't care about that,' she said. 'I never really wanted to be married, and I'm past caring what people say. Rebecca's made that decision for me.' She rubbed her hand down her face. 'And now this, this thing, is making decisions, too. It's no good pretending I'm making all the choices any more. I will need help, someone to care for me. I just wish it wasn't you.' She looked at him. 'I want you to love me Lawrence, not to nurse me.'

'Can't I do both?'

'I'm sure you can manage it, but I'm not sure I can.'

'What can we do?' he said. 'I want to care for you, not because you're a sick person, but because I love you.'

They sat in silence for a few minutes. The fire crackled in the range.

'I don't know how long we'll have, to be together, but I don't want to move,' she said. 'I know this house has its drawbacks, but it's my house. I need to keep something of my own, for now at least.'

'I can understand that,' he said. 'I'd probably feel the same.'

'And there's another thing.'

'Go on.'

297

'If you move in here with me, I want you to keep the rooms on the top floor as yours, or give them to me as my space, my own space.'

He smiled. 'You want to be able to live alone, and with me, all at once.'

'I know that sounds crazy, but I need somewhere that's mine.' She hesitated. 'And my own bed.'

He was quiet, remembering when Rebecca stopped sleeping with him.

'Do you want to think about it?' said Jessie. 'I told you I had to be honest. It's not that I don't love you, I do. At least, I think I do. But after all these years of being me, I can't give that away, not to anyone, not yet.'

'We live in this house, together, and one of us uses the top floor as a separate flat.'

She nodded.

'Does that mean you want to stop, you know, making love with me?'

'No! God, no,' she said, stretching out her hand to him. 'I love that. It's just the sleeping together I can't cope with.'

He squeezed her hand. 'That's a relief. It's so good, I couldn't bear to lose that.'

'We won't. We can take it in turns, my bedroom or your bedroom.'

'Or on the kitchen table?'

She laughed.

Lawrence was trying to envisage this unfamiliar domestic arrangement. 'What happens when people come to see us?'

'Do you think they will? We might be shunned by all right-thinking God-fearing folk.'

'Are you serious?'

'Of course not,' she said, laughing again. 'My family know how strange we both are, but Violet might need special dispensation from Father Price.'

'Talking of priests,' said Lawrence, 'what happened to the one from Maryport, the one I thought you were very friendly with?'

'Pat? I wrote to him saying I didn't want to be part of the "movement" for now. I'm not sure where we stand now. He's been a friend for a long time, but we seem to have drifted apart.'

'Does he know about you illness?'

'No. I need to tell him. And what about your children, Lawrence? Will you tell them?'

'About you or about us?'

'Both.'

'I'll tell them about things that affect them, but your illness is your business, not theirs, don't you think? I'm sure they'll be fine. If Rebecca and I can stay on reasonably good terms, they won't feel too torn between us. I've told them both so much about this place, and they know how welcome they'll be.'

'Well then, who else matters? When we have people to stay they can have the top floor, and we keep some privacy. Plenty of room in the big bedroom for an extra bed.'

'One bed for loving and another one for sleeping,' he smiled. 'Sounds pretty civilised to me.'

Jessie got up and held him close as he sat at the table, his head on her chest. 'If I didn't love you already, Lawrence Finer,' she said, 'I would now.'

When the morning cloud had cleared, and a northerly sharpened the outline of the Isle of Man on the horizon, Jessie and Lawrence wrapped up warmly and walked together along the beach. A flock of dunlins rose from the tideline in effortless unison and danced, brown and white against the pale sky.

If you've enjoyed the story, you may want to…

- Order another copy to pass to a friend.

- Read *A Good Liar,* Part 1 of the trilogy, also set in Cumbria. Tells the story of Jesse Whelan who risks career and independence with a love affair, whilst her secret past draws ever closer.

- Read *Forgiven,* Part 2 of the trilogy, set among the coal mines and fells of the Cumberland coast in the gloom of post-war rationing and cold. Jessie Whelan's struggle continues, caught between her secret and the possibility of future happiness.

- Follow Ruth Sutton's blog on *ruthwords. wordpress.com* and check her website *www.ruthsutton.co.uk* for latest news of her writing.

- Follow Ruth Sutton on *Twitter@ruthsutton* and on Facebook.

JESSIE WHELAN has always been a good liar, trying to protect her independence and her career as a teacher. But she risks everything when, after years of discreet loneliness, she embarks on a love affair. In the meantime, her secret past draws ever closer.

Ruth Sutton's powerful novel is the first part of her trilogy, *Between the Mountains and the Sea.* It is set in Cumbria, the north-west corner of England.

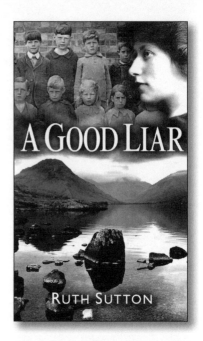

JESSIE WHELAN'S lies about her past are beginning to unravel and the truth could overwhelm her. In the gloom of post-war Cumberland she struggles to keep her job, the respect of the community and her hard-won independence.

Set among the coal mines and rugged fells of the Cumberland coast, *Forgiven* is the second part of Ruth Sutton's trilogy, *Between the Mountains and the Sea.*

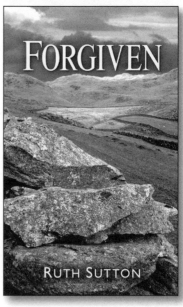